STATE OF THE ORBIT

THE DISTINCTION BETWEEN SCIENCE FICTION AND FANTASY has always troubled me. As a young reader, it struck me that fantasy was made-up stuff that happened in the past, while science fiction was made-up stuff that happened in the future. As I grew older I came to realize it's more complicated than that, what with the blending of fantasy and science fiction in *Star Wars* and *Doctor Who*, and most recently, *Jupiter Ascending*. Stories like these tend to get called "soft" science fiction, as opposed to "hard" science fiction. I don't mind the term "hard science fiction," since the examples I can think of off the top of my head (Connie Willis's *Blackout/All Clear*, Neal Stephenson's *Anathem*) are definitely hard stories. As in, they take focused concentration and dedication on the part of the reader, and lots of research on the part of the author, because the defining factor of hard SF is the degree to which it maintains scientific plausibility. And that is, in every sense of the word, hard.

What bothers me is the term "soft science fiction." Probably because this is the type of SF I write, and even though it is laced with improbable coincidences and fantastic landscapes and more magic than you might reasonably expect in an SF novel, I still take care to get certain aspects of the science right. Not necessarily correct, mind you, but right in the way that will satisfy the scientifically literate reader. This is still a high bar to clear, and I count myself lucky to be related to just such a person (my dad) who is always more than happy to point out when I have gotten my science wrong, or (gratifyingly) right enough that it delights him.

I am not a scientist or an engineer. I am a storyteller, and I work in a field that is malleable in the extreme. That doesn't mean I don't have enormous amounts of respect for actual scientists and engineers. I am enamored of them, to tell the truth, and though I will (probably) never discover a new type of bacteria or a comet or how to use epigenetics to treat cancer, I can write stories that inspire people to go into the fields where they might do just that.

I mentioned before that magic creeps into all my stories. This is because the act of storytelling is magic in and of itself. It is the magic that happens between a story and the reader's mind, where two things meet, and new ideas and feelings are formed. *Star Trek*, for all it is considered "soft" science fiction, inspired generations to go into astrophysics and space exploration. There is a material benefit to dressing up otherwise "hard" subjects like orbital mechanics and string theory and showing how they can play a part in an exciting story. And as long as you get the core essence right enough that it doesn't make people like my dad roll their eyes, you can put as much magic and talking dogs into your story as you like: it's still science fiction in my book.

Which brings me to the lead story in this issue of Apsis: "The Dogs of Canary Island" has a lot of "could-be" science. I took concepts and practices which are already well known (if not well understood) and ran forward several thousand years. Then I tossed Professor Odd and her crew into the middle of it. I took the liberty of borrowing the name of a real scientist for a purely imaginary particle. As the story is set several thousand years in our future, I figured either he or one of his descendants might have been responsible for discovering it. It is a small nod to one of many heroes working in the scientific canon to which my stories are merely science fan fiction.

"The Wolf and the Rabbit," in contrast, is pure fairytale, and in the Bouragner Felpz stories, "Moonfoot Problem" and "Case of Countess Baronia," we are thoroughly engulfed in my original definition of fantasy: stories with magic set in the past. Even so,

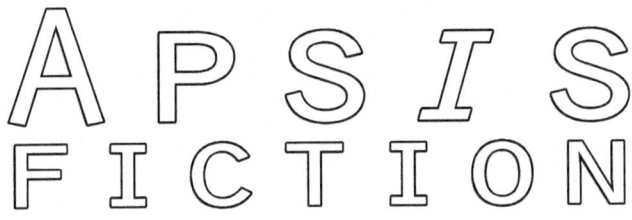

The Semi-Annual Anthology of Goldeen Ogawa

Volume 3, Issue 1 • Aphelion 2015

CONTENTS

author • illustrator • editor • book designer
GOLDEEN OGAWA

a HELIOPAUSE PRODUCTION

Apsis Fiction: The Semi-Annual Anthology of Goldeen Ogawa
Volume No. 3, Issue 1, Whole No. 5 (Aphelion 2015).
Published semi-annually by Heliopause Productions.

FICTION/Science Fiction/Short Stories

FICTION/Fantasy/General

First Edition 2015

ISBN: 978-06924668-1-0

working in a completely fantastical setting allows one to explore concepts which, brought into our present world, might be too hot for some folks to handle, and I have taken full advantage of that.

This issue closes with the sixth story in the *Driving Arcana* saga, "Missionary Man," which is as much a fusion of science fiction and fantasy as any high-wheeling space opera, only set in modern-day Kansas. With demons. And a somewhat battered angel. And even though there is a lot of magic in it—not all of it explained—the reader can be assured that I have taken as much care to keep it internally consistent and accurate as I do when depicting real, non-magical occurrences, like runaway diesel engines.

These are the stories of *Apsis Fiction: Aphelion 2015*—which our planet will reach at approximately 19:40 UTC on July 6th. Some of them have science, they all have a little magic, and though they aren't hard, they're certainly not soft either. Colorful is the term I use to describe my own work. I think it gives the reader a much better idea of what to expect.

—GOLDEEN OGAWA
California
May 2015

"The Dogs of Canary Island" is the seventh story in the Professor Odd *series, though it is the first of the second "season" of these episodes. It is preceded by the Season One finale, "The Monster's Daughter," which appeared in* Apsis Fiction's Perihelion 2015 *issue. All previous episodes are available as singles from Heliopause. Written in the fall of 2013, it will be followed by "Chronostrophe" in* Perihelion 2016.

The Dogs of Canary Island

Prologue

THE ISLAND HAD ORIGINALLY BEEN A VOLCANO. Once, it had been tropical. It was still one of seven islands off the coast of what the old maps called Africa and the new maps called "Dangerous, Do Not Enter." Now, however, in the Canine Epoch, after the Long Winter and with an overall cooler global climate, the island was solidly temperate. Cold, even, if you climbed to the peak of the caldera that marked the center of the island. Which was where Discovery Intent was headed. Scout Reiji had complained loudly how stupid it was that they had to climb back up the side of the mountain when they were going to be air-dropped from the transfer-cannon in Lis.

"Why not aim us right at the top?" he'd asked at their very first briefing. He'd chosen a grating, male Bostonian voice for his comsys, something Alpha Zora expected to change at the soonest possible moment.

Tech Ishin, looking awkward in his mission gear, nearly barked in agitation.

"We *can't* do that," he said, and Alpha Zora was relieved to hear he was using Science Division Standard. "The objective is at the summit! We can't risk damaging it."

Scout Reiji had grumbled at this, but didn't question further. Tech Ishin was a real Science Division member, and carried with him a residual aura of secrecy and covert research. It was Science Division that had predicted the end of the Long Winter. It was Science Division that had produced a cure to the radiation illness. It was Science Division that had built most of the gear they now took for granted—like the comsys. When Science Division wanted something, Arms Division and Exploration Division got it for them. Which was what they were doing now: Science Division wanted something that was apparently at the top of some manforsaken volcano island, and so members of Arms Div (in the forms of Ranger Omu and Gunner Xixuan) and Expo Div (Scout Shani and her partner, the talkative Reiji) had been pulled together under Alpha Zora (Arms Div) with relatively little explanation.

"Like I said," Alpha Zora repeated. "Our primary mission is to assist Tech Ishin in reaching the objective. Our *secondary* mission is to conduct observations and gather data on Canary 6. It was a heavily farmed area in the Sapien Epoch, and could yield a lot of new information."

Keeping his comsys low so as not to be overheard, Omu leaned over to his partner and muttered, "Would ya believe it? They gave us a barking sci-phile!"

Xixuan, big and shaggy and blue-lipped, shrugged. Shrugging was his primary mode of communication, even though, as a gunner, he was allowed to use Deep Male, the Arms Div's most coveted voice. Omu had, however, become pretty good at reading the various shrugs of Xixuan Lao over the course of their partnership.

"Just keep quiet and get it over quickly, eh?" he said.

Xixuan nodded.

They were marched out of the briefing room in short order, down a hall and across the complex to the Slingshot—which was the affectionate nickname the locals had given the transfer-cannon at Lis.

Scout Shani, conscientious as the partner of Reiji Shibo must be, looked around and frowned. "They did not assign us a medic," she observed.

"Acquisitions mix-up back home," Omu said from behind her. "Double-booked the Alpha's regular. Had to pull in someone from outside his pack. They're on their way."

But even as Discovery Intent settled themselves into the transfer shell, strapping into the impact harnesses that would prevent them from being pulverized upon landing, there remained an empty seat which went unfilled until they were practically ready to be loaded. Then there were raised voices outside. Someone barked. The shell rocked and a moment later the seventh member of their team climbed in.

She wore the red star of Arms Div above her white medic band, but aside from that she didn't look Arms Div. She was unnaturally tall and lanky, and her face was so long and narrow it looked like she could stab people with it.

"Aw cripes," said Reiji. "They sent us a flipping *Borazynes?*" There was a *thump* as his partner silenced him.

Their medic, if she heard, didn't respond. She scanned her tag at the shell's monitor and began briskly strapping herself in, carefully threading her long limbs through the harness.

"Medic Ksanos," she said, raising a deferential hand to Alpha Zora when he saw her. "I'm Sochi's replacement." Her comsys had a slight accent to it—clearly not Arms Div standard, but then medics didn't usually use the standard voice; it helped to separate them from the combatants.

"Charmed," said Alpha Zora gruffly. "Hope you know what we're getting into, Med, 'cause you missed the briefing."

"Canary 6," the medic replied. "I was told to expect the worst."

Ranger Omu laughed at that, but any further discourse with the newest member of their team was cut off by the sealing of the shell. Silence fell inside as it jerked and shuddered, the flight foils being checked. Alpha Zora flipped around in his harness and went through his pre-flight check with the ground crew.

Xixuan, resting on the knowledge that his alpha was the only member who needed to remain conscious during the transfer, went to sleep. He continued to sleep even as the shell was loaded into the cannon and the big countdown light began to flash.

"Hey, hey," said Reiji, "I just thought of something."

"You need to use a fencepost, Scout?" Omu growled.

"Nah, man, I'm a *professional*," Reiji said. "I was just thinking: they're cannoning us to an island, right? Well, it's an island that don't got no transfer-cannon of its own, right?"

"Please be advised, ignition will begin in ten . . . " the control tower's voice began the countdown.

"I was just wondering, once we're there—"

" . . . five . . . four . . . three . . . "

"—how are we going to get b—"

" . . . one. Launch sequence initiated."

Scout Reiji's last word was drowned in a monstrous *bang* as the cannon ignited and sent the shell rocketing out the barrel. Bursting from the muzzle it arched up into the sky leaving a small trail of flame in its wake before disappearing into the clouds.

Part One

THE ODDITY WAS A STRANGE, complicated place that Alister didn't pretend to understand, not even after all the time he'd spent living in it. The rooms were strange. The way new ones would come and go seemingly at random was downright unnerving. The table in the center of the place, though it was barely visible under the heap of junk and artifacts, never actually overflowed. And the cockpit . . . Alister didn't want to think about the cockpit. It was a wall filled with monitors and blinking lights and had fiber-optic cables running up and down either side. A narrow passage leading down to the front door split the wall in half, with a swivel chair on either side, allowing comfortable access to the banks upon banks of round, glowing, colored buttons—each of which played a different note when pressed. Alister gathered they worked a bit like a keyboard, but he was blowed if he knew how to operate them. The Professor and Elo—not to mention *Dave*—seemed to intuit their meaning, and banged away happily with hands, paws and tentacle-arms respectively, creating a sound which, though not unbearable, was not quite music, either.

Alister couldn't bring himself to touch it. He knew—just *knew*—that if he did he would do the transuniversal traveler equivalent of driving them off a cliff. The flashing lights were distracting, the *noises* the Oddity made as it traveled (or, " . . . brought universes of suitable compatibility close and integrated with their anchor points," as Professor Odd said) were unnerving. These were mostly *bongs* and chimes and tinkles, and gave Alister an uncomfortable, undecided feeling. And he simply couldn't make head or tail of the keyboard no matter how many times it was explained to him.

Currently it was Elo's turn, and she sat on her haunches on the floor with her front paw-hands on the edge of the keyboard and nosed Alister's left arm encouragingly.

"It's all a matter of figuring out what the colors mean to *you*," she explained patiently. "I see colors differently from the Professor, and she sees them differently from you. Dave probably sees something *completely* different."

"I CAN PERCEIVE A WIDER RANGE OF ELECTROMAGNETIC RADIATION THAN ALL OF YOU," came Dave's abrasive artificial voice from the direction of the kitchen alcove, where he and Professor Odd had been occupied for the last few hours working on something they were calling "Breakfast, sort of. Maybe. Hopefully one day. Elo, go take Alister and teach him how to drive, would you? It's far too crowded in here . . . "

Which was why Alister was now sitting uncomfortably at the left-hand console, listening to Elo try to explain the keyboard.

"Yes, anyway," said Elo with determined brightness, "just . . . let your mind relax. Stop imagining that the keys need labels on them to make sense. Figure out what they mean *to you*."

"What, you mean make something up, like?" Alister said. "Say, that's the key that makes it so all the other keys just play music? Or, *that* key is the one that searches for universes that don't contain dangerous things that will try to kill me?"

Elo laughed, her long canine mouth opening wide and displaying a mouth full of healthy, ivory-colored teeth. "Nothing so complicated. But you *could* maybe have a sequence of keystrokes that does that. Say, pressing *that* key means you want to change function and then hitting those keys over there in the red-blue-green order turns the bottom row into a piano keyboard, but hitting them in the blue-green-red order gives you a pipe organ. You need *layers* of function. Remember, you're working with the infinite multiverse, you need as many options as your brain can hold."

"But these are all *my* ideas," Alister said, trying to keep from wailing. "*You* don't have a 'change function' key, do you?"

"Sure I do," said Elo. "The Professor does too. We use ours to switch between sorting universes, viewing universes, and portal management. The Oddity does so many different things there's no way for one keyboard—or set of keyboards, in this case—to be able to cover it all."

"*But . . .* " said Alister, gripping the sides of his head—his hair was finally getting long enough to be graspable again— "*Your* 'change function' key is *a different key* from the Professor's?"

"Yes, exactly!" said Elo, and her fluffy golden tail thumped happily against the floor. "That's the thing about the Oddity. It reads its pilot's *intentions* and develops a new language for each driver. You just need to start building a language with it."

Alister groaned and rubbed his eyes. It felt like his brain was trying to escape through his ears. "What if I change my mind halfway through?" he asked.

Elo frowned, her ears drooping outward. "You *can*, technically. It's practically impossible to get your system absolutely perfect right from the start, but I don't recommend making any major changes—that could confuse the Oddity."

"I don't want the Oddity to become confused," Alister moaned, shuddering at the thought. It would probably lose his room and his carefully constructed wardrobe of not-too-garishly-colorful clothes.

"Look, it's not so bad," Elo insisted. "I'll walk you through the steps of making a portal, and you do the button pressing. Just . . . try not to think of it as operating a machine. It's more like . . . like you're *dancing* with someone. Someone who's *really good* at dancing but has never danced with *you*. You just need to show the Oddity how you dance, and she'll do the rest."

"Dancing . . ." said Alister, staring at the rack of buttons and feeling ready to cry in frustration. "Right."

"First you want to search for a suitable universe," Elo said.

"And how do I do that?" Alister asked, resigned.

"Well, where do you want to go?"

Alister sat back and thought about it.

"Somewhere nice," he said. "Like where you'd go on holiday. A tropical island, maybe."

"Oo, that sounds nice," Elo said. "Okay, so first you'll need a button to tell the Oddity you want to search universes. Pick one and press it."

Alister picked a big, blue button near the center of the keyboard. He pushed it delicately with one finger. It made a loud *bing* noise, and to his alarm all the lights blinked, and a faint hum started up from behind the console.

"That's okay," Elo said, patting his elbow. "It just means the Oddity is listening. Now, you'll want a button to tell it to search for worlds within that universe, and a button to tell it you want a world with a particular place."

Alister picked two buttons near the big blue button and pressed them. *Bing, bong.* There was also a faint tinkle of a bell that echoed in the distance . . . and kept echoing. It was like the Oddity was waiting for him.

"Right. Now the Oddity needs to know what *kind* of place you're looking for. So you need buttons to define a human-compatible world, what kind of climate you want, and what location you want. You can, of course, get more and more specific the better you get to know the Oddity, but we're just in basic introductions here so we'll keep it simple."

"Simple . . . " Alister repeated with a hollow laugh. He decided on a friendly greenish-blue button to mean he wanted an earth-like world, a warm orange button to mean he wanted a pleasant climate, and a bright yellow button to mean an island. He pressed them dutifully and waited.

A gentle vibration ran through the console, beginning under his feet before traveling up through the banks of keys, making the columns of lights shudder. The piping behind the light brackets filled with glowing liquid, making them shine in shades of gold and green, and a string of pure white lights sent a star shooting up from the far console, arching over the corridor, before falling down to land in an explosion of flashing colored lights beside Alister's right hand, leaving the white light blinking on and off. The blank blue screens that hung in walls studded with glowing buttons flickered to life and began showing different blobs of color, slowly shifting and flowing into one another.

"Okay, now you have your worlds. You can see them there," Elo said, pointing at the screens.

"All I see are bits of color," Alister said.

"Yes," said Elo. "Those *are* worlds. You just need to learn to *read* them."

"How do I do *that?*" Alister whined. "Can *you* read them?"

"Not these," Elo said cheerfully. "The Oddity's talking to *you.* I can only read it when it's talking to me—or the Professor. I'm pretty good at reading the Professor's code."

Alister fought the urge to collapse and rest his forehead against the nearest keyboard.

"How can I learn to read it if I don't have the faintest idea what it *means?*" he said instead.

"Well," said Elo. "Think about what you've done so far. What color and button choices you've picked to mean certain things. The Oddity builds its code off the choices *you* make. The more you tell it, the finer the code gets, the more detailed its descriptions will be. Right now these are pretty general, but you should be able to tell the difference between them."

Forcing his eyes upward, Alister examined the screens once more. There were twelve of them: two rows of six. Each one was currently showing morphing blobs of colors, twisting and spreading at random. After watching them for a while, Alister decided that the ones on the top row looked altogether warmer than the ones on the bottom, and the one in the lower right-hand corner was downright chilly looking.

"I can tell that some of them are different from each other," he said eventually.

"That's *great,*" said Elo, giving him an encouraging pat on the shoulder. "Now, the best way to learn to read the Oddity's displays is to go *see* the world. That way you can start to associate the Oddity's code with the *actual* world."

"Why can't the Oddity just *show me* what the world looks like?" Alister asked, realizing even as he spoke how petulant he sounded.

"It *is,*" insisted Elo. "It's just speaking in its own language, which is really much better at describing worlds than any picture, you just need to learn it."

Alister sighed and ran his fingers through his short hair, making it stand up comically in the front. This was the farthest he'd gotten driving the Oddity, and even though it felt like he was groping wildly in a sea of random colors, he was also excited at his progress.

"All right," he said, "how do I pick a world?"

"You'll need a button, of course," Elo said. "When I started, I used buttons next to the relevant screen. But it got tiring having to stand up to reach them. Of course, you're taller than me . . . " she trailed off as Alister reached up and pressed a deep purple button directly below the middle-bottom screen.

Immediately the Oddity began to shake. Lights spiraled out from the monitors, and the pattern of colors on the screen Alister selected flowed out to take up all the others, showing more and more details in the form of winking lights and tiny squiggles, like flowing roots, drifting in the clouds of colors.

"Okay, now you have your universe, world and location," Elo said. "From here you can move your location around as much as you like, but that's a bit more complicated so we'll just go with the entry point the Oddity has chosen."

"Thank *goodness*," Alister breathed.

"At this point we're not actually connected to the universe," Elo explained. "To connect, you've got to pull up on this lever here, under my paw."

Alister obediently reached down and grasped the handle that looked a bit like a parking brake. He pulled, and felt resistance.

"Right, now hold it there," Elo said. "You've got the portal breacher open, now you want to bring it into the native space-time continuum. To do that, pull down on that knob." She pointed at a bright red knob by Alister's right shoulder.

Keeping firm hold of the parking-brake lever, Alister grasped the knob and pulled down. It slid smoothly under his hand, and as it went he felt the pressure on the lever decrease. When the knob reached the bottom of its track all the lights flashed, and from deep within the Oddity a great *bonnnng* rang out.

"Aaand we're here!" Elo announced happily. "Er, you can let go now," she added, seeing Alister was still gripping both the knob and the lever as if his life depended on it.

Gently Alister unclenched his hands and backed away from the console so he could peer down the corridor to the front door. This was usually a matte-black square—when the Oddity was unattached—or appeared as the backside of whatever door the Oddity was using to connect with the given universe. Alister had seen it as battered wooden doors, metal grills, sliding doors, once even an aperture formed of tree branches. He had never seen it like *this*.

Where the matte-black door had been, now it looked like someone had put a light behind it so it glowed slightly. Alister was reminded of the frosted glass in lavatory windows. Through the Oddity's door he thought he could see a wide stripe of something pale, and something darker above that, and something paler above *that*. There was a distant sound of roaring, as of wind or the ocean.

"Huh," said Elo. "That's odd." She left Alister's side and went down the steps to the portal and stuck her head out.

"Wait—but—" Alister began, but Elo had already stepped outside.

She was only gone for a moment. Then she was back in, leaping up the steps, her voice breaking into a bark in her excitement.

"Professor, *Professor!*" she yelped. "You *have* to come see what Alister's done! It's *amazing!*"

"I . . . it is?" Alister stammered.

Professor Odd's head, wearing a vibrant magenta wig and with her tentacle curling under her chin, emerged from the kitchen alcove.

"Elo, *please*," she said. "Dave's *almost* got the noodles right—"

"But you *must* come and see!" Elo insisted, jumping up and down and wagging her tail. "Alister's made a *unanchored portal!* A *stable* one!"

Though Dave remained stalwartly parked in front of the stove, that got Professor Odd out of the kitchen in a hurry. Still wearing her apron (bright purple with equally bright red poppies printed on it and matching red frills) and carrying a wooden spoon half covered in white sauce she threaded her way neatly around the table, leaping clean over one of the chairs.

Alister, who had been in the act of getting up, was forced back down into his seat as the Professor and the wolf—*vroknaär*, he had to correct himself—went hurtling past. Only once their footsteps had banged down the stairs and out the door did he dare get up. Looking cautiously around to make certain Dave had not decided to follow, he walked slowly down to the front door.

Up close, the surface of the portal seemed a little misty, and it breathed cool air on him when he reached out a hand to touch it. Instead of meeting resistance, however, Alister's hand passed smoothly through, and on the other side he felt the firm pressure of a cool, gusting wind.

Reassuring himself that both the Professor *and* Elo were on the other side, and Dave was still safely occupied in the kitchen if something went wrong, Alister held his breath and stepped through.

It was like stepping out into a cool overcast day, and when he blinked at the comparative brightness and looked around he saw that was more or less the case.

He was standing on a narrow strip of whitish sand between a gray-blue ocean and a thick forest of emerald-green plants. In the distance he could see the arm of a peninsula jutting out on the horizon, and behind him a steep hill covered in greenery disappeared into the low clouds that swirled above his head.

The smell of salt water and plant life filled his nostrils, driven by a persistent wind. It cut clean through the light cotton shirt he'd chosen that morning (neon blue splashed with lemon-yellow tiger lilies—*thank you Oddity*) and Alister wrapped his arms around his midsection against it.

Finding the beach apparently empty he called "Hello?" and looked around.

"Yes?" came Professor Odd's voice at once, and she appeared from behind the ... the ...

Alister had seen many strange and inexplicable things during his time with Professor Odd. He had been slowly building up a higher and higher tolerance for the wildly unbelievable, but every now and then he saw something that left him reeling, something so far beyond what he considered possible that his mind threatened to quit on him.

This was very nearly one of those things.

The Oddity's portal, which usually wove itself seamlessly into doors, windows, or other apertures, was now a plain black rectangle standing in the middle of an open patch of sand.

It was . . . *wrong*. Wrong like the time Alister had been stuck in a dying pocket universe and had seen the world dissolve, dissipate into the void like ice melting into water.

This was a little like that, only firmer, smaller, and more contained. It still felt like someone had punched a hole in the fabric of reality, but this time it was a carefully constructed hole with hemmed edges that wasn't about to collapse. There was a faint distortion around the outside, like the surface tension in a glass of water when viewed from the side, and the interior was not so entirely black, now that Alister looked more closely. He could see faint patches of color inside it, and thought he could just translate that into the lights of the Oddity's cockpit.

Professor Odd came all the way around and clapped Alister on the shoulder.

"Well, well, *well*, Mr. Bane!" she cried, grinning hugely. "Congratulations! Congratulations *indeed!* Your first portal is *unanchored!*"

"I don't understand . . . " Alister mumbled. "What did I do wrong?"

"Nothing," said Elo, appearing from behind the black rectangle. "It's just . . . wow. It's nearly impossible to get the Oddity to make these. I mean, sometimes it'll make them on its own, but those are usually unstable."

"They move around randomly within the native space," Professor Odd explained. "Like the one that let us into the dying world. But this one . . . *this* one . . . " She gestured proudly. "Solid as a rock."

Frighteningly, that was the moment the black rectangle fizzed, flickered, and then disappeared, leaving them looking through the space where it had been to the low trees and shrubs of the island.

Alister felt his heart plummet.

"Oh *really?*" said Professor Odd, sounding more annoyed than anything else.

Almost apologetically, the rectangle flickered back into existence.

Alister didn't wait. Didn't think. He'd been trapped outside the Oddity before, and he had no wish to repeat the experience.

His feet dug into the sand as he shot himself toward the portal. Kicking up debris behind him, he threw his shoulders through the blackness, reaching out with his arms to catch himself on the stairs of the Oddity.

He lay there, gasping and trembling, only to find the portal was still perfectly live and functioning behind him.

A shadow crossed it, stopped, and put its hands on its hips.

"That was rather foolish, Mr. Bane," came the Professor's voice, slightly muzzy and distant. "What if it had gone off while you were passing through? You could have been severed. Not a good way to go. Not pleasant at all."

"I'm *fine*," Alister called back through the portal. "But I don't think it's so *stable* after all. Now get back in here before—"

Like a light going off, the pale glow faded and the door went black and dormant.

"That..." Alister said. "Before *that* happens! That was *exactly* what I was afraid of!"

He waited for another minute, just to make sure, but it didn't flick on again; the portal was gone.

He realized, as he got shakily to his feet, that the Professor did have a point: what *would* have happened if it had shut off *while he was in the middle of it?* He shuddered to think.

Of course, this was not much better. Now he was stuck inside, and Professor Odd and Elo were stuck *outside*, in the Oddity-knew-where. And Alister didn't speak Oddity.

Fortunately, there was someone who did.

"*Da-ave!*" he called. "Leave off breakfast, I need your help!"

"*See?*" Professor Odd said to the empty air where the portal had been. "*That* could have happened! And where would that have left you if you'd been in the middle of it, Mr. Bane? In two places at once, I should think, and not at all happy about it. Not at *all*." She put her hands on her hips and jerked her chin triumphantly.

Elo came and stood by her side. They waited. The portal did not come back.

"Sorry," said the wolf in a small voice. "I guess it wasn't as stable as I thought."

"For an *unanchored* portal it was *very* stable," Professor Odd said generously. "You were quite right to show me. It was *marvelous*—I didn't know the Oddity had it in her."

"It *does* leave us in something of a problematic situation," Elo allowed, looking around at the deserted beach.

"Not at all," said Professor Odd, feeling under her apron for the pockets of her baggy trousers (pinstriped electric blue today with matching braces). After some fiddling she produced something that looked like a compass with an extendable antenna. Pulling this out (for almost two feet), she held up the strange device at arm's length above her head and turned in a slow circle, then she brought her arm back down and inspected its little round face.

"Oh!" she said. *"Interesting . . . "*

"Oh, dear," sighed Elo, who knew what *that* tone of voice meant.

"No, no, everything's quite all right," said Professor Odd, pushing the antenna back in and slipping the device into her pocket. "Mr. Alister will get our Dave to open a proper portal, of course, so we'll need to head for the nearest proper *anchors*. We just have a bit of a *walk* ahead of us, is the thing. I know this universe, you see, and I know where we are in it."

Elo perked her ears and gazed expectantly at the Professor, who grinned.

"You'll *like* this," she said. "Well, maybe you won't. *I* think it's funny, anyway. Would you believe it? We're on one of the *Canary Islands!*"

Things began to go wrong rather before the shell landed, but only just. Good thing, too, Ranger Omu thought. If things had gone *really* wrong before they'd landed there would probably be very little of Discovery Intent left. As it was, the Alpha had been injured and everyone else badly shaken.

It was all a bit of a blur to Omu, who had been rudely awakened by alarm bells blaring inside the shell. He'd heard Alpha Zora shouting at them to get into crash positions and then . . . then *unpleasantness* had happened. He'd bit his tongue and heard Reiji, the stupid kid, screaming that stupid Shibo scream, and then they'd crashed.

Of course, shells were *supposed* to crash. They were built for that. Part of being built for that meant that they came equipped with a parachute to slow their descent and huge air balloons on the outside that inflated moments before impact. When everything worked *perfectly* the chute deployed and slowed the shell down enough that it didn't simply explode on impact, and then the balloons inflated and it crashed into the ground, bounced a couple of times, before finally rolling to a stop—with its contents relatively undamaged.

Omu wasn't sure if something had gone wrong with the chute or the balloons, but *something* had broken so they hit a lot harder than they should have. The shell cracked open and didn't so much *bounce* as thud into the ground and then skid for an awful long way, crashing through plant matter and tumbling over bumpy terrain. By the time it finally came to a stop both the regular and emergency power systems had been compromised, and instead of opening, flower-like, as it should have to let them out, it just sat there and steamed faintly.

It turned out to be just as well that the outer shell had cracked, because Omu and Xixuan, being the largest, had been obliged to pry the two halves apart so that Med Ksanos, being the *narrowest*, could slip out and open the shell manually. Omu had to crank up the speakers on his comsys all the way so she could hear his instructions through the crack, since the Medic hadn't been trained for emergency procedures with trans-cannon shells. He was in a thoroughly rotten mood by the time the side panel finally fell away and they were able to get out, and then they'd found out what had happened to their alpha.

The alpha of a group always sat in the pilot seat of a shell. This allowed them access to what rudimentary controls were available, but it was also the most vulnerable position in a crash. Alpha Zora had suffered for that.

They had set up a triage tent over the remains of the shell, that being the clearest, most level patch of ground, and Omu Akit had found himself suddenly thrust into the unwelcome position of temporary alpha. Worse, he wasn't sure exactly how *temporary* his alpha-hood would turn out to be.

When Ksanos had initially emerged from the triage tent, pulling off her gloves and smoothing down her long hair, she'd robotically announced that, although she had every expectation that Alpha Zora would make a full recovery, she was relieving him of command for the remainder of the mission.

"His injury, while not lethal, is physically incapacitating," she intoned. "I do not believe he will be able to function as a team leader on such an active mission. However, the reason I cannot allow him to continue in command is that his comsys has been irreparably damaged."

There was a low groan from the assembled team. A grunt could continue to work with a damaged comsys, since all they had to do was follow orders. But if an alpha couldn't give orders they couldn't be an alpha, and you couldn't communicate, let alone give orders, without a comsys.

"Would a transplant be possible?" he asked hopefully. Sometimes it was possible to transplant a lower member's comsys to a team leader, in extreme situations.

Med Ksanos shook her silky head. "The plug was damaged. I do not have the equipment or the personnel to conduct a full root transplant."

Scout Reiji groaned audibly at that, but the Boraznes's razor-thin head remained turned to Omu. "Ranger Omu, I believe you have seniority. I can assure you he is cognizant enough to hand over the mission orders concerning our objective. I will leave you two alone."

"No!" exclaimed Tech Ishin, jumping to his feet. Omu was so taken aback by his intensity that he sank back against the tree which was currently serving as his seat. "No, he *can't* be relieved of command! I . . . I can fix his comsys, I'm *sure!*"

Well, *that* was a relief. Omu relaxed again.

Ksanos narrowed her eyes at the smaller dog. "I cannot prevent you trying," she allowed. "But I'm still putting Ranger Omu in temporary command."

"*Temporary,* yes, *temporary,*" Ishin squeaked, sidling up to the loose flap of cloth which was serving as a door to the tent. Ksanos, who was still partially standing in it, moved aside but didn't leave her post.

Omu Akit glared at her, but kept a strong hold on his comsys so he said nothing aloud. Being temporary alpha meant he didn't have access to the mission orders; he simply had to keep everyone calm until the original alpha could take command again. Which meant . . .

"Well *shucks,* Alph," said Reiji, who'd been sitting comfortably in the crotch of a tree. "What should we do in the meantime?"

Omu felt his hackles rising at the familiar nickname. It was a brazen sign of insubordination, but he wasn't in a position to discipline Reiji . . . *yet.*

"*You* are going to do your job," he snapped. "You and Shani are going to scout us a perimeter. One kilometer radius from the triage tent. I want reports every hour. *Get!*" He raised the volume as Reiji's comsys lit up in advance of a reply.

Without a word his partner adjusted her light pack and disappeared into the undergrowth, and the little Shibo followed her.

"As for you, Xixuan," Omu said, not turning to look at his own partner. "Wipe that smiley face off your comsys and help me get the damn radio working."

Alister stood behind Dave's panvironment suit and said, as calmly as he could: "What do you mean you can't reopen the portal?"

"IT IS NOT MY PORTAL TO REOPEN," Dave replied testily. Of course, his synthesized voice *always* sounded a little aggravated, so Alister didn't consider it a good indicator of the creature's mood. A better one would be the fact that he'd had to practically drag Dave, panvironment suit and all, away from the kitchen. Warm smells of cooking food and the sound of bubbling still emanated from that direction, and Dave's external camera (mounted on a track so that it could look 360° around his barrel-shaped suit) kept swinging around to get a glimpse of it.

"Your soup or pasta or *whatever* it is you're making can *wait*," Alister snapped. "The *Professor's* stuck out there, *and* Elo."

"YOU MISUNDERSTAND ME," intoned Dave. "I CAN RE-OPEN THE PORTAL; IT WILL SIMPLY NOT BE IN THE SAME PLACE YOURS WAS."

Alister dragged a hand over his forehead and down past his eyes.

"How far away will your portal be?" he asked.

"I DO NOT KNOW," Dave replied. "I DO NOT HAVE EXACT COORDINATES FOR YOUR PORTAL. THE ODDITY IS NOT BEING COOPERATIVE. I WILL DO MY BEST."

His arms, all ten of them (octopus-like, but now encased in heavy-duty fabric) sprang through apertures arrayed in a line below the domed top of his panvironment suit, and began pounding keys. Alister stood back respectfully, keeping an eye on the front door.

After a moment the place gave a sort of shiver—it raised the hairs on Alister's forearms—and Dave slid the red knob down until the Oddity went *bonng*.

"THERE," he said, "THAT IS THE BEST I CAN DO. NOW PLEASE, DO NOT BOTHER ME; BREAKFAST IS A DELICATE OPERATION."

He turned and trundled off around the table. Alister barely stayed to watch him go. He fairly leapt down the stairs and then stopped, prudently, and examined the door that was now in place of the matte blackness that had been there before.

It was made of metal, rusted and streaked from water, with something growing under the bottom of it. Shrugging to himself Alister pushed down the handle and thrust it open.

Bitter cold air flowed inside. Alister caught a glimpse of a metal structure overrun with vegetation, and high above, a pale blue sky. Then he shut the door firmly and went back up the steps into the Oddity. He passed by the kitchen alcove, climbed up the ladder to the second story, and padded around the catwalk until he came to his room. He went in, went to his closet, and pulled out all the warm clothes he could find.

This turned out to be quite a lot: the Oddity had provided him with a hooded, fur-lined parka, boots with sheepskin on the inside, a variety of sweaters in obnoxious colors, and a wide selection of gloves, mittens, scarves, and hats. Alister picked the sweater that made him feel the least like vomiting (bright green with yellow zig-zags), a pair of pink gloves, the boots and the parka. He pulled on a knit hat made of wool dyed in the colors of the rainbow, and went back downstairs.

This time when he poked his head out the door he felt the cold only as a chill breath across his nose, and he stepped carefully into it.

He appeared to be on the outside of a building. It was tall and white—even now with rust showing through and vines creeping up through the crannies—and from where he stood Alister could look out over a railing and down to a patch of thick green forest, from which other structures jutted, in varying states of ruin.

Despite the chill the day was bright and sunny, and as Alister squinted outward he saw that he was standing on an island flanked by a sea of frothy white clouds. There was no sign of the real ocean, or the beach, and none whatsoever of Professor Odd.

"Well *bugger* this," Alister said. His voice rang out uncannily in the chill quiet air, and far away the noise set off a flock of birds hidden in the greenery.

"The Canary Islands weren't named after the birds," Professor Odd remarked as she picked her way through the thick, wet forest, climbing up gullies and over cliffs. "The birds were named after the islands. The *islands*—well, they all have their own names, really. But they were called *canary* because they were supposed to be home to huge dogs."

"Were they?" Elo asked from around the Professor's knees. With the rough terrain she was moving on all fours, following easily in the Professor's tracks.

"Not sure, actually," Professor Odd said cheerfully. "I've yet to find a universe of the proper age in order to see for myself. I *think* what the European explorers saw were what we call giant sea lions, actually."

"Canary…" muttered Elo to herself. "Canary, canari, *canine.*"

"That's the trick," Professor Odd said, gently lifting aside a plant with huge, frond-like leaves. It sent a shower of dew over both of them, and the Professor shivered involuntarily.

"Are you getting cold?" Elo asked, concerned. As she was naturally blessed with a thick, double-layered golden coat of fur and was on top of that wearing a practical denim jumpsuit, the island's cool temperature had come as a pleasant change. Professor Odd, on the other hand, had no such natural insulation, and was only wearing a pair of trousers, a thin cotton shirt, her apron and a wig.

"A bit nippy for me," she allowed, tiptoeing along a fallen tree trunk that spanned a ravine. "If I keep physically active, however, I should not become hypothermic. I hope. I've never *been* hypothermic as far as I can remember. It might be interesting!"

"I'd rather not find out," Elo was saying as they thrashed through the upper branches of the tree to get to firm ground. Then they came out of the foliage abruptly, and she had to suppress a groan.

Something had been through here and cleared the forest as effectively as a wrecking ball. Broken stumps and the pale underbellies of leaves showed unusually bright under the overcast sky, and some of them looked a little singed.

Professor Odd was standing in the middle of the wreckage, looking up and down the path left by whatever had been through.

"Huh," she said, and leapt nimbly up onto the remains of a large tree. Shading her eyes with her hands she peered around. "*Hmm . . .* " she said, frowning a little.

"Oh, no," said Elo, forging through the debris field to where the trees began again. "No, no . . . we don't have *time* to go exploring, Professor," she said. "By your reckoning the nearest door is at the top of the caldera—it could take us *all day* to get up there. Now let's just leave this . . . whatever *this* is . . . to the natives to handle. We don't have to get involved in every . . . " She trailed off as Professor Odd pivoted on one heel and went bounding down the swath of cleared forest.

"They went *this-a-way!*" the Professor called back over her shoulder. "Come *on,* I think they might be in *trouble!*"

Elo made a noise between a growl and *"Damnit,"* and slunk back into the cover of the trees. While the Professor had been looking, she'd been doing some smelling, and she hadn't liked what she had found. She hadn't liked it at all.

Tech Ishin was inside with Alpha Zora for a very long time. Omu Akit didn't mind. The radio package had been damaged in the crash, and it was taking all his patience not to throw the whole thing down the nearest ravine. There were plenty of ravines tempting him. All the Canaries had been (or were still) volcanic islands, and Canary 6 boasted a particularly large caldera whose top was hidden from view beneath a blanket of clouds. The ground—once fertile farmland during the Sapien Epoch—was now a rutted maze of overgrown rock, jagged and cracked. Some of those cracks went down a long way, and in their depths water still ran in the irrigation channels carved by the humans. Such a crevasse would make a suitable home for the infernal device that was currently resisting Omu's best efforts at repair.

"Would you like me to try?" Xixuan offered. After taking apart the battered box for Omu the large dog had stood aside and kept resolute guard. They were both watched by the narrow gaze of Med Ksanos, still standing by the triage tent, her arms folded and her comsys half shut down.

"No," snapped Omu, glaring at the mess of wiring on the radio's underbelly. Somewhere in there a wire had gone wrong, and he was neutered if he knew which one.

There was a violent crashing in the undergrowth, and Scout Reiji tumbled into the clearing, hackles high and comsys ablaze.

"Alph, *Alph!*" he shrieked, accompanied by an undignified yapping. "Code Blue! Red! Whatever means majorly serious! We got a *breach,* Alph! Someone's headed our way!"

Omu Akit looked up from the radio, perfectly ready and willing to bite the dumb Shibo's head off. Fortunately for Reiji, he was a safe distance away.

"Then what are you doing *here?*" he growled, backing up his words with a real growl from deep in his throat. "We're on a Class Six priority mission; why didn't you take them into custody?"

"Would have, Alph, *would* have," Reiji said. He was so excited he was actually bouncing from foot to foot. "But I thought it was better to hang back and *watch*—which Shani's *doing*, Alph, don't look so angry—because, you see, I think *they* are a *human*. That's why I came back to tell you . . . since the radios aren't working . . . "

"Oh *eat* the master-damned radio!" Ranger Omu shouted, throwing it down in frustration. "Reiji, there *are no humans* left on Earth. Haven't been since the before the Long Winter. They are an *extinct species,* Scout. And if you think this is some hilarious joke for your new Alpha, you've got another thing coming you pea-brained son of a—"

He froze. By the triage tent, Med Ksanos's narrow head had turned like a compass needle and now *her* hackles were rising too.

The wind had shifted, wafting a new scent into the crash-zone-turned-campsite. It was a strange smell—utterly foreign, potent, with an undercurrent of something that might have been . . . cheese?

Omu Akit was still puzzling over it when a piercing wail came up from the trees, in the direction of the trail of destruction left by the shell's landing.

"That's Shani's signal," hissed Reiji. "It's within two hundred meters now. Orders, Alph?"

"It's *Alpha Omu* to you," Omu said. "Xixuan, cover the tent and the Medic. Reiji, come with me, and *tell* me you know how to use your sidearm."

"I'm the top score in my sharpshooter club," Reiji said promptly, but without his usual cockiness. He seemed hesitant. "Um . . . we're not gonna *attack* it, are we Alph—Alpha? I mean, if it is *human*—"

"It *won't* be human," Omu declared, pulling out his shotgun and going to look across the battered and broken remnants of the shell. Like that he could look up the path it had cleared through the forest. He rested the barrel of his gun across a relatively flat piece of shell and waited.

The scent, clear and cutting and a little bit synthetic and— yes, that was *definitely* cheese—grew steadily stronger.

And then, over a line of broken stumps, something short and shaggy and bright, bright magenta came bobbing into view. It was followed by an oval head, a pair of rectangular shoulders, and below that a bipedal body wearing the most extraordinary clothes Omu Akit had ever seen.

"Great master . . . " he breathed, his grip on the gun going slack. "If *that's* a human, you can call me a saber-toothed *cat.*"

The not-human but human-like thing seemed to hear them. It quickened its pace and raised an empty hand, jerking it back and forth.

"Alpha," said Reiji in a small voice. "I think it's *waving* at us . . . "

"Hellooo!" called the thing, tripping closer through the wreckage of trees. *"Buongiorno? Konichiwa?* Are you lot all right?"

It was speaking. Through its mouth. Omu Akit had heard that humans had been able to do that. He stared in fascination, feeling his own jaw go lax.

Then the thing crossed an invisible boundary, and Omu's instincts took over. Snapping his gun to bear he put the volume of his comsys all the way up and directed the speakers in the creature's direction.

"Hold where you are," he commanded. "This is a controlled area. Identify yourself!"

The thing paused. It seemed surprised.

"Controlled?" it said. "By whom? I don't recall La Palma being inhabited at this point in your narrative."

"We are a team dispatched by the United Breeds of Euro-Asia, this is our territory—now *identify* yourself!"

"Euro-Asia?" said the thing. It put a hand up and scratched under its reddish-pink hair. "Then why are you speaking *English?*" To Omu's horror, a third limb had emerged to drape over its shoulder: this one was long, boneless, pinkish in color but speckled with green, and shaped like the arm of an octopus. Omu Akit had eaten octopus once. He hadn't liked it.

"If by *English* you mean *Human Standard*—" he began, then wondered why he was essentially conducting an interview across a wrecked trans-cannon shell and several meters of ruined forest. "Which isn't relevant to you. Get on the ground. Hands, arms—whatever you got—keep them in the open!"

"Oh," said the creature, its shoulders sagging. "Military. I see. Well, ordinarily I'd be *happy* to cooperate, but you see you're going about this *all wrong*. Now, why don't you put the gun down, and we can have a *nice,* civil talk about things. And maybe you could lend me a coat?"

"Get. On. The *ground!*" Omu Akit shouted through his comsys. The distortion coming out of the speakers was awful, but it was still understandable.

"You *really* don't want to do that," said the thing. "I only want to help you."

"Reiji, flank her," Omu snapped. "You! *Thing!* On the ground before I *put* you there!"

The thing put her hands in the pockets of the strange, frilly garment that covered her front, and sighed. "That's *really* too bad of you," she said, and seemed about to go on, when there was a crashing in the bushes, and Scout Shani stumbled into view.

She stumbled because she was being marched, frog-like, in front of . . . of . . .

Omu Akit felt his hackles go up and a growl swelling in his throat. Instincts he thought had been thoroughly bred out of him came welling up, his sight bleeding red, and the desire to fight—or to flee, he wasn't sure—took hold in his pounding head and rendered him frozen.

The thing that held Shani was *not* a dog. Not even an old, quadrupedal type. It reminded him of technical illustrations he'd been shown of *wolves,* but not quite: it walked on its hind legs, and its forepaws were clearly somewhere between a hand and a paw. It had deep golden fur and triangular ears—in that way it did not look unlike Omu Akit himself—but there was a leanness about its snout, a feral slope in its shoulders, and a stringiness about its limbs that screamed *wild.* Its head looked strangely naked, for it wore no comsys, and its blue cloth overalls had clearly been sewn to different standards than the uniforms he and the rest of Discovery Intent wore.

Omu Akit sniffed, and now he could smell it—half masked by Shani's own scent—it was something strong and pungent.

Like dog, but also so *not* like dog that it was frightening in its *wrongness.*

And then . . . *and then* . . .

Then the not-a-dog *opened its mouth* and *spoke.*

"Okay you *clowns,*" it said in a voice like a snarl. "Let's get one thing clear: we're gonna do this *my* way!"

It might have occurred to Omu to resist; to take some course of action other than simply rolling over on his back and submit-ting to this wolf—dog—*thing* . . . but Reiji had already thrown down his sidearm and come out from cover with his hands in the air.

"Okay, okay," he squeaked, his comsys-voice sounding tinny and weak compared to the wolf—dog—*thing's* full-throated growl.

Omu Akit reluctantly lowered his weapon but stayed behind the broken shell.

"Right," said the wolf—dog—*thing,* "I'm Marhütz Elo of the Black Thirteen Auxiliary, this here is Professor Odd. You lot seem to be in a bit of a pickle. We'll help you out—but you need to put down your guns *right now.*"

He shouldn't listen to him—her?—but something in the way she spoke her orders—*spoke!* With her *actual mouth!*—made him want to curl into a little ball and submit.

"Xixuan," he projected over his shoulder. "Stand down. We got unknown factors incoming, and they have a hostage."

"Elo, what on all the earths do you think you're *doing?*" Professor Odd asked, but without rancor.

Elo, still concentrating on keeping the wiggly anthropomor-phic dog in a firm grip, grunted. "Moving things along," she growled. "You would have been standing off with that stupid Akita *all* day otherwise, and it probably would have ended with someone getting shot."

"I didn't think so," Professor Odd said. "He seemed reason-able enough. Isn't he reasonable, your boss?" she directed this last question at the dog still in Elo's grip.

She was significantly smaller than Elo. She had a shorter, fox-like face and almond shaped brown eyes. She was light beige, mostly, with white markings around her face and down her neck. She wore a camouflage flak jacket and trousers and a harness on top of that. The most curious piece of equipment, however, was the contraption strapped to her head.

Part helmet and part headset, it had a collection of wires and electrodes that rested against her forehead and behind one ear, speakers mounted on the front and sides, and a small liquid-crystal display on her cheek under one eye. At the Professor's question this contraption lit with little blue lights, and a voice spoke from the speakers. In clear, clipped words it said:

"I am not authorized to divulge that information." Below her left eye, the LCD display flashed a simple emoticon; a colon, followed by a bar.

"Well, I suppose we can ask him soon enough," Professor Odd said cheerfully.

They were approaching what looked like the remains of a crude aircraft. A ravaged metal exoskeleton was partially visible under swaths of cloth and plastic that looked like deflated airbags or a parachute, or both. This then was the object that had made the track of broken plants and leaves. As they came around its side, Elo could see that part of it had been pried open and a small camp set up among the flattened foliage. There was a triage tent and a partially assembled communications center. There were also four creatures like the one she was currently frog-marching: things that walked on two legs, had opposable thumbs, and yet for all scents and appearances were, essentially, *dogs*.

One of them, the one that had been shouting at the Professor, was significantly larger, with a healthy ruff around his neck. His fur was an earthy tan, save for a darker splash across his face. He also wore one of the headset/helmet things, and his LCD currently had the universal angry face. Behind him, positively quivering, was another, smaller dog, similar to Elo's captive, but where she was beige this one was a vibrant reddish brown.

There was a low whining sound, and a heavy *thunk* of something hitting the ground. This had been made by the largest dog yet—a huge, red dog with a squashed-looking face and a thick, lion-like mane—dropping what looked like a small rail-gun. He had blue lips, and his face was so wrinkled his eyes were visible only as little twinkles in dark crevices. Like the others he wore a flak jacket, though his was dark green, and he also wore a heavy harness which had until recently supported the huge gun and its racks of ammunition.

The fourth dog stood behind the huge red one, squarely in the way of the entrance to the triage tent. Like her comrade she wore a dark green uniform, only hers had a white patch with a red cross sewn to one sleeve. She was tall, narrow, with laid-back ears and long, silky fur the color of silver snow. Her headset was more complicated than the others, and its LCD was blank.

"*Well,*" said Professor Odd, taking in the scene with her hands on her hips. "This is truly remarkable. You really *are* dogs, aren't you? Shiba Inu, if I'm not mistaken," she said, gesturing to the beige one in Elo's grip and the red-and-white one cowering behind the taller dog. Professor Odd's finger swung to him next. "And you're an Akita, I think. That's a *songshi quan,* or Chow Chow, depending on your country. And *you,*" she said, rounding on what was clearly their medic. "A sight hound, I'm pretty sure. Borzoi?"

The dogs stared back at her, nonplussed. Professor Odd grinned at them implacably. "*So,*" she said, clasping her hands together, "what seems to be the problem here?"

This was why you didn't give command—even *temporary* command—to natural-born betas, Ranger Omu thought bitterly as the human—creature—thing that called itself Professor Odd sat down cheerfully by the radio and began snapping pieces together and braiding wires like she did it every day. Perhaps she did.

He had no idea where they had come from. All the sources and reports from Sci Div were resolute in their assertion that *homo sapiens* was an extinct species on Earth, and yet here *was* one—or something very close to one. Omu Akit had to admit that perhaps humans had changed themselves as much as they had changed their dogs. After all, they had hardly any solid records from the events of the Long Winter. No one knew exactly what had become of the humans—only that they were not *here* anymore.

Then there was the *wolf*. She kept talking. *Without* a comsys. It gave Omu chills.

"Is someone injured?" she asked Med Ksanos, practical and businesslike.

Ksanos narrowed her eyes at the wolf. Combined with her already narrow face Omu thought it must be like staring down a knife, but the wolf was unperturbed.

"Our alpha," she said shortly.

"I thought *he* was your boss," said Professor Odd, jabbing her tentacle-arm at Omu.

Ksanos looked pointedly at Omu.

I should have handed over command to her, he thought miserably.

"I'm only the temporary alpha," he explained. "Alpha Zora was injured in the crash. His comsys was broken so he had to be relieved of command. Our tech is trying to fix it."

"I'm sorry?" the wolf said. Her face kept twisting and twitching as she spoke, and it gave Omu the impression that she was telling him more than just her words, but he couldn't understand what.

Just in case the break in communication was two-sided, he explained:

"The comsys"—he tapped his own—"is our only way of communicating. A leader who can't communicate can't lead . . . "

The wolf's pupils rolled skyward, revealing her white sclera, stained dark in the corners. Omu thought she might have been having a seizure, but then her eyes focused on him again and she snorted.

"*What?*" she said. "That's ridiculous. Let me talk to him."

"I cannot allow—" Ksanos began, but Omu had had enough.

"Stand down, Medic," he snapped. "I'll accompany her. If she can get through to the Alpha then it'll be worth the breach of security."

"We're sorry about that, by the way," Professor Odd called. "We promise not to tell anyone else, if that helps."

Omu Akit sighed inwardly and stepped up next to the wolf. Her smell rolled off her: fresh, heady, *fierce*. It was like standing beside a wild animal. A wild animal that talked and was as intelligent—as *sapient*—as any of them.

"Stand aside, Med Ksanos," he ordered.

For a moment it seemed the Boraznes wouldn't. She wavered, her arms crossed defensively, and then like an icy veil she stepped slowly aside.

Tech Ishin, who had clearly been eavesdropping, leapt away from the tent's entrance just a moment too late. Omu Akit caught him by the collar.

"We've got some unconventional assistance," he said. "Get *out*."

"But it's . . . it's—" Ishin, clearly excited and frightened, made a darting gesture, as if he wanted to take hold of the wolf and study her.

Omu remembered what the wolf had done to Shani—and *she* was a trained combatant—and stopped the tech just in time.

"*Out!*" he ordered, and shoved the little white Shibo forcefully toward the door.

Elo knelt by the reclined form on the makeshift bed. He was another of the smaller, fox-like dogs, but where the others were beige, reddish-brown and white, he had bold black markings over his head and tan patches under his eyes that contrasted sharply with his white muzzle. He appeared to have a broken leg, and the remains of his headset/helmet—*comsys*—lay scattered on a nearby table.

Elo left them for now. She was good with electronics, but at the moment she was more interested in what the injured dog was saying in a language that didn't use words—not as humans would recognize them.

The language of Elo's people—the *vroknaär*—consisted not only of a lexicon of grunts, barks, growls and howls, but was combined with an array of facial and body expressions, each as telling and communicative as their vocalizations. Whole conversations could take place using these silent words, and the unspoken language varied as much as the audible one when it came to dialects and accents.

Still, a certain amount was ingrained instinct, and learning to speak in expressions had given Elo exceptional sensitivity to other canine body language. So she took a seat at the head of the stricken dog and said, quite frankly:

"Now, I believe you can understand what I'm saying. You don't know me, and I don't know much about you other than your name's Zora and you're supposed to be the leader of this little pack. I'm Elo. Marhütz Elo. I'm not a dog, as you can see. I'm not a wolf either. I come from a place where wolves evolved into something else. We call ourselves *vroknaär.* I think, whatever you are, that we've got about the same level of basic intelligence, but we've come to it by different means. We'll leave that for now. The point is: I'm trying to help, but to do that I'm gonna need to know some things."

She waited a beat, then continued.

"They tell me your communicator is broken, and you can't speak. That doesn't matter. There's lots of ways to talk without audible words. I'm talking with them right now. I don't know if you can tell."

Can you understand me now? she asked, slipping into the simplest form of visual *vroknaär*-speech she knew. She watched the dog carefully as she spoke, and was disappointed to see his face register only bewilderment overlaying mistrust and fear.

She sighed to herself. Time to take another tack.

"Okay, how about this," she said, switching back to English. "I'll ask you the questions, and you just react in the most natural possible way. Don't *try* to do anything, just relax and let your muscles do the work."

The dog—Zora—gave her the universal look that said: *Huh?*

"Okay," Elo blazed on. "What is your pack, er, team, doing here?"

Searching, said the dog. *Objective. Secret. Only one knows. Secret. Scary. Frightened.*

It was like listening—or, in this case, watching—someone talk in the most basic, primal language. Elo had to do a significant amount of interpretation, but the dog's expressions were so clear and unguarded she was satisfied he was telling the truth. He had never been taught to speak body language, and as a result, had no idea how to lie in it. She went on:

"Where are you from? Do you want to go home?"

Big land. Colder. Mountains. Yes. Home. Yes. Home good. No— no must complete objective. No home until objective. Sad. Scared.

"Why are you sad?" Elo asked, making the Akita next to her jump. "What's scaring you?"

Tech. Tech scares. Orders. Orders were not told until arrival. Did not know. No go home now. No go home.

"How do you know he's *sad*?" the Akita asked, his synthetic voice a jarring contrast to the vague expressions Elo was trying to read.

"Because he told me," she snapped. "Zora, what are your orders? Why can't you go home?"

"What do you mean he can't go home?" Omu asked.

Elo ignored him. At her last question Zora had stiffened visibly. His shocked expression and rigid muscles tried to keep his face still, but the words slipped through anyway.

No extraction. No extraction. Objective more important. Only tech goes home.

Elo leaned back on her haunches and regarded him gravely. She wished she knew more about their world—about their society, about their history—but she was slowly piecing together a picture of the situation, and it was not pretty.

"Omu, who is the tech?" she asked.

No. No. No tell. No tell anything! Zora practically shouted with his face. To Elo's intense interest, Omu Akit seemed entirely oblivious to his words.

"You mean Tech Ishin? He's . . . er . . . he was the little white one . . . "

"Better go get him," Elo said. "He's important. And I've got questions for him."

Omu Akit looked uncertain, but he seemed to already harbor some doubts about the tech, and he ducked out of the tent without objection.

No, bad. No, bad, Zora was saying when she turned back to him.

"Don't worry," Elo said soothingly. "We'll get this sorted out and then you can go home."

No way. No extraction, Zora said.

"We have a way," Elo said, and thought: *it's just a little awkward to get to.*

The tent flap shook violently as Omu Akit stuck his head back in, his comsys ablaze with lights.

"Tech Ishin has *gone*. Disappeared! Took his gear and *left*."

Elo resisted the urge to turn and stare, because Zora had started speaking almost at once.

Gone for objective. Tech knows orders. Always knew orders. Tech can go home.

"Alpha Zora," Elo said, and the dog's attention snapped to her. "What were your *orders?* The ones they didn't let you see until you got here?"

Both the dogs went immediately on edge. Elo wished she could turn to see what Omu Akit was saying with *his* face, but she was too busy concentrating on Zora.

Assist tech. Only tech matters. Only tech's message matters.

"*Where* are our orders?" Omu Akit was saying as he poked around in the corners of the tent. "They weren't in your gear, Alpha. By rights, I need to see them."

Tech took orders. Only us authorized to see them. Only tech matters.

"We don't need to see them," Elo said. "Your alpha just told me."

"*Told* you? But he can't *speak*. I've *been* here. He hasn't said a word!"

"There's more than one way for a dog to talk," Elo said. "Seems to me, you lot have gotten so dependent on those *com-sys* you all wear, you've forgotten how. Mostly. Okay, one last question for you, Zora, and it's in your best interests to answer clearly: *where* is this objective?"

Alpha Zora stared at Elo in a mix of horror and resignation. At the same time, he said:

Summit. Old buildings. Old human *buildings. Objective there.*

"Right," said Elo. "Omu, tell your medic to get back in here. She needs to get Zora ready to travel."

"What, *travel?*" Omu was so surprised he let out a small *yip.*

"*Yes,*" said Elo. "Turns out, your objective is in the same place as *our* objective. That's where your tech has gone, most likely. So we're going too. *All* of us," she added, turning back to the injured dog. "We're going to figure out this *objective* of yours, and then we're sending you home."

* * *

The camp was in an uproar when they emerged. Reiji and Xix-uan were accusing each other of letting the tech slip away. Only Shani had remained at her post, with *dash, full-stop, dash* planted firmly on her comsys. In the middle of it all, Professor Odd was happily fiddling away with the radio. She was now draped in Xixuan's all-weather jacket, and there was a bright pink tinge to her cheeks as she looked up at them.

"So, what's up? It was the tech, wasn't it?" she asked.

"How did you know?" the wolf asked, a little deflated.

"His uniform was different," Professor Odd said, turning back to the radio. "I think you may be in a bit more trouble than you thought," she said, sideways, to Omu.

"Not *now*," Omu said. "Med, we're moving. I need you to get the alpha mobile."

"I'll help!" shouted the Professor, jumping to her feet. "Your radio's fixed, by the way," she added. "What good that is. You know, I don't think it was an accident." As she spoke this last she looked past Omu, at Med Ksanos. Omu felt stymied.

"Just get the alpha ready," he said. "Reiji! Xixuan! Cut that out before I confiscate your comsys!"

Like a silver-and-white shadow, Ksanos disappeared into the tent, followed by the bright red dash of Professor Odd's wig. Reiji backed sulkily down and Xixuan turned to Omu.

"I did not realize the tech was under surveillance," he said reproachfully.

"Neither did I," grumbled Omu. "But it turns out the wolf is a mind reader."

"That's actually my cousin," the wolf said matter-of-factly. "I'm just multi-lingual. Right. Now, I think half your problems have come from people keeping secrets, so I'm just going to say this for everyone to hear:

"You were sent here simply to insure that your tech—this Ishin who's run off—reaches the objective. Near as I can tell, you're not expected to return. There may be some arrangement made for Ishin, but I'm not sure how it will work. This *objec-tive*"—she continued over Reiji's shouts of "I *knew* it! Didn't I say there's no way for us to get *back?*"—"this *objective* is at the summit of this island's caldera. That's where the only remain-ing human installations are, and as it happens, that's where the

Professor and I are heading. Because we *do* have a way home. So we'll accompany you, help you achieve your objective—whatever that is—and then we'll send you all home. Any questions?"

Reiji raised a reluctant paw.

The wolf snapped her attention to him. "Yes?"

"Does this . . . uh . . . " the little reddish Shibo glanced nervously at Omu, "does this mean *you're* the alpha now?"

Shani turned to him, an angry face displayed on her comsys.

"Careful, Scout," Omu Akit said, backing it up with a growl.

The wolf gave him a strange look. Omu Akit found himself wishing, not for the first time, that she wore a comsys. It was impossible to tell what she was feeling.

"Only if Alpha Omu wants me to," she said. "For now, consider myself and Professor Odd your unofficial civilian advisers."

As if in response there was an uproar from the tent—a distressed *yelp!*—and Med Ksanos shot out of it like a bullet. She leapt clean over Elo's head, landed on all fours and then leapt again, all in one graceful movement, then disappeared into the trees. There were a few rustles, and then nothing.

"Permission to pursue!" Shani shouted.

"Permission barking granted," Omu Akit snapped. "And keep in *contact* this time! Remember the radio!" he shouted after her disappearing tail.

"She won't catch her," Xixuan said dourly. "Barking *Boraznes.*"

"Don't underestimate Shani," Reiji said, swelling in defense of his partner. "She always wins at the agility trials."

"The *medic,*" said the wolf, not seeming to hear. "Of *course.* Why didn't I see it before! Professor—" she broke off, having turned to the tent and seen what was sitting there.

Professor Odd was crouching in a tight knot, knees up in her chest, and holding the end of her tentacle-arm squeezed between both hands. Between her fingers red blood was slowly seeping.

"Yes," she said, a little out of breath. "The medic. Don't worry, your Alpha's fine. But I hope you lot get regular vaccines."

"She bit your *arm,*" the wolf said, sounding appalled.

"It'll heal," Professor Odd said, and brightened. "She left all her equipment. I'll tie it up while you guys pack. We need to move. I've just realized what your objective must be."

Omu Akit came and stood in front of her, putting his hands on his hips.

"Talk," he said. "What do you know?"

"Quite a lot, actually," said Professor Odd with an apologetic smile. "I'll explain fully once we get going. It's just—this . . . Canary 6. It's La Palma. The summit you're heading to, that's the site of the *Roque de los Muchachos* observatory. They had some pretty big telescopes up there back in the day. And later, there were *other* things." She shot the wolf one of those *looks* which Omu Akit couldn't understand. But he could understand the way the wolf's ears turned back and her hackles rose.

"Oh," she said. Then: "*Oh. We gotta move.*"

Three dogs ripped through the cold rain forest. The white one, significantly ahead of the other two, ran low to the ground and followed a map laid out on an extension of his comsys. He was weighed down somewhat by his pack, but he was young and athletic—that was one reason he'd been picked for this mission. He moved swiftly up a ridge, climbing up and up into the clouds.

The second dog, far behind but slowly gaining, followed a path half-remembered from her youth. She was older now, tiring more easily, but her long legs were strong, and her spring-like back carried her over the rough terrain. She was unladen, and she slipped through the foliage like a fish through a jungle of seaweed, a flash of white and silver through the greens and browns.

The third dog ran hot on the trail of the second, keeping her nose trained to the scent. Her small, compact form shot through gaps in the undergrowth like a bouncing arrow. Though sometimes she lost ground she would always gain it back again. She was in her element, and after the humiliation she'd suffered at the hands of the wolf her eyes blazed with determination. This was what she'd trained for. What a millennia of breeding had scored into her bones. She ran.

* * *

Alister sat on the metal stairway outside the Oddity, wrapped in his coat and muffler, wearing the least offensive pair of sunglasses the Oddity had provided. These looked rather like they belonged to the windshield of a model jet fighter, and their lenses had a rainbow quality, like that of an oil slick. Alister felt a right fool in them, but the brightness made them necessary.

It must have been morning when they'd come through, because he'd waited for hours before the sun finally reached its zenith. When it was well on its way down again he'd gone back inside and managed to snatch a loaf of bread and a jar of peanut butter from between Dave's waving arms ("I MUST HAVE COMPLETE AUTONOMY WHILE IN THE KITCHEN, PLEASE REMOVE YOURSELF") and now he sat, carving off hunks of bread with his pocket knife and smearing peanut butter over them, feeling the sun warm his face while his back, cast in shadow, remained chilly even through the layers of clothes. He sipped warm water from a thermos and considered what to do next.

By far the safest thing would be to wait where he was. But then, he worried, how would the Professor find them? How was she to know where the portal had opened? And even if she did make her way up here (Dave had assured him this was indeed the same island) how would she find *this* doorway, when it looked as though there were many dilapidated and ruined buildings cowering under the cloak of green-and-brown foliage?

Alister finished off the loaf, wiping the blade of his knife on his sleeve before closing and pocketing it. He drained the last of the water from the thermos, getting to his feet and stepping back inside. Once there he left the thermos on the table and climbed up to his room where he got out his everything bag (one of the few possessions he'd taken from his home universe) and packed a length of rope, a thermal blanket, a first-aid kit, a compass and some flares. Then he went back down the ladder and made another dash into the kitchen to refill the thermos.

"I'm going out," he told Dave. "I'll be back before dark."

"BREAKFAST WILL LIKELY BE READY BY THEN," Dave informed him as he left.

Outside, the afternoon sun lit the tops of the trees, making it look as though they were crowned with green fire, a bright contrast to the shadowy world beneath. They were smallish trees,

Alister realized as he descended the stairs, considerably more sparse than the ones down by the coast. From a few steps above the ground he could still get a pretty good view of the area: a wide, tree-covered plain that sloped gently off toward the north, and disappeared steeply to the southwest.

Far from striking off for the next nearest structure, Alister contented himself by exploring the one the Oddity had attached itself to. From the ground, it appeared as one sheer, white wall, but the area around it was sufficiently flat that Alister was able to hike out far enough to look back at it. From there he was astonished to find that the end of the building rose up into the wide, white globe of an observatory. Monstrously huge and impossible to miss from a distance, it had been entirely cut out from his vision by the angle of the building. And though vines and other climbing plants now traced dark lines across its surface, the overall shape was intact. Now Alister looked, many of the other buildings in the distance had similar, bulbous outlines.

"They're *telescopes*," he murmured to himself.

Adjusting his everything bag so it hung securely against his back, he retraced his steps to the side of the building and began making a slow circuit of its outer wall, looking for a way in.

He found several doors, but they were all either locked or fused shut. One had a tree grown over it: the vine-like branches curling sinuously into the cracks of the door, forcing it open, but now the tree sufficiently blocked it. At last, after he had almost completed his circuit, Alister discovered a wide, square aperture at the base of the wall. It looked like it had once been a vehicular loading dock, but was now so choked with plants it was almost unrecognizable.

Taking out his flashlight Alister stepped cautiously into the building, making soft rustling sounds as he slipped between the plants.

These ended abruptly just inside, like the vegetation line at the entrance to a cave. Alister found himself standing on old, split asphalt with moss growing in the cracks. Above him was a concrete ceiling with ominous water stains, and—yes!—there was a stairway leading up. It had originally been blocked by a metal gate, but Alister easily climbed over this.

The stairs were metal, like the ones outside, but in considerably better shape. They clanged softly as Alister passed over them. They ended in a landing with a fused door, but this one appeared to have been forced open some time in the past, leaving a gap wide enough for Alister to get his arm through. Like that, he was able to nudge it open far enough for the rest of himself to follow.

He found himself in a large, high-ceilinged room lit by long windows. Stripes of vegetation grew in the path of the sunlight, which was currently casting one patch into bright yellow and green. Alister saw the movement of tiny, white-winged insects humming over the leaves and small flowers.

One side of the room appeared to have been a reception area, with wide stairs leading down to a pair of doors that Alister knew he had passed on the outside. The other side ended in a blank wall.

This bothered Alister. Aside from the sunless cave from which he had just emerged, everything here had a dirty, overgrown appearance. This wall was plain and white. *Too* white. Too *clean*. Alister approached it warily, a frown gathering on his forehead.

Something about this place was triggering some unpleasant feelings deep inside him, but he couldn't say what exactly. He reached out a hand to brush against the wall . . .

He saw the red light down in a corner near his foot. He saw it *turn green* . . . and that was all the warning he got before the wall gave a little *grunt* and began to *roll up*, opening at the bottom.

Alister scrambled backward and stood in the doorway of the exit, fighting the urge to run down the stairs screaming. His heart pounded audibly in his chest and his hands shook against the door frame.

The wall was, apparently, fake, and now rolled up and away to reveal an even bigger chamber, dim and shadowy. As Alister watched, fluorescent lights flickered on in the depths, illuminating the base of a giant telescope, which in turn was surrounded by a strange tube-like structure. There was writing on this, spray-painted red through a stencil.

When the wall had stopped moving and silence descended—and more importantly, *no one jumped out of the cracks and attacked*

Alister—he reluctantly left his post by the door and crept up to the newly revealed room. With every step his legs screamed at him to run away, the unpleasant feeling growing stronger and stronger. But he had to know.

Standing on the white line left in the dust and dirt from the retracting wall, Alister could lean in and just read what was spray-painted on the side of the tube.

Somehow, he was not surprised. Somehow, the fear in him had known. And he read, with perfect clarity and horror, the awkward, large capitals:

PROPERTY OF

And below that, in smaller but still legible italics:

The Canary Company

Alister did run then. Rather, he stopped holding his legs back. Out the door and down the metal stairs—*metal stairs!* That had been what had tipped him off!—and out of the cave into the afternoon sunlight. Now every odd shadow, every rustle of branches, seemed to Alister to herald unfriendly people in white hazard suits. Likely with guns. He didn't know how they came to be in this world, which was clearly not his own, but— they had transuniversal technology—they could have found a way . . .

Before he knew it he was clattering up the steps to the Oddity and throwing himself inside, slamming the door shut behind him and leaning his back on it, panting.

"*Dave!*" he gasped. "Dave, we have a *problem.*"

The rattling noises from the kitchen slowed, then stopped altogether. There was a whisper of treads on carpet, and then Dave appeared at the head of the stairs. All ten of his arms— normally tucked safely inside his panvironment suit—were out, encased in their thick cloth sleeves. One of them held a measuring cup, while another held a wooden spoon. All of them were frozen at odd angles, as if he hadn't bothered to move them since leaving the kitchen.

"WHAT PROBLEM," he began, restrained fury leaking into his synthetic voice around the edges, "IS SO GREAT THAT YOU MUST INTERRUPT ME *AGAIN*—"

"The *Canary Company,*" Alister gasped, not waiting for Dave to finish. "The ones that captured you—*and me*—the ones that put you in a tank and cut bits off. They've *been here.* Or they *are* here!"

Part Two

THE DOGS MOVED IN SINGLE FILE through the thick forest, their leaders rotating every few minutes. The humanoid, Professor Odd, remained in the rear and pulled the sled they had strapped together for Alpha Zora to lie on. Omu Akit had been uncertain about it, but since it freed Xixuan up for lead duty it meant they made overall better time: the big chow hurled himself at the foliage like a wrecking ball, hacking at the undergrowth with a vengeance, as if it had done him some personal insult. Reiji was less effective, being smaller, and Omu found himself having to take out the higher branches that would have otherwise inconvenienced the Professor. He did his best to make up for it when his turn came, but it was the wolf—*Elo,* that was her name—who truly made the difference.

She took Med Ksanos's standard-issue knife and wielded it like an extension of her body. *Snick, snick, snick,* it went, and the branches fell away. And though Omu Akit held the compass and was in charge of triangulating their route, Elo had the best sense of how to navigate the steep gullies and short cliffs they ran into.

On his back, Omu felt the radio pack sit hard and heavy, but no word came from Scout Shani.

They made surprisingly good time, but they couldn't keep it up forever. The sun sank before they even breached the thick layer of clouds, and the light dimmed further and further. A little after 18:00 Omu Akit called a halt and had them raise a bivouac. They had spent most of the day climbing, and now they sat just beneath the cloud line with what would have been a magnificent view down the side of the mountain if there had been light to see it by.

Reiji and Xixuan set up camp, rigging a tent against a solid tree for Alpha Zora, and a stand of LED lights so they could see to unpack the food. Professor Odd plunked herself down in a soft bed of leaves and split Ksanos's ration with Elo ("Dried beef? They *do* feed you well!") while Omu Akit checked in with his stricken alpha.

Zora was a fit dog in his prime years and seemed to be taking the physical stress about as well as could be hoped. Ksanos had set and cast his leg and left him with a generous supply of pain killers, and he'd probably had the easiest time of any of them. He grunted in recognition as Omu sat down next to him, then with some effort he raised one paw and pointed at the wolf.

"She's something, that's for sure," said Omu. "Don't quite know what to make of her. Do you think they're from Sci Div? Some special, secret branch?"

There was a sharp tug on his sleeve, and he looked down to find Zora staring intensely at him. He pointed again, jabbed his finger in the direction of the wolf, then pointed at himself.

"You want me to go get her?" Omu guessed, surprised.

Alpha Zora gave him the thumbs-up.

"Hey, wolf—er,—*Elo!* Alpha wants a word with you. Or something."

Elo turned to look at him, her expression even more un-readable as she was backlit by the harsh lights. But she got up and padded slowly over, using all fours to navigate the uncertain ground. She sat down next to Alpha Zora and looked at him thoughtfully.

"It's not me he wants to talk to," she said. "It's *you,* but he can't talk to you. He's asking me to translate."

"You can do that?" Omu said.

Elo shrugged. "If you'll trust me. Though I think if I get it wrong he'll let you know. You should watch too; it's a criminal shame you've lost your language. Maybe you'll pick something up."

"Language?" repeated Omu. "What *language?* We're *dogs.* We can't talk without the comsys."

"Not like *humans* you can't," Elo said. "What you do with your comsys, and what I'm doing right now, is talking like humans. But you don't need to *speak* a word to talk like a dog—or a wolf, or a *vroknaär.* I'm doing a lot of talking with my face *right now* that apparently you can't read. So watch *his* face and see if you can read what he's saying, like I can."

Omu Akit felt his hackles rise at being lectured, but he moved aside so the alpha's face was no longer in shadow, and looked dutifully down at it as Elo asked:

"Now, what was it you wanted to say?"

He saw the muscles move, saw how Zora's lips bunched and his ears twitched. It meant nothing to him, but then Elo said:

"It seems your medic—Ksanos, you called her?—is a spy. She was the one who sabotaged your uh . . . uh . . . I'm not sure. The thing you used to get here."

"The transfer shell?" Omu Akit exclaimed. "But that could have killed *her* as well!"

"Doesn't . . . doesn't seem to matter," Elo said, still watching Zora's face. "He thinks she's from . . . something. A secret group? Dissidents? Rebels? Does that mean anything to you? Your physical language is quite rudimentary—I'm doing my best," she added, speaking to Zora now. "You could help us a lot more if you'd tell us what exactly your objective is . . . but you really don't know? He really doesn't know," she finished.

Alpha Zora sank back onto his bed, winced, and shut his eyes.

Omu Akit looked up to find Elo had leveled her intent brown-eyed gaze at *him* now. "You know, it'd help *us* a great deal if you told us more about your world."

He stared at her, speechless. "What *are* you? A time traveler?"

"Sadly, no," Professor Odd called from across the camp. She was tucked snugly up against Xixuan's side and wrapped in all the spare jackets. "This is not a temporally flexible universe. Though it does seem to be relatively advanced."

Xixuan started, turning to look at her. "You mean to say you're—" he began, but Reiji cut him off.

"You're from another *world?*" the Shibo asked, coming down from his watch post. "How did you *get* here? How are you getting home?"

"Get *back* to your post, Scout," Omu snapped.

"Two other worlds, actually," Professor Odd said cheerfully. "How we got here isn't important—yet. What's more important is for Elo and myself to understand the series of events that led to *your* being *here*. In the broadest way possible."

Omu Akit came and sat under the light tripod, trying to keep a handle on his temper. "So, what? You want a brief history of our *world*?" he said.

"Only the last few thousand years," Professor Odd said serenely.

Omu Akit looked around and found that Elo was now watching him expectantly as well. He heaved a great sigh and began to explain—simply, as though to a litter of puppies.

"Well, when the Sapien Epoch ended and the Long Winter came . . . "

"How long ago was this?" Elo asked at once.

Omu Akit growled. "We don't know," he admitted. "Dogs weren't in a position to access records in those times. We only know that the humans left—taking some of the dogs with them—and then the Long Winter came. Our ancestors lived out that time in the old bunkers, underground. We were primitive savages then, fighting over what little technology had been left behind."

"But you were *intelligent*." Professor Odd interrupted this time. "That is, you were *sapient?*"

Omu Akit blinked. "Oh, yes. The forerunner dogs died out during the Long Winter. Those were the dark ages; most of what happened before and during the Winter Sci Div has had to reconstruct through archeology. What we do know is, eventually the Thaw came, and the beginning of recorded history. Back then there were no divisions; instead we were all separated into nation-states according to breed."

"I'd been wondering about that." Professor Odd spoke up again. "If you've been without human interference for what must have been *at least* ten thousand years, why are your breeds still so evident?"

"The Breeds were how we were created," Reiji answered, much to Omu's surprise. "They were the ideal forms the humans left us with, along with our intelligence and the comsys. It's a horrible taboo to interbreed."

Professor Odd and Elo looked at each other then, and another expression flashed between them. Omu wished he knew what it meant.

"We're not *breedists,* though," Reiji continued. "Most of us aren't, anyway. We don't believe there's a single superior breed—that's *stupid.* But each breed has a purpose and is the best at what they do. Except Shibos," he added, puffing out his chest a little. "We're the best at *everything,* and we're some of the longest-lived. Akits and Chows are good too," he added quickly, as Xixuan's comsys flashed red lights and a capital D, colon, lesser-than bracket appeared on its display.

"Fascinating," said Professor Odd.

"Sickening," said Elo, but she said nothing more.

"Tell me about these *divisions,*" Professor Odd said.

With relief Omu Akit moved on. He had not wanted to be pushed to the point of admitting that his great-grandmother had mated with a Deutschguard. Not that there was anything *wrong* with Deutschguards . . .

"The three Divisions," he explained. "Those came about in my great-great-grandfather's time. We have Arms Division, Exploration Division, and Science Division. Me and Xixuan, for example, we're Arms Div. So is our alpha. We're trained in weapons and tactical strategy. Arms Div also oversees trauma medicine, so Med Ksanos was Arms Div too. Reiji and Shani are Expo Div. They're also given arms training, but it's secondary to navigation, exploration, and fact-finding. Then there's Science Division . . . "

"You're afraid of Science Division," Elo said suddenly. "Why is that?"

Omu Akit didn't even bother to ask how she knew this time.

"Sci Div was the first Division. They developed the current communication systems and pretty much all of our technology, even a lot of our weapons. They're at the forefront of all the medical breakthroughs—the average lifespan of a dog is almost thirty years now—and they get all the findings from Expo Div to use in their research. The three divisions are supposed to work together, but it's more like Expo Div and Arms Div work for Sci Div."

"And your tech . . . what was his name?" Elo prompted.

"Tech Ishin," said Omu. "He was Science Division's representative here. We were supposed to escort him to the objective and then await further orders."

Professor Odd tapped the end of her tentacle-arm against her lips, thoughtfully processing this information.

"And you?" Omu said. "What's *your* story?"

"Long," said Elo, tiredly. "And complicated. Suffice to say we're . . . travelers. We stumbled into your world because I was teaching one of our companions how to drive our . . . erm . . . *car.* Uh . . . *transport device.* It's really an accident we're here at all."

"But a happy one," Professor Odd chipped in. "I think you'll find, before the end, that it was a good thing you met us." And she snuggled deeper into the fur-lined coat and closed her eyes. "Elo, tell them they can shut off the light now."

The three dogs on the run spent an uncomfortable night at varying points up the side of the mountain. The first dog, still ahead of the other two, curled up in the branches of a tree and slept fitfully. The second, driven on by desperation, slept in one- or two-hour increments, moving herself slowly forward through the night. Her tracker, the scout Shani, did the same, resting whenever she came to a newly vacated site. It grew cold.

Alister and Dave spent the evening watching the sun set from within the safety of the Oddity. Dave had stored his in-progress meal, which forced Alister to scrounge for snacks while he placidly drank orange juice through a straw. He had a special aperture in the side of his suit for this purpose, and Alister couldn't help but wonder how he ate the juice once it mixed with his panvironment suit's liquid-filled interior.

He had other problems to worry about, however.

"And you're *sure* the Oddity can't see any activity?" he asked Dave between bites of a cold chicken sandwich that he barely tasted.

"THERE IS NO EVIDENCE OF ADVANCED HUMAN AC-TIVITY CONGRUENT WITH THE OPERATIONS OF THE CANARY COMPANY," Dave said. He sidled up closer to Alister, who was sitting on the bottom step and staring out onto the darkening landscape. "IT HAS, HOWEVER, DETECTED MOVEMENT ON THE NORTH-BY-NORTHEAST OUTER SLOPE OF THE CALDERA."

"Could that be the Professor and Elo?"

"I EXPECT SO."

Silence fell between them. In it, there was a slurping, gurgling sound as Dave finished his orange juice.

"ARE YOU CERTAIN WHAT YOU SAW WAS EVIDENCE OF THE CANARY COMPANY?"

"It *said* 'Property of the *Canary Company*,'" Alister replied, a little snappishly. "If you don't believe me, why don't *you* go see for yourself?"

"I INTEND TO," Dave said. "TOMORROW. WHEN THIS AREA OF THE PLANET IS EXPOSED TO ITS STAR. *AFTER* I HAVE EXAMINED THE ODDITY'S REPORTS MORE THOROUGHLY."

"Right," said Alister. "Why don't we disconnect then, so you can slip us forward in local time?"

"THAT MAY CAUSE PROBLEMS IF PROFESSOR ODD ARRIVES WHILE WE ARE DISCONNECTED."

"Aye," Alister conceded. "That would be bad."

"I CALCULATE IT WOULD CAUSE HER TO BE CROSS WITH US."

So they slept—or at least, *Alister* slept; only Dave knew what Dave did at night—with the Oddity still anchored to the door of the observatory. It was not a pleasant experience for Alister, who kept waking up and worrying that the sounds he heard seeping in through the shut door were padded footsteps on the stairway, and any moment unfriendly people in hazardous environment suits would come bursting inside to drag him and Dave away to who-knew-where.

He woke early in the morning—he could tell from the birdsong drifting upstairs—and for a moment the sounds were so incongruous with the void he usually found outside his window that he felt completely discombobulated.

There was clattering from downstairs and the smell of something baking.

"Is that . . . *breakfast?*" he asked as he descended the ladder a few minutes later.

"NOT YET," said Dave from the alcove. "I GIVE IT ANOTHER SIX HOURS. IN THE MEANTIME, HOWEVER, WE HAVE WORK TO DO."

"*Six* hours?" Alister exclaimed. "What in the worlds are you—what do you mean *we* have work to do?"

"THE ODDITY'S ADVANCED EXAMINATION OF THIS SITE TURNED UP SEVERAL NARRATIVE ANOMALIES," Dave said, rolling out of the kitchen.

"I almost understood that," Alister said. "Unfortunately I'm not Elo or Professor Odd . . . yet. You'll have to try again."

"IT FOUND THINGS THAT SHOULD NOT BE IN THIS UNIVERSE," Dave offered.

"Oh," said Alister, feeling rather like he did when at the dentist's being told he'd got a cavity. "What do we do about them?"

"TREAD CAREFULLY. WHICH IS WHY YOU MUST ASSIST ME."

Which was how Alister found himself sitting once more at the Oddity's controls, staring despairingly at the banks of buttons.

"It was my driving that got us *into* this mess," he pointed out.

"YOU WILL NOT BE DRIVING," Dave told him. "YOU WILL FOLLOW MY INSTRUCTIONS: KEEP THE PORTAL NEAR MY POSITION—I HAVE SET IT TO AUTOMATICALLY RE-CENTER WHEN *THIS* BUTTON IS PRESSED." He indicated the big orange one which, in Alister's mind, meant a nice place to go.

Sighing, he rubbed at the short fuzz of his hair. "Anything else?"

"YES," said Dave. "IF I AM COMPROMISED, YOU MUST DETACH THE PORTAL *AT ONCE.*"

Alister looked around at him, but all he could see was the blank blue dome of the creature's panvironment suit.

"You think . . . it might come to that?" he asked.

"NO. BUT IT IS BEST TO HAVE A CONTINGENCY FOR EVERY SITUATION."

Alister shook his head. "I still think this is going to go horribly wrong," he said.

"I HAVE A CONTINGENCY FOR THIRTY SUBOPTIMAL OUTCOMES," Dave assured him, and began descending the stairs. He did this by tipping bodily sideways so the tractor treads that encircled the waist of his barrel-shaped suit were able to roll him sedately down the steps, moderated by interference from his many arms. When he got to the bottom he put out five arms on his lower side and with an almighty heave pushed himself upright. Then with a clang and a creak of dry metal he was out the door, leaving it open behind him. Alister watched him tip sideways again out of sight and listened to the clanging as he descended the metal stairs outside. He shivered at the draft of cold air and pulled his parka closer about his shoulders.

Tired and aching, Tech Ishin at last reached the summit: a wide expanse of low forest rising majestically above the thick blanket of cloud. He was in time to watch the sun peek above this, shooting streaks of gold out across the frothing sea of white, turning its depths to purple and blues tinged with pink.

The natural beauty, however, was lost on him. The objective was near at hand, and he consulted the cipher map he'd carried tucked against his side the whole way. Using the special augmentation on his comsys, he overlaid the cipher upon the landscape around him, and quickly located the largest and best-preserved dome. He had been told this was, in the days of the Sapien Epoch, the home of one of their largest optical reflecting telescopes. Primitive and clumsy compared to the tech developed since, but invaluable now that it had been adapted into something entirely different. The fact that it still functioned as a telescope and aided in observing and therefore calculating the optimal time of conjunction was just an added bonus. In reality, Tech Ishin suspected his pocket gammascope would be of more use, considering the time of day. Optimally, of course, he was to wait for night, but circumstances demanded immediate action.

Tucking the cipher back against his side, the little white dog took to all fours again, and began trotting wearily across the plateau toward the largest dome.

Medic Ksanos, resting under cover of the topmost wisps of clouds, licked a protein patch and checked her armaments. She hadn't had much time, and most of her tools had been left behind with the rest of her gear. But she still had her microgun and hipknife, and most importantly, she had the information drilled into her mind.

The payload must not be allowed to reach the objective. Not at any cost.

Swift and silent, Ksanos took off on the last leg of her journey. She followed a slightly different route than Tech Ishin, one that bypassed his stopping point and headed straight for the observatory. With luck, she would reach it before him . . . and if not, then there was the microgun.

Hot on her scent, Scout Shani paused at the discarded protein-patch wrapper. Scenting the air and tuning her ears carefully she picked out the sounds of feet dashing away into the distance. Climbing a nearby tree she surveyed the landscape, scanning for the minutest of movements among the gently rustling branches. After a while she climbed back down and, at last, got out her radio.

Professor Odd was on her feet and fumbling for the controls of the radio before Ranger Omu was fully awake, but he heard clearly enough the sound of Shani's crisp female-standard voice crackling through the static.

"Discovery Intent. Come in, Discovery. This is Scout Sigma. Do you copy?"

"Shani?" Professor Odd asked. "Is that you?"

The radio crackled for a moment, and then Shani's voice came back, sounding annoyed.

"Who *is* this?"

"Professor Odd," said Professor Odd. *"You* know, the one—"

"Go ahead, Scout," Omu Akit said, coming to sit beside the Professor. "Have you reached the objective yet?"

"Not yet Ranger—sorry, Alpha," said Shani. "But it looks like Tech and Medic are almost there. If I've calculated their courses correctly, the objective's exact location should be at 28° 45' 23.8" north, 17° 53' 31.3" west. I've yet to measure elevation, but it must be a little over two thousand meters."

Professor Odd sat back on her heels at this. She looked across Omu to where Elo was just climbing down from her watch post.

"The *Gran Telescopio Canarias*," she said. "Only it's not just a *telescope* anymore."

"You'll have to explain," Omu said.

"Oh, I *will*," said Professor Odd. "While we walk. At this rate we'll miss the show."

The globe of the observatory shone in the morning sun like a second moon, and Tech Ishin had to pull down the visor function on his comsys against the glare. Off to his right and a little downhill was another, smaller dome, but the cipher had been quite clear: the large one was his objective. On weary legs he stormed up the final slope and edged along the base of the crumbling concrete pier the structure was built on. Scrambling up an eroded embankment he emerged onto a plateau where, in prehistoric times, humans had parked their mobile transport machines. Huge hangar doors, welded shut, were visible across the plateau on the building's face, but Ishin knew from the cipher that there was a smaller door around the corner, and he had the key to it. He set off at a rambling trot, taking care not to trip in the many cracks and crevices that had spread across the pavement like a spiderweb.

There was a sound like *whuff,* and pain exploded in his left shoulder, the force knocking him sideways and off his feet. He screamed, a high, inarticulate wail that distorted the speakers of his comsys, and at the same time let out an instinctual yelp of agony.

Dazed, and aware of the deep, cold precursor to a much worse kind of pain, Ishin scrambled to get his good legs under him and made a desperate dash for the nearest piece of cover.

Med Ksanos clipped her microgun back into its holster in disgust. She'd *missed.* After all that, with a perfectly clear shot, she'd *missed.* Whether her eyesight had gotten worse than she'd thought or the fatigue of the journey had hampered her muscle control didn't matter at this point. She bounded across the plain toward her wounded target, growling subconsciously.

Alister, listening carefully from within the Oddity, heard the scream-turned-yelp, and ran to the door to see a canine form fall to the ground, flailing. His heart leapt into his throat and without thinking he was out the door, clattering down the stairs and wrenching a branch off a nearby tree to serve as a makeshift weapon.

"Elo!" he shouted, almost missing the last step in his hurry. He stumbled, and when he looked up he saw that it was *not* Elo. This dog was significantly smaller, dirty white and wearing a grayish blue uniform with a lumpish pack strapped to its back. It was struggling toward him now, heavily favoring its left foreleg. It wore a strange contraption on its head with a tinted visor that obscured its eyes and what looked like speakers mounted on both sides.

Alister skidded to a halt, uncertain, and then *another* dog burst from the undergrowth on the far side of the decaying parking lot. This one was huge, with long silky fur, and it bounded like a cheetah toward them, its teeth bared in a feral snarl. It wore a khaki-green suit and a similar headpiece, though this one didn't have a visor.

Every instinct in Alister's body told him to *run,* but the higher functioning part of his brain said: *if you run, it will chase you.* So he planted his feet firmly apart, leveled the branch at the approaching dog, and bellowed: *"No! BAD dog!"*

The attacking dog was so shocked its front legs went out from under it, and it did a somersault over one shoulder, long legs flailing. The wounded dog, who was almost at Alister's feet by this point, stopped as well and stared up at him. Then with a mad scramble and a pitiful yelp it tried to back away.

"Stay where you are," Alister told it firmly. "You're hurt. *Dave!*" he shouted. The creature couldn't have got far. *"Dave get back* here!"

The larger dog had got itself right side up now, and was staring at Alister as if it couldn't decide whether to bite him or run away.

They were not quite like Elo, Alister saw. They looked like they would be more comfortable on two legs than four—whereas Elo's unusual anatomy was equally suitable to both—and where Elo was lean and wolf-like, these animals were certainly *dogs.* They had that soft, puppyish look that wolves simply didn't have, even though Alister could see they were both adults. But like Elo they had expressions that normal dogs didn't have either, and it was this—more than their clothes or obviously high-tech headgear—that convinced Alister he was dealing with intelligent creatures.

"Look," he said to the bigger dog, lowering his stick a fraction. "I don't want to hurt anyone. Ah . . . but I can't let you fight. Oh great, I hope you speak English. Can you understand me?"

Slowly, the large long-haired dog rose onto its hind legs—it was perhaps an inch taller than Alister that way, and he found himself taking an involuntary step back.

"Identify yourself," said a canned voice from the direction of the dog's head. Alister had to take a moment before he realized it was the dog's *headset* that was speaking, not the dog itself.

"Am . . . " he said. "I'm Alister Bane. I'm not really meant to be here and I don't want to be a bother, but I can't let you tear this guy apart. Who are *you*, if you don't mind my asking?"

"If you are not a master, you cannot let him reach the objective," said the larger dog, and darted forward.

Alister thought it was going for his throat, but then he realized the small white dog had, while he'd been distracted, made a valiant effort to reach the locked door at the side of the building, and the larger dog was going after *it*.

They were both stopped, however, when the door burst open and six of Dave's arms came flying out, followed shortly by the barrel of his panvironment suit.

The little dog yelped and cowered. The large dog was so surprised it overbalanced and sat down hard on its rear. Dave surveyed the scene with his usual implacability, slowly retracting his arms.

"I SEE," he said, though Alister hadn't the foggiest notion what *that* meant. "YOU TWO," Dave continued, folding his two remaining arms across the front of his suit, the ends tapping impatiently, "HAVE A LOT OF EXPLAINING TO DO."

"The *Gran Telescopio Canarias* was one of the largest reflecting telescopes humans ever built . . . on *Earth*." Professor Odd spoke briskly as they hacked their way through the jungle. "In *most narratives* that was all it ever was. But in a few worldtracks the observatory was repurposed to house some rather unconventional equipment."

They were passing through thinner forest now, the steep, jagged terrain leveling out into a wide, high plain. Though the going was easier they were now at a high enough elevation that Professor Odd had to pause occasionally to catch her breath.

"And by *unconventional* I do mean just that," she went on. "It wasn't the sort of stuff that would have existed, conventionally, in this universe."

"*What was it?*" Elo snapped from the rear, giving voice to their collective question.

"That depends on which exact narrative this is," Professor Odd replied. "But we could make an educated guess based upon what we already know."

"But we don't *know* anything," Omu Akit said.

"On the contrary, my good canine," Professor Odd said cheerfully. "We know a great many things. We know, for example, that your Med Ksanos knows what this thing is. How? Well, she knew where to go even without a map or any equipment. That tells me she has been here before. If she was here before, then it means these sorts of *missions* have happened before. *Haven't* they?" she called back to Elo, who was walking behind Alpha Zora's sled and could read his reaction.

There was silence from behind them, and then Elo's voice was raised in surprise.

"*Yes,*" she said. "Yes, they *have*. It was never recorded though because . . . because . . . oh dear. Because no one ever comes back from these missions."

"How come *I* was never told this?" Reiji demanded.

"Because you're a scout and it's none of your business," Omu Akit told him. "It was none of *our* business either, until this thing went nipples-up."

"But *someone* must," Professor Odd mused. "Didn't he say the *tech* would be extracted?"

"He says that's what was in the orders," Elo informed them. "But he's not sure how truthful his orders were. He's never heard of a tech coming back from this mission."

"Define *this mission*," Professor Odd said. "Does it have a name?"

"Well," said Omu. "Our team's designation is Discovery Intent but—"

"No," Elo cut him off. "The mission doesn't have a name. Or if it does he doesn't know it. All he knows is . . . oh, this is tricky. *Gaps*, did you mean? Yes, gaps. Places where there ought to have been reports, but there were none. Not even casualty reports."

"And how often do these *gaps* occur?" Professor Odd asked.

"Every eight or ten years," came back Elo's prompt response. "He noticed the pattern in the records because . . . oh I *see* . . . he went to check them when he was assigned alpha of this team."

They walked for a time in silence. They were in the thick of the clouds now, and had to stop and re-triangulate often as it was impossible to see further than a dozen meters.

"Then consider this," Professor Odd announced after one such stop. "Med Ksanos is not a medic at all, but a former *tech*. She was the tech on the *last* mission to the *Gran Telescopio*, and for whatever reason, she thinks it would be a bad thing if your mission succeeded."

"A *very* bad thing," Omu Akit grumbled. "If she thought it would be better if we all died in a shell crash."

"Which tells me she knows *exactly* what this mission *is*," Professor Odd went on. "So all we have to do is find her and ask her. But until then, let's consider the relevance of the time between missions. Eight to ten years, you say? That's too short for a comet—a natural one, anyway—but it might be some other celestial conjunction."

"How do you know it has anything to do with *outer space?*" Omu asked.

"There's lots of isolated places in this world," Professor Odd remarked. "Lots of secret places to run secret experiments. Why choose one with such an *impeccable* view of the *sky?*"

She threw her hand up in illustration, and as the dogs turned their heads skyward they saw for the first time a hint of blue in the whiteness.

"It may also be worth mentioning," Professor Odd remarked, "especially in light of what became of the previous teams, that at least in *similar narratives,* the unconventional equipment usually had something to do with *teleportation.*"

"Trans-dimensional or local?" Elo asked at once.

"I don't know!" Professor Odd said. She sounded unbearably cheerful.

The radio—strapped to Elo's back—fizzed to life. Omu Akit doubled back from his position and fell in behind her.

"Come in Discovery Intent." *hhrrrkh* *"Come in, Discovery. This is Scout Sigma, over."*

"Scout, this is Discovery," Omu said. "Report."

"The tech and the medic have reached the objective." *hhrrkh* *"They were intercepted by what seems to be a human. And a robot in a barrel."* *hrrrkh*

Elo stopped dead in her tracks, and Omu nearly crashed face-first into her back.

"What *happened?*" she yelped.

"Who is this?" *hhrrkh* Shani asked cagily.

"That's Elo," Omu Akit sighed. "You know, the *wolf*—"

"Vroknaär," Elo corrected him.

There was an unfriendly silence over the radio.

"Continue, Scout," Omu Akit said.

hhrrkh *"They have entered the structure. Tech was injured. Robot in the barrel seems to have been expecting them. Advise next course of action, Alpha?"*

Omu Akit had absolutely no idea what to do about this.

"Friends of yours?" he asked Elo.

"The thing in the barrel is *not* a robot," Professor Odd called back. "He is a very remarkable person. We call him *Dave*. The human's name is Alister. She should try to help them."

"And how do I do that?" Shani's comsys sounded even more irritated cut with the radio static.

There was a thoughtful silence from the two interlopers. Then Elo said:

"Ask Dave. He'll tell you what to do."

"You mean . . . " *hhhrrrkh* *" . . . the robot?"*

Dave's synthesized voice clanged off the interior of the observatory, making the dogs wince. It grated on Alister's nerves as well, but at least *he* didn't have such sensitive hearing.

"FOR THE LAST TIME," Dave was saying. "I AM *NOT* A ROBOT."

They were assembled in the foyer area, which Dave had assured Alister was "SAFE AND DEFENSIBLE," and Alister was currently crouched over the smaller, white dog, attempting to perform first aid while the larger dog, held at bay by Dave's immovable shape, seethed quietly. It was she—Alister was fairly certain it was female—who had called Dave a robot.

"Give it a rest, Boraznes," said the white dog, and whined involuntarily. The whine was the only sound that came out of its mouth; the words themselves came from the strange device strapped to its head. Alister found it rather disconcerting.

He'd been afraid the poor animal's wound would be much worse, but after he'd drawn out the small projectile lodged in the dog's shoulder—very long and thin it was, more like a needle than a bullet—and put a wad of cotton against the wound to stop the bleeding, the dog began to look better at once.

"Thank you," it said when Alister had finished rather clumsily wrapping its shoulder. "This is indeed a surprise: I had no idea your people would send a representative. Does this mean you can take the payload through? Or are the other five still necessary?"

"I'm sorry?" said Alister, wondering if the dog's speaking device was malfunctioning. *"Other five?"*

"Our alpha was injured, it may be difficult to move him. *She's* a spy, a saboteur, or something. And there was more . . . an unexpected occurrence."

"Your comsys is babbling again, Ishin," said the tall, thin dog. She was sitting very still, watching them with the intensity of a cat watching a bird in the grass, and Alister was grateful for the solid bulk of Dave in a metal can between them.

Dave's optical receiver spun around to glance at the dog on the ground, then back at the one sitting before him.

"I SEE," he said. "WE HAVE APPARENTLY CROSSED PATHS WITH YOUR NATIVE SEQUENCE. ORDINARILY WE WOULD NOT IMPEDE YOU, HOWEVER THERE IS TECHNOLOGY HOUSED AT THIS LOCATION THAT AFFECTS US DIRECTLY."

The tall dog's ears flicked, and she looked from Dave to Alister sharply.

"Don't tell me," she said. "You're a part of *her* lot, aren't you? The wolf and the pseudo-human?"

"You've *seen* Professor Odd?" Alister exclaimed. "And Elo? Are they all right?"

"For better or worse," said a new voice. It was high, clear, but Alister could tell from the quality of the sound that it came from a *comsys* device.

He turned to find another dog—more or less the size and shape of the white one, but light brown—standing in the open doorway with some sort of projectile weapon trained on the tall, thin dog. She continued speaking as she advanced slowly into the room.

"And they're on their way *here*, Boraznes, along with Reiji and Xixuan and Omu *and* the alpha, so don't you think of pulling another stunt like yesterday's." She came up beside Dave, still covering the tall dog—Boraznes—with what appeared to be a small rifle. She inclined her head toward Dave's dome. "Scout Shani, s'ram, Professor Odd and Temp-Alpha Omu instructed me to do as you say."

"WELL," said Dave, "THAT IS A RELIEF." An arm snaked out of his suit and plucked the gun neatly from Scout Shani's hands. "YOU CAN TELL ME WHAT YOUR TEAM WAS GOING TO DO WITH THE SHORT-RANGE LOCAL PORTAL EMBEDDED IN THE OTHER ROOM."

"I'm sorry," said Shani. "That *what?*"

"It's a *portal?*" Alister spoke up from his position on the ground by the white dog. His mind immediately flew to the stencil on the side of the tubing: *Property of the Canary Company.* The Canary Company, which had access to extra-universal technology. Perhaps *this* was one of their "extra-universes." In which case they might not be here *now,* but they *could* show up at any time. He looked down at the dog in his arms. "Is *that* what you meant about taking a payload through?"

The dog stared back at him, blankly.

"He can't tell you that," said Boraznes. "Neither can the scout. They were not given clearance."

"BUT YOU CAN," Dave stated.

Boraznes put her head on one side and cocked an ear at them. Her gaze traveled over the scout, Shani, to Dave, then to Alister and finally the injured dog. "I might," she said.

Dave made an angry whirring noise within his suit.

"Look," said Alister, "I know we must seem pretty strange and all, barging into your world like this. But you should know, the portal—or whatever it is—that's in the next room, it's being used by a . . . a *company* that's not at all nice. I don't know whether you're working for the Canary Company, but if you're not, I wouldn't recommend sending them any payloads—and I *certainly* wouldn't recommend trying to talk to them."

Boraznes went very still and locked her eyes on Alister. Lights danced across her comsys and her nostrils flared.

"You know about the Canary Company?" she said quietly.

"Aye," said Alister, "Dave and I both have been quite intimately acquainted."

"UNPLEASANTLY SO," Dave added.

"So I think it's in your best interests," Alister ventured, "to tell us *exactly* what's been going on, and *who* you're working for."

Boraznes hesitated further, but then the radio on Shani's harness cracked into life.

"Come in, Scout Sigma. This is Discovery Intent. Over."

"Scout Sigma here," Shani said. "I have achieved contact with the Professor's allies. I would have taken Medic Ksanos into custody, but my weapon has been confiscated."

"Was that Dave?" said a new voice over the radio.

"YES IT WAS," said Dave.

"Professor?" cried Alister.

"Hallo, all," came Professor Odd's cheerful sing-song voice. *"Listen, sorry if I've got the wrong end of the stick here. But Dave, if you've got Ksanos there you might ask her the reason for the intervals. Eight to ten years between missions, according to Alpha Zora's records . . . or lack thereof I might say. Ask her what happens every eight to ten years. Must dash now, see you soon!"*

There was some confusing noise from the radio, and then silence. Shani looked at Dave, who looked at Boraznes, who narrowed her eyes at them.

"RECURRING MISSIONS ON AN EIGHT TO TEN YEAR INTERVAL," Dave said. "TO VISIT A *LOCAL* PORTAL THAT HAS BEEN REQUISITIONED BY AN *EXTRA-UNIVERSAL* AUTHORITY." He let the last words ring out around the room and waited until the clanging echoes had faded. Then his optical dish slid around to look at Alister, and he said: "THIS EXPLAINS *EVERYTHING*: THEY HAVE AN ORBITING WORMHOLE."

"A *wormhole*," Professor Odd said as they ran, zig-zagging, through the thinning forest. She was breathing rapidly and heavily but still managed a few gasping words. "I *bet* it's a wormhole!"

"You'll have to—explain—better—" Reiji gasped.

"Wormholes," said Elo, who was keeping up easily, "are naturally occurring transuniversal portals. But they're usually *perfectly* stationary. Which means they appear to move around—because the entire *universe* is moving around *them*. They *can* be anchored to a particular place—usually using gravity, but their presence also creates a field of compromised reality that can be problematic to things living near it. Hence you wouldn't want to anchor a wormhole on Earth."

"I bet," gasped Professor Odd, "that they've anchored it to a *comet*. Something that regularly passes—close enough to Earth—to be reached by a . . . a *short-range* local portal!"

"So, every eight to ten years, when your wormhole-bearing comet passes within range of the local portal, you have a short window of time in which to send or receive things transuniversally." Elo finished. Then added: "Though eight to ten years is awfully short range for a comet."

"Likely—human-built," Professor Odd panted, "specifically for—this case—carefully timed and—engineered."

They had reached a high plateau, and Elo could see on the horizon a huge white dome peeking out over the tops of the trees. Reiji checked his instruments, scented the air, and determined that that was the objective. He insisted they wait for Omu and Xixuan, who were working in tandem to pull the alpha's sled. No sooner had they come into sight, however, than Professor Odd took off again.

Medic Ksanos Boraznes scratched behind one ear and regarded them thoughtfully.

"I was never given exact information regarding the conjunction," she said, "even after I joined the Neo Canii. All I knew was that it happened on a regular schedule, and during the conjunction the Canary Portal would open, and a team had to be there to receive the orders that came through—and to deliver whatever had been ordered during the previous conjunction."

"You're *Neo Canii?*" Shani said, sounding disgusted. "I should have *known.*"

"You should be *thanking* us," said Ksanos coldly. "Because of interference from the portal our culture has been handicapped for *years.* You think Sci Div has created great things? Well, they've done *even more* that they've been required to send through the portal instead of sharing with the rest of you. And not just inventions: data and studies. When I was sent to Canary 6, a part of my payload was a detailed genetic simulation that proved crossbreeding *strengthened* the population by decreasing susceptibility to congenital diseases and deformities. But the masters wanted exclusive access to anything like that, and so people have kept on enforcing these archaic standards of *pure breeding* that's been causing such trouble for the Grandanes—not to mention the *Boraznes*. It's not so bad for your lot, you're *Shibo*," she gave a little snarl in the direction of Shani and Ishin. "But *both* my parents died of gastric torsion, and all my children had it too. *I* have mild cardiac arrhythmia, and I probably won't live much past the age of twenty-two."

"Could you *possibly* begin at the beginning?" Alister asked timidly. "Why are you here in the first place? What is this payload, and what exactly do you do with it?"

Ksanos cocked an ear at him, and the lights of her comsys flashed.

"The payload varies," she said. "Last time it was study reports and simulation results. Sci Div sends a team to the Canary Portal every conjunction with a payload. Their agent—usually a tech—sends the payload through along with the rest of the team. Then the tech waits for a reply, which includes instructions for recalibrating the portal to their home destination—in my case it was Sci Div headquarters. The Sci Div agent then takes the orders and uses the portal to travel home. I do not know what happens to the payload or the rest of the team, and I have never seen a Canary Company member, but it is presumed they are human." Her eyes, very large and brown and rather sad, turned to Alister. "I took you for one of them at first. I am sorry. But you say you have been in contact with the Canary Company? Did you see any dogs with them?"

"Aye," said Alister heavily. "But no dogs. Other things, though. Whatever happened to your team, I don't think it was pleasant."

At this, Shani rounded on Ishin, who cowered backwards against Alister's shins. "And *you* were going to hand us over? Just like *she* did?"

"He was likely told the same thing I was," Ksanos said before the tech could answer. "That the others were being called home to serve the old masters. That they would be taken care of." She snarled. "It is a pleasant *fiction*. But I *saw* the orders they sent us. This time they wanted weapon schematics and the access codes to all our defense systems. When I got back I also did some research into the contents of previous payloads: they've taken historical records, ancient artifacts, one-of-a-kind vaccines and *more*. And it's been going on for *decades*. When I tried to bring this up publicly I was shut down. They revoked my clearance and probably would have shipped me off to the Old Farm, but I escaped. Went and joined the Neo Canii. When I told them what I'd learned we decided that *this* payload must be prevented from going through at all costs. With it, if the Canary Company decided to invade us, they could take out our infrastructure with a single comsys. We may be *dogs*," she said, raising her chin and looking Alister straight in the eye. "But we're not *slaves*.

"I volunteered to be the plant. I'm old; I've had my litter, and I know the terrain. Plus I'd had medical training in Sci Div, so it was easy for me to take on the role of an Arms Div medic. Getting me on the transfer shell, that was a trick. But since Sci Div locks the team out of communications after launch there wasn't much else needed to be done. Arms Div is probably getting royally raked over the coals back home, now they've discovered a fake medic got on a top-secret operations team.

"Now you know as much as anyone on this island," Ksanos finished and folded her forelegs across her chest, her comsys going dark.

The little white dog whined in Alister's arms, and he stroked its neck unconsciously.

"I think you're right not to send the Canary Company any more payloads," he said. "But we can't help you if you keep running around trying to hurt people."

"Not to mention sabotaging our transfer shell!" Shani piped up.

"That was a legitimate accident," Ksanos said primly. "I take responsibility only for Alpha Zora's comsys and Tech Ishin's shoulder."

"Even so," Alister began, but was cut off by a clang from the front of the building.

"AT LAST," said Dave, and left his post in front of Ksanos and began rolling toward the front of the building. "WHAT TOOK YOU SO LONG?"

A flash of bright magenta, and Professor Odd sprang into view. She was still wearing her frilly purple-and-red apron, but was bundled snugly in an ill fitting coat with a fur-lined hood. Behind her was Elo, and behind *them* a small, reddish-brown-and-white dog dressed like Shani. There was more crashing from outside, and a pained *yelp* and synthetic voices raised in argument. Soon two larger dogs entered, carrying a third between them. This one was small, black and white, with its hind leg in a cast. Its supporters were a beige wolf-like dog and a large fluffy red one with blue-black lips. They were talking over each other as they made their way inside.

"What do you want me to *do* about her? She doesn't listen to *my* orders."

"You are probably the least effective alpha ever."

"Shut *up*, Xixuan."

Things got rather confusing after that. Alister felt loath to leave his post above Ishin, and as a result caught only snatches of the conversation, with Dave's loud clanging voice drowning out all the others.

"It *is* a wormhole, isn't it?" Professor Odd was asking.

"THE CANARY COMPANY HAS BEEN EXPLOITING THIS UNIVERSE."

"Let me *at* that barking medic. I'm gonna throttle her!"

"I CANNOT ALLOW ANY FURTHER VIOLENCE."

"Oh *will* you all just *sit down* so we can talk this out like civilized animals?" Elo's voice howled above the others.

Surprisingly, this was more or less what happened. Between Dave's loud, clanging voice and Elo's natural authority they managed to herd the pack of dogs into the open area in front of the door to the observatory dome and got everyone sitting in a circle. Introductions were exchanged, and at last the whole story came together: Alister learned how the Professor and Elo had stumbled upon the team of dogs, how first Scout Ishin and then Med Ksanos deserted them, ("I am sorry for biting you," Ksanos said diffidently. "I have been under a great deal of stress." Professor Odd waved her bandaged tentacle and laughed. "Completely understandable, given the circumstances.") and of their cumbersome ascent up the side of the mountain. Dave explained, with Alister's help, how they had found themselves at the summit, how Alister had discovered evidence of the Canary Company, how Dave had detected the presence of a portal, and how they had intervened when Ksanos had tried to kill Tech Ishin. ("I apologize for that as well; it was only in the line of duty.") Finally Ksanos told her story all over again, then sat back and asked:

"Now that you know the whole truth, and since my efforts have been compromised, I can only ask, what do you intend to do *now?*"

A profound silence followed this question. All the dogs looked toward their leader, the only one aside from Elo who didn't wear a comsys, who in turn glared back at them. Professor Odd folded her legs, tapped her chin with a finger and hummed.

"If I might make a suggestion," Alister said tentatively. "I don't think it would be a good idea for you to continue sending payloads—let *alone* living dogs through the portal. The people on the other side—well, I can't imagine they have the best of intentions towards this universe or its inhabitants."

"I CONCUR," Dave announced.

Ishin, who had been sitting quietly, curled against Alister's side with his head in his paws, said: "But we *need* their directions. After the payload is sent through, we receive instructions. They tell Sci Div what we're supposed to *do.*"

"And Sci Div tells the others what to do—yes I see the problem here," Professor Odd remarked.

Alister was flabbergasted. "You mean you've been following the orders of the *Canary Company* all these years?"

"We are *dogs*," Ksanos said, though she did not sound particularly proud of the fact. "It is what we *do*."

For her part, Elo looked around at the assembled pack in outright frustration. "Oh . . . *bollocks*," she said. "You lot do *know* what the only real difference between *wolves* and *dogs* is?"

When all this got her were blank stares she growled and went on: "*Dogs* are just *wolves* who haven't grown up yet. You don't have to change who or what you are, you just have to *grow up*. Take *responsibility* for your species!"

"Easier said than done," said Omu glumly.

"I never said it would be easy," Elo replied briskly. "But it *is* possible. And better, I think, than being *pets*. Which is what you're still clinging to—you've clung to it so hard, even after all your native humans were gone, *extra-universal* humans were able to come in and boss you around. Get that subservient mindset out of your heads and you'll do much better."

A resentful quiet descended on the group after this outburst. Alister suddenly realized that all the dogs were focusing their attention on him, though they would not look directly at him. They seemed . . . almost expectant. It was such a clear illustration of the problem Elo had put her paw on that it made him uncomfortable.

"Oh for goodness *sakes*," he said, making them all jump. "If it makes any difference, you certainly have *my* permission to, am, to *disobey*."

There was . . . not quite a sigh . . . more like a collective release of tension among the dogs. Omu looked at Xixuan, Reiji looked at Shani, and Ksanos and Ishin glanced at one another. The alpha—Zora—whined and plucked at Elo's sleeve. Elo looked around at him.

"Say that again," she said. "You're getting better, but I wasn't looking for the first bit. Oh." She turned back to address the group. "Alpha Zora says he'd like to . . . um . . . *get that in writing*, as it were. Because, if it was up to him, he'd order us to shut down the portal."

"Get *what* in writing?" Alister said.

"Your 'orders'," Elo said, holding up her paws and making air quotes. "You're a *human*." She rolled her eyes. "And if they have something to show I'm sure it'll make the massive overhaul of their culture and society a bit *less* of a disaster."

"I got a question," Reiji said, raising a paw.

"Of *course* you do," Omu said, but his comsys was on such low volume he was drowned out as Reiji barreled on:

"If we're shutting down this portal, *how are we going to get back?*"

Professor Odd picked her head up from where it had been resting on her hands. "Oh," she said happily. "We'll get you sorted out, don't you worry."

Night fell on the ruins of the Roque de los Muchachos observatory, and the stars—piercingly bright in the clear, black sky—gently illuminated the round white dome of the Gran Canarias telescope. The gentle rustling of the wind in the sparse treetops was broken by the sudden groan and creak as the dome began to slide open, revealing a deep black slice in the otherwise smooth, white globe.

Inside the dome, Reiji was dancing around Professor Odd and Dave, who were standing crouched over the controls.

"Yes, yes, but *why do we have to see how it works?*" he was saying. "Why can't we just blow the place up? Xixuan's got enough firepower!"

"Because I *want* to see how it works," Professor Odd said amicably.

"IN ORDER TO DEACTIVATE IT THOROUGHLY," Dave added.

"Well, *technically* what we're doing is creating a mutual lock," the Professor explained, leaving Dave at the console and going over to where Xixuan, Omu and Elo were working to align the telescope according to Ishin's instructions. "Make it so they can't send anything through to you, and you can't send anything through to them. This way you can *keep* the technology of the portal and use it however you want, without worrying about running into them. It's incredibly useful stuff, is portals."

"We've got it, Professor—it's just as you said!" Elo yipped excitely. She had made a trip to the Oddity and come back with an armful of cables and monitors, which she had hooked up to the digital output from the telescope. Now the dogs clustered around her gave a collective gasp, and Alister got up from where he had been drafting the message for Zora and went over to look.

The screen showed a fuzzy black-and-white image slowly coming into focus. At first it looked a bit like a comet—it had a streak of white trailing behind it—but as the picture solidified he saw this was the actual shape of the structure.

For structure it was: a vaguely wedge-shaped contraption with eight arms arrayed out like a starfish in front, centered around a deep black patch that made Alister's head hurt to look at.

Professor Odd, bending over the backs of the assembled dogs, shook her head with a smile. "This was at one time a highly advanced piece of astronomical observatory technology," she said ruefully. "And we're using it to look at something only a little father away than the moon."

"What *is* that?" Alister asked. He didn't like the look of the black spot; it seemed unnatural.

"That is a gravity anchor," Professor Odd said. "On what appears to be a metal frame of some sort. Looks like an *extremely* short-period artificial comet. Even so, it's much farther away from Earth than any other human-crafted satellite. It would have to be, considering what it's carrying."

"That . . . black spot?" Shani asked, pointing to the display.

"It's not black," said Professor Odd. "That's just the telescope being unable to recognize the radiation it's putting out. Really, wormholes are *all* colors, some gamma rays and a few quataert particles. Quataert particles aren't conventional matter or energy, and I don't think you have anything in this universe that could see them. Hence, black."

"And that," Omu said with a frown, "that leads to the *Canary Company?*"

"Or some place they have access to," Elo said. "Likely, they have some sort of similar relay on their end, to prevent damage to their world from the wormhole."

"Yes. Explain about this relay system," Omu said, jerking an elbow in the direction of the huge white tube running around the interior of the dome. "How does *that* work?"

"Oh, that's just the short-range, local-portal device," Professor Odd said dismissively. "It can't take you across universes, and its range is probably in the neighborhood of eight hundred thousand kilometers—which is why you have to *wait* for the gravity anchor to pass within that distance of Earth. You can then use the local portal to transport items from Earth to the mouth of the wormhole, which sucks them down and spits them out the other side. But because of the orbit of the gravity anchor it only comes within reach every eight years or so—hence Alpha Zora's periodically missing reports. Your missions to La Palma—er, Canary 6—have to coincide with the anchor's closest approach to Earth—probably on one or the other side of its perihelion." She looked around at them, glowing with excitement. "Does that make sense at all?"

But the dogs were silent. They were looking at the screen with a sort of cold horror. At last Ishin said:

"I was supposed to send my *team* through that thing."

Professor Odd's smile faded. "Yes," she said reluctantly. "But if you calculated the opening of the portal correctly and the receiving portal was open when they arrived, there was a good chance they would have survived the journey."

Ishin did not appear comforted by this.

"How do we destroy it?" he asked instead.

Professor Odd's shoulders slumped. "You *can't* destroy a wormhole," she said. "You can wait for it to die, or you could destroy the anchor and let it drift free. Destroying the anchor is probably the closest you could get, but considering it was built to withstand the phenomenal forces exerted upon it by the wormhole, you'd need the equivalent of a small star."

"Is there any way to, I don't know, sabotage the anchor's orbit so it falls into the sun?" Omu asked.

Professor Odd turned a bright smile on him. "You know, I believe there *is*, Ranger Omu. It's a bit beyond my means at the moment, but I think that's something *your* people could figure out how to do on their own—given enough time."

"That does not help us now," Ksanos pointed out. "How do we destroy it in the immediate future?"

"WE WILL NOT DESTROY IT," Dave said. He had planted his panvironment suit by an aperture in the tube and was working on a small circuit board there. "WE WILL DEACTIVATE THE LOCAL PORTAL. WITHOUT THE LOCAL PORTAL TO ACT AS A RELAY, ANYTHING THAT COMES THROUGH THE WORMHOLE WILL BE IMMEDIATELY DESTROYED BY THE NATURAL FRICTION OF THE WORMHOLE MEETING CONVENTIONAL SPACE. IT IS AN EFFECTIVE DEFENSE."

"Hold up a moment," Alister said. "You mean if there's no portal to pick up whatever comes through it gets destroyed? What is the Canary Company doing then? Just sitting there with their portal open?"

"Oh, they probably wait until they calculate the window for this portal's efficacy is open," Professor Odd said with wave of her hand. "Then they leave theirs on until they receive the payload, send back their new orders, and then close up shop until the next time."

"So . . . " Alister said slowly, to be sure he got this right. "They probably have their portal open *right now*, because *here's* the team and *there's* the wormhole." He gestured at the dogs in the room and then pointed at the screen.

Professor Odd turned and gave him a penetrating look.

"What are you suggesting, Mr. Alister?"

"Oh," said Alister, suddenly uncertain. "Well . . . I was thinking. If we're going to do this properly, oughtn't we to send them one last message? You know, tell them to back off?"

"I DOUBT THE EFFECTIVENESS OF SUCH A COMMUNICATION," Dave said. "BUT A PART OF ME AGREES IT WOULD BE POETICALLY SATISFYING."

Alister turned to the dogs. "Well then," he said. "Is there anything you'd like to tell them, before we deactivate the portal?"

Unsurprisingly, they all had suggestions. It was decided in the end that everyone would write a note, and they would put them all into the metallic case that Ishin had been given to carry to the payload. Elo, Dave and Professor Odd all declined to write notes, but Alister, after some thought, carefully tore a square of paper off of Reiji's pad. Using the floor of the observatory as a hard surface he carefully folded it into a paper bird and, with a borrowed pen, printed, LEAVE THEM ALONE on the underside of one wing.

Feeling unreasonably triumphant and just a little naughty, Alister tucked the paper bird in with the rest of the notes (he didn't read them all, but Reiji's said something about "go hump a barbwire fence"), closed the case firmly and handed it back to Ishin.

The little dog turned to Professor Odd, holding the case in both paws.

"Now what?" he asked.

Professor Odd grinned.

The white tubes running around the interior of the observatory did not make a complete circuit: there was a break just by the door to the rest of the building, where the ends of the tube terminated in smooth, domed faces of naked metal. Professor Odd ushered the lot of them through this gap, out of the observatory, before arranging them in a semicircle facing the aperture. Dave remained within, where he jump-started the generator and slowly brought the portal online.

The was a flickering in the air between the two metal faces, a high humming sound that made Alister's ears hurt, and Elo and the dogs clapped their paws over theirs. Then the portal snapped into existence.

It did not look like the other portals Alister had seen. It was not fixed to a physical aperture, for a start: it existed as a twist of light between the ends of the tubing, and gave off a faint fizzing sound. As one the dogs backed away, and Elo looked at it critically.

"I wouldn't fancy going through *that,*" she said.

"YOU MAY SEND YOUR MESSAGE THROUGH NOW," Dave announced from beyond the twist of light and noise. "I HAVE CALIBRATED THE DESTINATION LOCATION AS PRECISELY AS THESE INSTRUMENTS ALLOW."

"That's your cue," Professor Odd said, turning to Ishin.

The little white dog, holding his injured arm close to his side, awkwardly lobbed the slim metal case into the fizzing twist of distorted light. Electricity arced from the metal domes, striking the case, and for a moment it was completely surrounded by a blaze of lightning.

Then it was gone, leaving behind a burning afterimage and a faint smell of scorched metal.

The humming sound faded away, and the light with it, until there was nothing left. Then there was an abrupt crunching sound, and Dave rolled into view holding the control panel in three of his arms. From the way it had twisted and the broken wires trailing from its underside, it looked like he had pulled it violently out of its socket.

"NOW IT IS DONE," he said.

"And well done, I think," Professor Odd said. She turned to the assembled crowd of tired, hungry, and marginally injured dogs, and said brightly: "Now we'll see about getting you lot home. In the meantime, would anyone like a little *breakfast?*"

Epilogue

THEY ATE BREAKFAST—or was it dinner?—gathered around the table in the main room of the Professor's ship.

"Only it's not *really* a ship," Elo tried to explain as she cleared the table, carting away queer bits of machinery, weapons, monitors and stacks of data discs by the armload. "It's more of a *place*. A place that *moves* around. Anyway, that's not so important. The important bit is that door—" She nodded to the little door where Ksanos was currently overseeing Alpha Zora being carried up the steps. "We can open that pretty much anywhere in your world. Once we've eaten we can drop you off wherever you like!"

Feeling like he was being plunged even further out of his depth, Omu was relieved when Professor Odd changed the subject by pushing whole piles of stuff off the table.

Breakfast turned out to be a strange combination of egg-filled pastry with buttery flakes, crispy strips of fried meat laid over slices of fluffy brown bread with jam drizzled on top, and warm creamy cereal with sweet crunchy bits. There were also baked apples covered in cheese, which, Omu realized, was what he had first smelled on the Professor.

"You made . . . all *this?*" Alister exclaimed.

"I WAS HUNGRY," said Dave.

Omu glanced sideways at the thing that insisted it was not a robot. It still *looked* like a robot to him, but he had never heard of a robot that *ate food,* and it was currently stuffing an egg-filled pastry into a little hole in the side of its barrel and held a cheese-covered apple in one of its long, curling appendages. Omu shrugged to himself and added it to the growing list of things he personally considered to be above his pay grade. He was perfectly happy to let Ksanos and Ishin (who seemed to have resolved their differences) confer with Professor Odd over where exactly to drop them off.

"It would be ideal if we could arrive within walking distance of a Neo Canii satellite base," Ksanos was saying. "They will be the most receptive to our report. We can reach out to Arms Div and Expo Div from there."

"Give Sci Div a chance," Ishin protested. "We're not all zealous humanists."

"I will trust your judgement, Ksanos," Professor Odd said. "But would you not prefer to come through *in an actual base?*"

Ksanos looked shrewdly at the door and around at the flickering lights. "I think, if we could come through where there are unlikely to be *witnesses,* then we can more readily concoct a less incredible story."

"Suit yourself," Professor Odd said with a shrug. "Alister, would you like to try driving for this part?"

Alister looked up from his meal, the pink draining from his face and leaving him papery white. "Absolutely *not,*" he exclaimed.

On a wide, windswept plain of pale green grass under a high, gray sky, a small hut of the sort used in ancient times by shepherds crouched low and dark at the base of a huge power pole, supporting a dozen gently dipping wires that swooped across the sky to the next pole, nearly a half mile away. The only other sign of civilization was a small cluster of buildings just peeking out over the horizon.

With a creak the aged wooden door swung open, and a small reddish-brown canine head poked its nose out into the brisk wind.

"Oh *thank* the merciful makers!" Reiji cried, throwing himself out the door and onto the ground, where he began to roll exuberantly. "Back, back, we're *back!*" He paused, all four legs in the air, and then twisted himself upright again. "Um . . . *where* are we?"

Ksanos Boraznes stepped gracefully out of the door, ducking her narrow head to clear the lintel. She carried a heavy pack strapped to her shoulders; it contained the remains of the control panel Dave had ripped from the portal machine back on Canary 6. "Two kilometers outside Neo Canii Base North," she said. "Follow me."

In a slow, staggered line, one dog after another exited the hut and began making their way across the barren gray-green landscape.

As Tech Ishin left the hut, his wounded arm now held in a sling, Alister stopped him and passed him a folded piece of paper. "Your return message," he explained.

Ishin took the paper reverently, but did not open it. "What . . . er . . . what does it say?" he asked.

Alister looked surprised. "Just . . . 'no further orders,' of course."

The little dog nodded to himself, and tucked the message into his breast pocket. With the support of Scout Shani, he began walking resolutely after the retreating figures of Ksanos and Reiji.

Omu and Xixuan, maneuvering Alpha Zora down the stairs and into the wheeled contraption Elo and Dave had set up outside, were the last to leave the Oddity.

"Much better than that wretched sled," Elo assured him. She gave him an encouraging pat on the shoulder. "Good luck," she said. "Or, as my people would say . . . "

And then she did something with her face. Its meaning went clear over Omu's head, but he *saw* that it had meaning this time. He felt his face move instinctually in response.

"There," said Elo. "You're getting the hang of it."

She nodded to Xixuan, bowed to Zora, and then disappeared back into the hut.

"Good luck everyone," Professor Odd called from the door, waving to them as she pulled it shut. There was no great noticeable difference, but Omu Akit knew that, if he were to open it, there would be nothing but a damp, dirty shed on the other side.

He shook his head and looked down at his alpha. "What on *earth* are we gonna tell them back at HQ?" he asked.

And Alpha Zora looked up at him, his face strangely plain and naked without the comsys, and he smiled. A real smile, not the pixelated icon Omu was used to seeing on the comsys display. This was similar, but altogether more complicated. The alpha patted his soldier on the arm, as if to say: *Don't worry, I'll think of something.*

"I certainly hope so," Omu said, and began to push the wheeled chair across the ground. It rolled surprisingly easily.

Beside him, Xixuan's head jerked up.

"Oh, *no*," the big dog said. "Don't *you* start now!"

At the expression on *his* face, Omu Akit found he couldn't help barking a laugh.

Professor Odd will return in
"Chronostrophe"

Originally written to accompany the illustration of the same name appearing on the cover of this issue, "The Wolf and the Rabbit" is a sort-of folktale that introduces the Luck Rabbit, which has gone on to become a recurring motif in my work. First published online in 2008, it has been refined for its first print appearance.

The Wolf and the Rabbit

M ANY YEARS AGO, in a great, dark, wood, there lived a wolf. He was strong and clever, like most wolves, but also incredibly unlucky. The sheep he caught tended to be sick, and the farmers he offended very good at throwing stones. In this way he was often hungry, and smarting all over from bruises.

One day, when he was prowling the wood, hungry and grumpy, he came upon a plump, white rabbit sunning itself on a rock. The rabbit regarded him warily but did not run away.

"What a pleasant surprise," said the wolf. "I have found someone who is even more unlucky than myself! You, my plump little morsel, must be the most unlucky creature in this forest, so bright and white in a world of browns and greens. How is it you have lived so long?"

"I am not unlucky at all," replied the rabbit, cheerfully. "Quite the opposite, in fact. I am the luckiest rabbit in the world; so lucky that my fur shines with it."

"What a load of sheep sick," said the wolf. "Be that as it may, your luck has just run out, for I am tired and hungry, and I think I will make you my lunch. That will teach you to trust your precious luck."

"I wouldn't recommend that," said the rabbit, remaining calm even as the wolf edged nearer.

"Why not?" asked the wolf. "Are you sick as well?"

"Not at all," said the rabbit. "But if you eat me, I promise I will turn all my luck against you. The next sheep you eat will infect you with stomach rot. The next farmer who sees you will have a gun and not a rock. Your pack will desert you, and you will die, painfully and alone."

"Such is the life of my kind," said the wolf with an uncaring shrug. "I have lived with bad luck all my years, a little more doesn't scare me."

"But," said the rabbit, sitting up on her hind legs and spreading her little white paws. "If you choose not to eat me, and instead become my friend, and protect me from other wolves and from eagles and all the other nasty things that like to eat *my* kind, then I will share my good luck with you, and your life will be much more pleasant."

The wolf sat down and thought about this.

"No more sick sheep?"

"None at all," said the rabbit.

"No more farmers with stones?"

"I shall see that they all will miss."

The wolf chewed on his lip a while, mulling it over. The rabbit waited patiently.

"How can I know you're telling the truth?" the wolf asked.

"You must trust me and see for yourself," said the rabbit.

Now, how this story ends will depend on who is telling it. The farmers will tell you that the wolf ate the rabbit anyway and was killed by hunters the next day. But if you ask them why the hamlets are filled with stories about a great black wolf with a white rabbit riding on its back who prowls the forest, who takes the plumpest sheep, whom even the sharpest marksmen cannot hit, and who no trap can snare, they will go very quiet and change the subject.

If you are hearing the tale from the witches in the mountains or the hermits in the wood, however, they will tell you that the wolf took the rabbit at her word, and indeed his luck did change, and they have been inseparable ever since.

And, if you hang out in the hamlets at the borders of the forest, in the dusk and early morning, you might, just as the rabbit said, see for yourself.

Though it is the eighth story in the second volume of The Adventures of Bouragner Felpz, *"The Moonfoot Problem" (which appeared in* Apsis Fiction: Perihelion 2015) *stands on its own sufficiently to be read out of order. It was written over the course of a crowded week in the middle of November 2013.*

THE MOONFOOT PROBLEM

THE OTHER DAY I RECEIVED A LETTER from Felpz. In it was a clipping from the *Times* of Redling, containing an obituary for Lord Farrod, Earl of Moonfoot, and a note attached in my friend's own hand saying: *I think it's high time you told the story of Lord Nickel and Medrova. They are well beyond the reach of Kyrish law, and it can't hurt that terrible old man now.*

I was surprised and a little excited by this, as I had thought those events would remain buried until the time of my grandchildren or later. I was still skeptical of Felpz's assurance—being that the events in question compromised the virtue of a very grand old Kyrish family—but since the last lord of that line is cold in the ground, and having ascertained that the only people living whom this story could touch are safely on the other side of the world, I feel relatively comfortable in recounting them now.

Shoveling through my veritable snowdrift of notes, I find it was in the summer of 2322, over ten years ago, that my attention was brought to the astonishing murder of Lord Nickel Kellsbrook, only son and heir to the Earl of Moonfoot. To say this was where the story began, however, would be misleading. In truth the first I heard of the curious string of events—though I would not connect them until later—was at a casual lunch with my old friend Milky.

"Mrs Grissom told me the most incredible thing," he mentioned offhandedly one afternoon at Valaire's. We had taken to meeting there for lunch about twice a month, as otherwise our lives did not intersect save on the occasions when we were both caught up in Felpz's adventures, and then there was no time for innocent pleasantries. It was through these regular visits that I first learned of Mrs Grissom, the tailor who rented the shop next door to his carpentry business, and his other mercantile friends: Mrs Dolnir, a potter, and Miss Valaire, who ran the very same Valaire's Café and Chocolaterie where we held our semi-monthly meetings.

It amused me that Milky, despite cultivating friendships with mature and intelligent women, had managed to remain perennially single throughout our acquaintance. It could be argued that this was *because* they were mature and intelligent women. I certainly had no inclination to marry anyone, not even Milky—fond as I was of the man I had had enough of marriage to last a lifetime, and though I confess I did puzzle over what *his* reasons for singularity could be, I never was impertinent enough to ask.

I was, however, happy to listen to his recounting of Mrs Grissom's tale, which he told with an odd mix of amicable irreverence and acute attention to my reactions, as though he hoped to read something more out of them than what I would openly say.

"She has a remarkable new client," he told me. "A foreign gent, but she tells me no more of him. 'Parently he has been in and out of her shop for the past few months, always ordering some fine new garment or other, but with the most exacting measurements."

"That cannot be so unusual," I said. "A gentleman will want his suits to fit as perfectly as possible."

"Ah, but they're not *suits*, is the bargain of it," Milky said, dipping into his old slang in his excitement. "They're all *dresses*. A lady's wardrobe, from what Mrs Grissom can tell. Which wouldn't be so strange on account of itself—a man's got every right to order fineries for his lady to wear—but if these dresses are for a woman then she's a very peculiar shape."

"Why?" I asked with a laugh. "Have they got an extra sleeve or some such?"

Milky frowned at me, as if pondering how best to phrase his next words.

"Nothin' so fantastical," he said at length. "It's just . . . well, Mrs Grissom explained it better, bein' a tailor and all she knows about the shapes of people's bodies, and *she* says they don't seem like women's dresses. Something about the hips being mighty narrow and the shoulders unusually wide . . . also, whoever they are for, it's someone nearing six feet."

"That can't be so astonishing," I said, pouring myself another cup of tea. "Women are not cut out of dough by the same stamp, as you should well know, and some of us are quite tall."

Milky wriggled uncomfortably and appeared to hide behind the teapot.

"You cannot mean to suggest that you believe these dresses are being ordered for the gentleman *himself?*" I asked.

Milky, if possible, shrank further behind the pot.

"Not the gent what's been in there," he mumbled. "Mrs Grissom says he's a completely different size—much smaller than the measurements."

"Oh . . . " I said, thinking the matter over. In truth I found the idea of a man in women's clothing somewhat less shocking than my peers did. Having been exposed at a young age to women who preferred to dress in traditionally male costume, I now supposed that the reverse might also be true. I said as much to Milky, and added: "Though why a man would voluntarily submit to being laced into a corset and to wearing layers of cumbersome petticoats is beyond my imagination. Why not have a nice suit made with a few frills and floral patterning as a compromise?"

To which Milky laughed, and all the tension went out of the air. Our conversation turned down other avenues, and soon we were engrossed in picking over the reports, freshly appearing in the day's papers, of the extraordinary and gruesome murder of Lord Nickel Kellsbrook—the odd eccentricities of Mrs Grissom's clients clean forgotten.

Since it has been so long I see no reason why I should not recount the details here—though in their full and validated form, and free of the speculation added into accounts of the time for drama.

Lord Nickel Kellsbrook, as has been mentioned in this narrative before, was the only son and heir to Lord Ferrod, Earl of Moonfoot. A popular young lad, clean and handsome and dazzlingly charming, he had long been notorious for cavorting around the Redling clubs and getting into all manner of scrapes—though these were always of the amorous, rather than violent, variety. Even so it was a known shame to his father, who was rendered beside himself with grief and fury when the young man eventually fell ill as a result of his wanton lifestyle. The Earl responded by having the lad sent away for a year's voyage in the south seas, which the doctors prescribed as the best medication for his ailment. Much to the surprise of fashionable society (and the delight of Lord Moonfoot), young Nickel returned from this voyage fully recovered and with a much more sober bearing. He had arrived back at the family seat of Moonfoot Manor the summer previous, and to all appearances seemed content to remain there—eschewing his former haunts in the city and concentrating on fulfilling his duty as the heir of a major estate. Indeed, little had been seen of the young man since his return to Kyreland, and some rumors speculated that he had not in fact recovered from his illness and was on his deathbed at Moonfoot Manor.

The rumors proved both false and true, after a fashion, when his body was discovered, clubbed to death and throat cut, on the floor of the manor's dining room. The young man was certainly dead, but just as certainly due to no illness. Unless, as some of the more irreverent papers proclaimed, it was the illness of having half one's brains scattered across the hearth.

It was a shocking state of affairs, and the country was waiting eagerly for the report of the necromancers, who had descended upon the corpse like vultures the moment the Earl declared he wished to have the case settled as soon as possible. It had been two weeks, however, and not a word from any of the necromancy houses either in Redling or in the country.

"I wonder what Hydegan would have made of this," I pondered, referring to our old friend who had been instrumental in popularizing the use of necromancy in murder investigations.

He had long since retired to raise bees in Duscany but had left behind a force of young necromancers to take his place. Their practice had proved useful in cases where the victim had seen their attacker—though some legal gymnastics had to be done before courts would accept the testimony of a dead person—but not useful at all where the murderer had succeeded in hiding themself.

In this case, however, there had been no word—either of useful testimony or lack thereof—and the public's opinion of necromancers was becoming a trifle strained.

"I can't begin ter imagine," sighed Milky. "As I can't know what's stopping the ones we've got now. If it were the fact that his head was compromised that's preventing his corpse from talking, then I 'spect they'd 'ave just said so. What could be flummoxing them so good that they can't even *admit* they're flummoxed is beyond me. Though I'da guessed that, were it a really bad tangle, Hydegan as likely have sent off for Felpz by now, asking for help. But I fancy these new ones are too proud. It would be like running home to mother to get her to sew yer trousers shut. Nice thing to be able to *do,* but no one likes to admit it." He shrugged, and there we left the matter for the day. Milky retuned to his shop to finish a commission, and I returned to my own lodgings, looking forward to a pleasant afternoon spent writing in the seclusion of my study.

Which plans were dramatically overturned the moment I stepped into our entry hall and found Felpz lying in a truly alarming posture at the foot of the stairs. I shall not describe it, for I shall be describing enough unsettling sights herein, and I do not wish to torment my readers with ones which turned out to be completely benign.

At the moment, however, the sight of my oldest and dearest friend, apparently dead of a broken neck, sent my heart plummeting and a terrible wail out of my throat. Gone were any assurances that Felpz was a magical immortal whose physical form could endure the onslaught of centuries, scorching fire and freezing cold, for there he lay on the floor—as clearly deceased as a carcass at the butcher's—and all I could find it in myself to do was scream and scream, turning my head away as if to deny the universe this truth.

"Well at least *you* find it convincing," said the voice of Felpz from the top of the stairs.

I whipped my head around and there was my friend, full of life and light and wearing a deep plum-colored suit with matching leather shoes, filling the space at the top of the stairs with his warm, commanding presence.

"*Felpz,*" I gasped, my voice a mere rasp. I was not certain whether I wished to embrace or shake the man. Not being close enough to do either I shook my fist at him as I struggled to catch my breath. "Felpz—what is the meaning of this—*this*—" I gestured at the terrible form upon the floor.

"You mean my simulacrum?" Felpz asked, waving a hand. As he did so his fallen double dissolved into a dusky purple mist and then vanished altogether. "I wanted to see if I could make one in that state. Not something I've ever had to do before, but that is the joy of our ever-changing world: new sights, new challenges, new *tricks*. Oh, step up here my dear Corianne, I did not mean to shock you so. Come in and I will make you some tea. Then I will explain the matter in full."

I must have appeared more upset than I felt—indeed I mostly felt anger at Felpz for his insensitive behavior—for my friend turned hennish for a few minutes, guiding me gently to an armchair and seeing me comfortably settled. When I had gotten over my shock and began to snip at him like an impatient horse, he took the cue and cast himself back across our sofa with a grand sigh.

"Oh, it is all due to this blasted Moonfoot case, Corianne," he moaned. "If you must blame someone, blame those wretched, incompetent necromancers!"

"They have asked for your help," I remarked, with only a little surprise.

"If only they had been so deferential," Felpz snarled, unbuttoning his coat and casting it open so he could stretch his shoulders. "No, I have been retained—*retained*, Corianne, like a civil servant!—on behalf of the Great Kyrish Police, to sort out the mess *their* necromancers have caused by botching what should have been a simple waking. It has taken me *days* to work back to this solution, and I am still not sure it is the right one. Pray, do you feel strong enough to bear the weight of my unburdening?

I feel I must talk this through with *someone*, else my head will explode."

"By all means," I said, settling back in my chair and sipping my tea. Now that the shock had worn off—Felpz being so vividly and clearly *alive*—I was dreadfully curious about the whole matter. It was not often Felpz volunteered such candid discussion of his work before a problem was solved, and I relished the opportunity to attempt to solve it with him.

"Pray," I added with a grin, "leave nothing out."

Felpz smiled shortly, a brief flash of humor before his face fell back into gravity. "You may not thank me for that. Well, you must by now have heard of the unfortunate demise of the young Lord Nickel?"

"Oh yes, Milky and I were just discussing it," I assured him.

Felpz gave out a little *hmph* noise and twined his fingers together. "Then I shall pick up with events that first included *me*. You may recall, dearest and most long-suffering Corianne, how I was summoned away quite abruptly after dinner some weeks ago? Well, that was at the behest of our old friend Cullins—you remember Constable Cullins, who was so impetuous as to bring me in on the matter which you so fancifully titled *The Twisted Unicorn*? Well, he is *Captain* Cullins now, and quite a grand old captain he is—who more less begged me to have a look at a matter which stumped his necromancers. 'They are very good at getting the dead to talk, but if they *don't* talk then they're little more useful at solving a murder than kittens.' I protested that where specialists such as necromancers had failed he could hardly expect a general practitioner such as myself to have better luck. To which he replied that that was *precisely* why he wished for my assistance. Do you know what he said to me, Corianne? It was perhaps the most flattering thing I've ever heard: 'You are only a *general* practitioner,' he said, 'inasmuch as your specialties cover every vein of magic under the sun. You may not fare better than a necromancer at coaxing words from a corpse, but *you'll* see things in the situation that they, lacking your universal knowledge, would miss.'

"As you can imagine this outpouring of praise disarmed me, and I agreed. Much good it has done me to succumb to flattery." He twisted his face in disgust. "So I found myself summarily

briefed on the state of the investigation. Which, for your ben‑
efit, is this:

"They are relatively certain of the time of the murder, the
time of death being the one thing the necromancers were able
to divine from the body, and from the testimony of the house‑
maid, who heard a ruckus in the dining room at a little past
eleven. Since it sounded especially violent she, being a sen‑
sible young woman, fetched the butler and a footman before
leading them into the dining room. By the time they arrived,
however, the deed had been done, and Lord Nickel was already
dead. Cullins told me a full examination of the room turned
up a wealth of footprints and the residue from a sharp blast
of magic—presumably behind the blow that destroyed the poor
man's head. A few obvious valuable pieces—plate and a pair of
ornamental swords—were also missing, and as the man had no
known enemies the whole mess was presumed to be the work
of burglars. Moonfoot is known to be a wealthy estate, and the
earl is not particularly popular with the townsfolk, so it seemed
to fit well.

"Seemed, I repeat. The chief inspector on the case, a small
shrewish woman named Halfway, was puzzled over the matter
of the footprints. *She* felt there were too many of them, consid‑
ering the size of the room. Something about diverting forces to
act as watchdogs. Anyway, that point is not immediately rele‑
vant so I will leave it for now. What *is* relevant is what happened
when they brought the body back to the necromancers. I must
admit, on the whole they have not been too much of a disgrace
to Hydegan's name, but three young and impetuous—if largely
talented—individuals do not make up for the careful purity and
grace of form that marked Hydegan's work. They also have the
regrettable tendency to argue amongst themselves. So it hap‑
pened that the initial examination of the body, as it was reported
to me, was a fractured affair—each necromancer having scrib‑
bled their own notes over the official write‑up, and sometimes
over their colleagues' notes. They do seem to agree, however,
that the damage to the head, though quite extensive, was recon‑
structable provided they could recover all the pieces of brain
matter. As this was not the first time they'd been asked to wake
the victim of a head trauma, the request had been anticipated

by Inspectrix Halfway, and the missing pieces duly provided. And do you know what they found when they'd got the head reassembled and the corpse awake and talking?"

"Pray tell me," I encouraged him.

"Nothing," said Felpz. "Nothing whatsoever. The corpse rose, all right. It took breath and it answered their call, but of its life it would say *nothing*. Not even that it had no knowledge of its death. *It could not even tell them its name.*

"Well, at the time the necromancers understandably assumed that the problem lay in their reconstruction of the head, so they promptly put him out again and messed around *some more*. They tried this three times, and each time the corpse would say *nothing*. Finally they tried a fourth time, and that time they failed. The corpse would not stir. At this point Cullins thought to call me in, and though it is flattering to be considered a universal specialist, I can't help but wish I had been there from the beginning.

"I did, however, strive to learn from the mistakes of the necromancers. Rather than attempt a simple waking of my own, I approached the body as if I had been first called to the scene. I made an entirely mundane examination of it—just as doctor would have done—and I discovered a number of interesting things that had not made it into the official report.

"For one, the devastating blow to the head—which was no doubt the cause of death—was not the young man's only injury. Far from it. He bore a great number of smaller, yet altogether more sinister wounds. Multiple bruises around the ribs, a few of which felt broken, ranged from old and fading to brilliant and purple to new and red. And there were other marks: the small, circular holes caused by that of a hat pin or a needle along his upper arm and down his thighs, and multiple scars from similar wounds, long healed over."

Felpz leaned back upon the sofa, his twining fingers gone tense and angular. "All situated such that, when clothed, nothing would be visible. Indeed, since necromancers are not in the habit of stripping their subjects—in fact it is considered a terrible violation in their profession—they had no knowledge of the extent of the abuse the man's body had suffered. At the time I was hard pressed to say how it related to his ultimate fate, and

I was as stymied as they were. Eventually I came to the decision that, as his death was of no help to me, I might as well make a study of his life. For if his death had been as random and violent as it appeared there was nothing I could do. If, on the other hand, there had been something in his life to precipitate its violent end I might unravel the mystery that way.

"In this matter I was aided with surprising vivacity by Inspectrix Halfway, who, being neither mage nor necromancer, had lighted upon my train of thought from the very first, and was delighted to have the assistance of one versed in the magical arts at her disposal. She brought me over to Moonfoot Manor and showed me around the crime scene, carefully reconstructing it over the cleaned and tidied room. She showed me photos of the prints they had been able to isolate, and I had to agree they were a curiously diverse and varied selection of burglars, ranging from a great, striding heavy fellow, to prints as light and delicate as a child's. She also had me interview the servants who had found the man, and here I ran up against a curious thing: though they were all more than forthcoming about the events of the night—and with such ardent honesty I could not doubt them—they were singularly repressed when it came to matters of the *house*.

"'Was Lord Nickel often up late?' I asked.

"'Why sir, I couldn't say,' was the answer, and this coming from the man's *valet*. And a thread of fear ran through them all, as though they were intentionally shielding someone—not out of loyalty or love, but out of *fear*. I confirmed this when I asked after the relationship between the earl and his son, and they all but shut down on me.

"'Was the earl a loving father?'

"'I'm sure he was, sir.'

"'Was there ever any disagreement between father and son?'

"'I really couldn't say, sir.'

"The more I questioned the more I became convinced that they were holding something back, a dark secret that they dared not reveal for fear of losing their livelihoods. I shared this suspicion with Inspectrix Halfway, and we found ourselves in complete agreement. She had in fact already interviewed the earl and come away profoundly unimpressed.

"'He speaks of his son almost as though the man were a horse or hunting dog,' she confided in me. 'He mourns his loss, but only because it is an inconvenience since now he must find a new heir. As though he has lost a piece of *property*, not a member of his family.'

"'Grief does manifest itself in a myriad of different ways,' I allowed.

"'Wait until you've met the old boulder,' she told me firmly.

"Before I continue, let me give you my first impression of Lord Moonfoot, so that you may judge what transpired in context. When Halfway described him as an *old boulder* she was not being entirely poetic. The man struck me as having a hard, cold, immovable quality, and he is indubitably quite old. His son Nickel was the only offspring from his third marriage, which ended in divorce when the lad was sixteen. He has, in fact, three daughters from the two previous wives, all of whom were grown and married off before the son finally arrived. So the boy was raised as an only child by a string of nannies, as his mother was a sickly woman, and as soon as she got her strength up she left the old man—though she had to leave her son behind to do it. All this may give you a singularly uncharitable view of his character, but I can say that it would pale next to the revulsion you would feel were you to actually meet him.

"He is, it must be said, a handsome old man, with a fine head of silver hair and bright blue eyes. But whatever superficial beauty he has managed to retain is spoilt by his icy and venomous character.

"'I must wonder what a *magician* thinks he may accomplish in a matter not even the necromancers can untangle,' was his way of opening our interview. He then proceeded to ask me what my qualifications were, how I intended to catch his son's murderers, and whether I had found his missing valuables yet—as though I were coming to him in supplication, requesting the honor of serving him. I answered these questions with as much honesty and as little anger as I could manage, the result being that he took an immediate dislike to me. Perhaps this was unwise of me, for if I had bothered to curry his favor he might have been more forthcoming when I began bombarding him with my own questions. Then again, he might not have, and as it happened I learned a great deal more from his reactions and sub-conscious movements than I ever did from his words.

"When I asked, for example, how his son had come to be covered in small, hidden injuries, there flashed across his face as strong a look of contempt and guilt as I had ever seen. He made some excuse, of course, about his son's wild youthful adventures and not being able to exert the steadying influence that had been required. I became convinced, however, that he knew exactly who his son's tormentor was—if it was not in fact *himself.* When I pried more about the nature of the illness that had necessitated a year-long voyage for recovery he began elaborately obfuscating—at times contradicting himself. When I continued to press the matter he eventually allowed that it had been an illness of the *mind* rather than of the body, leaving me to assume that his son had been caught in some horrifically perverse act and only by removing him from Kyreland was a scandal averted. As an honored member of the peerage a *scandal* was to him a disaster even greater than losing his son entirely.

"I left his study, where our interview had been conducted, with the feeling of having been thrown against a board of nails, and was tempted to examine my own person for wounds similar to those of the dead man. Yet I now had a picture in my head of what Lord Nickel's existence in the manor must have been like, and I had to wonder if he had not bashed his own brains out as a means of escape.

"How all this leads to me creating a dead simulacrum of myself is a labyrinthine path so follow closely: I returned to Redling at this point, uneasy in my mind about the matter. It could yet have been a simple robbery and murder, for I am no expert at unraveling crimes, but I found I had become deeply interested in the life of this young man who, it seemed clear to me, had suffered a miserable existence in his short time. I felt immense sympathy for him, and wanted at least to uphold the truth of his fate, so that he might in death receive a validation that he had been denied in life.

"To this end I began to examine his history in more detail. I hunted down his old nannies, and found them for the most part to be good, kind women who—being no longer in the employ of that prickly old man—were altogether more willing to talk about Lord Nickel than any of his servants. To his credit the young lord had kept in touch with them, so from them I was able to glean a picture of an intelligent, sensitive young man with a taste for fine things and an appreciation of the arts. What did they think of his amorous exploits in Redling? Vicious lies, they said. Dear Nickel would never debase himself in such a way. Who spread them? There they were at a loss. Not his father, surely, for it would serve him no purpose. Perhaps some jealous peer who envied his popularity with the young ladies. So he was popular with the young ladies? Oh, *very* popular. Did he ever show them any favor? Nothing beyond what propriety would allow, he was a *perfect* gentleman. Then why was he sent away under such dubious circumstances? Well, there they hesitated, for he had never said—and they had heard nothing from him since he embarked on his voyage, but the consensus was that he must have fallen in love with some unsuitable woman. Perhaps a maid, perhaps a simple flower girl. For whatever reason she was not the woman his father wished him to marry, and in order to separate the two he had drummed up the story of his son's illness and sent him away. They feared at the time that his father would try to isolate him from all his old friends, and this fear was borne out by the events that followed. Lord Nickel returned, but not to the regular correspondence with his old caregivers that he had previously enjoyed. Their letters went unanswered, or were returned unopened. They were quite dejected about the whole matter. Had they any suspicions surrounding his death? There they were confounded. They all agreed that the old man held no great love for his son beyond that of a possession, but they could not believe he would have the boy murdered—as it would not serve his interests.

"I left them in no greater a state of enlightenment than when I had found them. In fact I felt myself heavily weighted by all the information they had laid upon me. It was at this point, dear Corianne, that I disappeared for a few days. Did you happen to notice? You *did?* Well, I hope I did not worry you. Anyway, it was during this time that I found myself drawn back to the problematic body—both of my own accord and because the Kyrish Police were anxious for me to resolve the matter and would not stop pestering me.

"I came into the necromancer's workshop late at night, when the place was deserted, and sat there alone with the corpse for some hours, turning over all the information in my head. I considered what I now knew of this man and what I knew of his family, and I decided the only way to untangle the mess for good would be to *talk* to him. You may point out that this is what the necromancers were trying to do from the beginning, but it is actually another thing entirely to summon the *spirit* of a dead person and converse with it, rather than simply to re-imbue a dead body with enough life that it may answer your questions. It is much more difficult to do the former, for example, and requires a certain elasticity—a disregard for the rules of life and death—on the part of the summoner, which not all magicians possess."

"But *you* do," I pointed out.

"Yes, *I* do," Felpz sighed, running a hand through his hair. Today this was a salt-and-pepper mix of dark brown and streaks of grey, but I knew it could turn all white or all brown at the whim of his mood. The same could be said for the bags beneath his eyes and the wrinkles of his brow. All could be gone and his face young and smooth were the right stimulation to be had.

"Even so it is not an easy task, and not something to be undertaken lightly. In this case, however, when all else had failed, I deemed it worthwhile. I set about summoning the spirit of Lord Nickel Kellsbrook, and do you know what happened?"

"I cannot imagine," I admitted readily, only wishing for the next piece of the story.

"Nothing," whispered Felpz. "Nothing *at all.* There was no answer from beyond the wall—not even a *rejection* of my summons. It was as if . . . as if I were summoning the spirit of one who was still tied to his body. In other words, the spirit of someone who was still *alive.*"

"But the body!" I cried.

"Yes!" Felpz echoed, leaning forward eagerly. "The *body!* Suddenly I looked at it again, really *looked,* and found myself doubting for the first time whether or not this was the *right* body. What if, I thought, Lord Nickel had faked his own death, and the corpse on the table was not, in fact, *his?* What if it had been tampered with, somehow, so that it could not speak and thus reveal its secrets? The best way to find out, I decided, would be to put the body back into its *original* state, *before* its head had ever been clubbed open. I could not bring it back to life that way, but I could at least examine it for signs of disguise—magical or practical. You may remember the magic I used ten years ago to restore the gold hair of that Cairdrian ghost?"

"I shall never forget," I assured him.

"Well, I did more or less the same thing to the corpse. It was significantly easier because the time that had elapsed since its death was not as much as in the case of the ghost. It took effort, yes, but I managed to run events backwards, effectively undoing the necromancers' muddling and reconstruction of the head. I saw it come apart, go back together, come apart, over and over, until at last it came apart and stayed that way. This time, however, instead of the careful dissection used by the necromancers, it was violently smashed open. A few pieces of skull and gore had even deposited themselves around the room, in effect recreating their positions in the dining room at Moonfoot.

"I then proceeded to do what I imagine Hydegan would have done from the start: I rolled time back *further,* so as to force the head into its original form, whole and intact. This is an even more difficult thing to do, as it requires crossing back into a time when the body was alive, but I expected I could hold it that way long enough to get a good look at the undamaged body.

"In this, however, I failed. Not through any lack of skill or power on my part, but because the body, when forced back along its own timeline to its form prior to that horrible blow, did not reconstruct itself as it should have. Instead . . . it *dissolved.*"

I started in my seat, nearly spilling my cold tea.

"I'm sorry," I stammered. "It *dissolved?*"

"Into a cloud of mist and vapor of pure, undirected *magic,*" Felpz said, his eyes shining with intensity. "The reason the necromancers hadn't been able to get a word out of it was because it wasn't a body at all—it was the *simulacrum* of a body! Like the one you saw me produce earlier. The reason it had been so difficult to push it back beyond the state of the head trauma was because that *was* its original state. It had been *created* dead. It had never *been* alive and so had no living memories to relay. It had no spirit. No . . . nothing. All its original, base components were simply this nebula of magic which, when I ceased to hold it, reshaped itself into the form of the murdered corpse once more."

"Why, Felpz," I gasped. "This is most extraordinary! But . . . what does it *mean?* Beyond the obvious, I should say, that there apparently has been no murder after all."

"And I reckon there were no burglars either," Felpz said, leaning back and smoothing down his hair. "As I think these events through I fancy more and more that the items really *were* stolen—but not by burglars. By Lord Nickel himself."

"To escape his abusive father," I said, speaking as the thoughts came to me. "He faked his own death and made off with a few valuable items, perhaps to aid in starting a life elsewhere."

"And that is where this whole matter breaks down!" Felpz cried, springing up from the sofa and beginning to pace about the room. "The motive and the evidence all points that way, but the *means*—where is the *means* by which he constructed such an incredible simulacrum?"

"Pardon?" I asked.

Felpz made a snatching motion with his hand, his fingers snapping, as though to catch the words he needed out of thin air. "To disguise the body of a real person would not be so remarkable," he said. "Distasteful, but it would be doable by the sort of disreputable jobbing wizard who might take such a commission. Where the body would be obtained is a further problem. But that is not what happened in this case. Here the body was constructed purely from magic, out of scratch and ether, and in such detail that it fooled all the best police officers and the necromancers *and me.* We all knew there was something wrong with it, but it never occurred to any of us that it was not real. To make something of that quality, that fine craftsmanship, with that sheer *realism*, would require a truly masterful magician. I know, because I've spent the last day trying to make one myself. The best result I managed was what you discovered on the floor when you entered a few hours ago, and that was after several attempts. If it is so difficult for *me* . . . then what magician could Nickel Kellsbrook have convinced to make *his?* For it would have taken a magician of my caliber to create such a thing, and I happen to know that there is maybe . . . *one* other such magician in all of this hemisphere capable of such a thing, and Nimbastula is such a wholesome soul I can't imagine her stooping to such a level. I have written and asked anyway, but I seriously doubt she had anything to do with this. You see . . . " and here he paused, having come around to rest himself against the back of the sofa. Crossing his arms he nibbled nervously at his fingertips for a moment before snatching them away. "In order to make a truly accurate simulacrum, one that recreates *exactly* the body it is meant to imitate . . . well, the magician in question must have intimate access to that body. Just as an artist who wishes to make an absolutely realistic portrait needs a life reference from which to work. I could make a convincing simulacrum of *my own* corpse, but I could not do the same for any other person—not even you or Milky. One would require a degree of knowledge of the subject's body that . . . well, to put it frankly, Corianne, the kind of knowledge that only mothers know of their children or lovers do of each other—and then only the most trusting and uninhibited of those." He shrugged unhappily. "I know exactly what I am looking for," he continued. "A extraordinarily talented magician who is intimately related to Lord Nickel and who has somehow *escaped* my notice. For be sure if one had been born in Kyreland, nay, anywhere across Thamber, I would have felt it."

"How are you so certain it is a *human* magician?" I asked. "Could not a fairy do something similar?"

"Oh, if it were a fairy that would broaden our prospects greatly," said Felpz. "But no, alas. From the feel of the magic I know the caster to be human. A young human, too, which inclines me to believe it is *not* the boy's mother. Though female magicians have, through sad necessity, become quite good at hiding their powers. Which leads me to believe . . . "

"His unsuitable lover?" I suggested.

"It does have a singularly romantic ring, does it not?" Felpz said, managing a grin. "A pleasant reversal of the knight in shining armor. Here we have a prince, not a princess, imprisoned and helpless, and a brave hero come to rescue him—not with arms and armor, but with clever spells and creative magic. But why did it take her so long? A full year he was away at sea—

surely to someone powerful enough to create a simulacrum of that quality, crossing a mere ocean and stealing your prince away off a boat would have been much easier! It is what I would have done. No . . . wait . . . *yes!*"

Felpz raised his head, and I saw his eyes were shining brilliantly. "The *boat!* Of course! It would explain why I have no knowledge of this mage! Ha *ha!*" he cried jovially, and danced around, gripping my arms and sweeping me to my feet. He kissed me on both cheeks and danced away to the door before I'd caught my breath.

"Oh, talking candidly to you is the best for clearing a troubled mind," he said, pulling down his hat and dusting it off.

"I am glad I could assist," I said, sinking back into my chair. "But Felpz, where are you going? Have you solved the mystery yet?"

"The *boat,* Corianne!" he cried, now halfway out the door. "The *voyage!* It all began there! Expect me back in time for supper—order enough for four, we shall be having guests tonight."

"What?" I said, bewildered. "Who?"

"Why, Lord Nickel Kellsbrook, of course," said Felpz. "And his brave enchantress!"

And with that he was out the door and down the stairs, leaving me alone and almost as confused as when the afternoon had begun.

Nevertheless I did as my friend had asked, pondering over what he could be up to. When dinner arrived I set it out while I puzzled over the implications of his last words.

"The lord must have met someone on the ship," I said to myself as I laid out the plates. "But if he were so madly in love, why not fly off there and then? Why come back to his father—who sounds like such a brute? Perhaps they didn't realize just how in love they were until later? *Pah.*"

At last I heard a touch of the bell, but when the housemaid showed the visitor in it turned out to be a pagegirl, who bobbed her head eagerly before handing me a letter.

It was a note from Felpz, and read as follows:

C, please bring dinner to the dockyards at Shiner's Head. Will be wait-ing for you aboard the Emmiran. *Say your name and the captain will let you aboard.*

~F

"*Oh!*" I broke off in frustration. "And I just got everything unpacked!"

There was nothing for it, however, but to re-pack the food and hire a cart.

The docks, calm in the steeply angled sun of that summer evening, were a particularly beautiful sight: the ships sitting like dark waterfowl upon a river that shone golden in the reflected light. I found the *Emmiran*—a steamship of modest size—after only a little difficulty, and the captain—who surprised me by being a stern woman with brick-red skin—let me aboard with a gruff welcome, leading the way to one of the larger cabins. There I found Felpz, sitting with his feet up on a dining table reading a novel of all things. He leapt up at the sight of me, and thanked the captain profusely before helping me lay out the dishes all over again.

"You left me at something of a chasm in your narrative," I chided him. "Surely you could string me a bridge now, as it were."

"Yes," said Felpz, distractedly straightening the silverware to his satisfaction. "I suppose we do have the time. Although we won't know the whole story until our guests arrive—they are not due aboard until nine o'clock—but I can tell you my train of thought, and how it influenced my actions of this evening. Please, sit."

"When I last saw you, Corianne," he continued once we were seated at the far end of the table, facing the door. "I left you with a somewhat confusing reference to a ship and a voyage. You may have already connected the loose threads yourself, and will not be surprised to hear that I suspected that this unusual mage who facilitated Lord Nickel's improbable disappearance was someone whom he met while on his voyage. Naturally the first thing I did was go down to the docking office to check the passenger man-ifests on all the ships during that time, and soon found the one that carried the ailing Lord Nickel. The *Nabasca*, it was, out of

Minton's Yard. She made a cruise down through the Shinasian Strait and around Idria before working her way north again around the far east coast of Aurasia and thence back to Kyreland. A straightforward enough journey, and no unusual hardships. The *Nabasca* has been in and out of Redling's docks five times since, and—according to Minton's records—is currently somewhere in the Ardaman Ocean, heading south for Soloran. This brought my line of reasoning up short, as I had assumed the timing of Lord Nickel's disappearance—if his confidante was indeed someone he met at sea—would coincide with the *Nabasca's* presence in Redling, and therefore the presence of that person. Was it a fellow passenger then? That would have made things rather difficult. However, I thought to examine the crew of the *Nabasca* and discovered that, though its officers are all the same as they were two years ago, one member of the crew left not long after Lord Nickel's voyage. Imagine my excitement when I discovered it was none other than the ship's *wizard*. One Wizard Medrova, according to the crew's list. Tracking this wizard's movements from ship to ship, I discovered that she has not been back to Kyreland since the *Star of Idria* docked here three months ago. At that time she transferred to serve the *Emmiran,* but as that ship—*this ship*—was currently en route from Azo, she was obliged to spend the last few months on shore. This puts her firmly in Kyreland during the time of Lord Nickel's supposed murder—and more, it allows her time to have planned this admirable stunt. Her being a ship's wizard also explains why I should be unaware of her presence—for I have been unable to discover any clue as to her nationality."

"I see," I said. "So you believe Lord Nickel fell in love with his ship's wizard, but still returned home?"

"I can only imagine the condition of their parting," Felpz remarked, "but I can suppose that, when she discovered the deplorable condition of his home life, this enterprising lover struck up a plan to free him. To that end they faked his death and now intend to flee the country. I checked, and indeed Wizard Medrova is bringing a guest with her on this voyage—though, no doubt as a means of subterfuge, they are listed on the passenger manifest as one *Miss Brodelia Summers*. It is for this couple that we are now waiting."

I found myself looking around the cabin with renewed interest—and not a little bit of alarm.

"If that is indeed who you are expecting," I said, "then why have you not brought Captain Cullins along?"

Felpz raised a curious brow. "Why, because I do not see how this concerns him," he said blandly. "No one has *actually* died, after all. I seriously doubt Lord Nickel is leaving against his will—though if that is the case of course I will prevent it. At this point I merely wish to meet this remarkable magician. Mostly just to see if I am *right.*" His eyes twinkled, and I suddenly thought: *there must be something more! He suspects there is more, otherwise he would not be here!* And I felt a thrill of nerves run through me, tingling in my limbs and making me feel momentarily weightless.

The evening wore on, the sun finally sinking below the horizon. Felpz lit the lamps, and we waited in their soft, warm glow. The little room rocked gently as the boat rode the swell of the river's current, and I began to grow drowsy from the motion. I was just beginning to worry that the dinner would be spoilt from the cold when there was a noise outside and we jumped to attention.

I was aware of voices on the other side of the door, too indistinct for their words to be made out, and then the handle turned and a couple bustled into the room.

A woman and a man, they appeared. He had the same brick-red skin as the captain, with short curly black hair and a clean-shaven chin; he wore a neat blue suit with the silver cloak of a sea-wizard thrown over one shoulder. The woman was a striking creature of unusual height with a delicately coifed head of golden hair and beguiling dark eyes. She was wearing a remarkable gown and a coat of fine brocaded cloth. Though both fit her well and were quite flattering, they were also clearly brand new, and were something of a contrast to the wizard's well worn coat.

They stared at us in shock, and for a moment I had the terrible feeling that we were in the wrong room and that we had interrupted a honeymooning couple—for they had that air about them of newlywed lovers—and Felpz was staring back in equal surprise. But then he leapt to his feet and beckoned to them in welcome.

"Come in, come *in*," he said. "You will forgive the intrusion—but I saw no other way in which we could be certain of meeting you. I am Bouragner Felpz, and this is my friend Corianne Birch. Please be assured we come here in all goodwill, and grant us the pleasure of your company at supper. You must forgive me," he continued, coming around the table to approach the wizard. He made a short bow. "I had no *idea* you were Azoan, and your name quite threw me off. Corianne, if I ever give the appearance of being an insufferable know-it-all, please remember this as one of the times I failed *utterly*. I got entirely the wrong impression of you, Wizard Medrova."

I found my gaze snapping around to the wizard, and then across to his companion with new shrewdness. Now I looked closer I noticed all over again her height, the broadness of her shoulders, and the somewhat awkward way she gripped her handbag. Then I looked back at the wizard, recalling that peculiarity of the Azoan language, where their boys' names were long and fancy, and the women's short and blunt.

"*You* are Wizard Medrova?" I couldn't help gasping. "But then—" I cut myself off before I said something regrettable.

"I *am* Wizard Medrova," the young man said, straightening his shoulders. "This is my fiancée, Miss Summers, and I'd thank you to remove yourselves from our private quarters, *sir*," he added, casting a scathing look at Felpz. He spoke Kyrish well, but there was an odd clip to his words and a cadence which I'd never heard before.

"Oh, well that is too bad," Felpz said. "I had hoped to hear the story from you, as I could never be sure otherwise. One question, then, and we will make you an engagement present of this dinner."

Wizard Medrova raised his chin challengingly. "Ask it," he demanded.

"Was it your idea, or Lord Nickel's, to use an inert simulacrum to fake his death?" Felpz asked, all innocent curiosity.

The effect of his question, however, was dramatic.

Wizard Medrova sucked in a breath so sharply it whistled, and the tall lady—whom I was beginning to suspect was a lady only in dress—made an involuntary motion as if to flee. Finding herself caught by the wizard's hand, she cast her head down and murmured something in his ear.

"No," said Medrova in answer. "I expect he has constables lining the gangplank."

"What?" said Felpz. "Nothing of the sort! If you're determined to be so unfriendly we will, naturally, leave. It is only I've never *seen* such a fine simulacrum, and I just *had* to meet the magician who created it. Of course, I am also curious as to what has taken you so long to leave the country. You've run quite a risk, staying so long after you pulled that magnificent stunt."

The two looked at each other, and I noticed how Medrova was not really so short; it was only the extreme height of his companion that made him appear so. Then with a sigh Medrova turned and shut the door firmly behind him and released Miss Summers's arm. Miss Summers, now putting herself to no effort to appear ladylike, fairly dumped her handbag on the table and drew out a chair, roughly grabbing her skirts to yank them out of the way as she sank into it.

"Well Med?" she said, in a voice so rich and deep it rivaled that of Felpz. "Why not just give him the whole story, if he's so persistent? Knowing him, if he wanted us caught we'd already be in shackles."

Wizard Medrova still hesitated, and his eyes went distrustingly towards me.

"I'll tell them then," said the lady, who I presumed was actually Lord Nickel. "The truth is, we had planned to wait until the night before the *Emmiran* sailed. We would be halfway to Azo before your necromancers puzzled out his simulacrum—which was *his* idea, by the way. Med is quite a brilliant magician, you know."

"Downright extraordinary," Felpz agreed. His head snapped around to gaze searchingly at Lord Nickel. "What happened?"

The man—and I could see clearly that it was a man now—sighed heavily, then winced a bit. "Well, I suppose I should begin at the beginning, otherwise you'll keep peppering us with questions, won't you?"

"Let me," Medrova said, coming around and laying a protective brown hand on Lord Nickel's shoulder. The man looked up at the wizard and then put his own hand over his companion's, holding it as if it gave him strength. Perhaps it did.

"I'd better tell the first part, though," he said softly. "It is mine to tell." He shrugged, a little sadly. "Whatever you have heard of me, or perhaps read about in the papers, I assure you it was all lies. My father saw to that. He would have preferred any lie, no matter how distasteful, rather than the truth."

"Which is what, Lord Nickel?" Felpz asked gently.

Lord Nickel tilted his impeccably coifed head and raised a perfect eyebrow, as if wondering why Felpz would even ask such a question. "I should think that would be immediately obvious," he said with a wry smile. "I shall not inflict upon you an account of the miseries of my childhood, however. But I will say this: I was never ill, and I never mistreated a woman. I *believed* I was ill for a time, and I tried—I tried very hard—to please my father. To find a wife. But the fact of the matter was, though it was laughably easy for me to befriend charming young ladies, I could never stomach the thought of marrying one. I backed out of several arrangements, which angered my father—he had it put about that I had committed some . . . indiscretion. Anything to cover up what was really going on. I managed this way for some years, simply putting off the inevitable, when at last I took a fall. I made an overture—an act of desperation, more like—to someone I thought I could trust. I was wrong about him, however, and he went straight to my father. The result was . . . well, according to the papers I had either contracted syphilis or had gone mad, when in truth I had only developed an unwise infatuation with my valet. The upshot was my father packed me off onto a wretched little boat for a year with a hand-picked counselor. His purpose was double-ended, you see—get me out of the public eye, and away from any friends or influences. I confess the first week was terrible. The counselor was very persuasive, and for a time I thought I really was going mad. Then . . . then I met Medrova." Lord Nickel looked up at the wizard adoringly, and gently brought the hand from his shoulder to his lips and kissed it, before letting go.

Medrova, not leaving his post, squared his shoulders and turned to Felpz. "I wasn't aware what was happening at first. Azoans have a different attitude toward male lovers, what with the way our marriage system works. I suppose you could call it *polyandry,* but that's a bit of a simplification. Let's just say, there's many Azoan women who prefer some of their husbands to show interest in *each other* rather than themselves. It's nothing to be ashamed of, as long as you don't deceive anyone about your preferences. It was something of a shock to me to discover foreigners who held quite negative views on the matter. I was still feeling my way around the crew of the *Nabasca* when Nick came aboard, and I'm sorry to say I didn't wise to what was going on right away."

"Oh, but you put a stop to it as soon as you did," Lord Nickel said, smiling ardently up at him. "He was so very clever about it, too."

"I am sure," Felpz said, a twinkle in his eye. "Please go on."

"Well," said Lord Nickel, casting his gaze aside, and blushing such that he almost looked like the maiden he was dressed as. "We became friends," he said. "Very close friends."

"We became lovers," Wizard Medrova said dryly, gazing across at us as if issuing a challenge. "It was not in the best judgment of course, but . . . " he sighed. "I still cannot bring myself to regret my choice."

"Darling," said Nickel with gentle reproach. "I do not believe there was much choice about it. On either side. Oh, but it was *wonderful.* And right under that dreadful counselor's nose, too. We got to see such sights: calling at ports all throughout Aurasia and Idria—I even got to ride an elephant. I wished the voyage would never end."

"But it did," said Felpz, and looked accusingly at Medrova. "And you did not take him away with you. Why?"

Medrova, after a moment of shock, pursed his lips. "I was in no position to offer him a good life," he said. "I'm a ship's wizard, not a captain. And at the time I was serving on a *Kyrish* ship. And . . . and he's a *lord.*"

"Not anymore," Lord Nickel pointed out happily.

"You were *then,*" Medrova insisted. "Frankly, sir, I didn't know what kind of life he would be returning to. I thought . . . well, I don't know what I thought. I certainly never imagined it would be this *bad.*"

"We did agree to see each other whenever he put into port," Lord Nickel said. "It was my sole consolation. But I thought, with that, I could manage. I went back to Moonfoot and redoubled my efforts to please my father. None of which were sufficient, however. I think he knew I had not changed. He hadn't, either. In some ways it was even worse than before, since I now had thoughts of Medrova constantly on my mind. It made seeing the prospective brides even more painful, because I recognized in them the same desire I had for love and affection—and I knew all of mine was already bound to another, oh, it was *awful*. I couldn't; I just couldn't, and it made me sick inside that my love was somewhere out on the far seas. My father knew it, and he ... well ... he expressed his displeasure."

"If you discovered the simulacrum," said Medrova coldly. "Then you no doubt examined it close enough to see the evidence."

"Oh, I saw," said Felpz quietly.

"He was worse when I found him," the wizard went on. "Two years I'd been out of Kyrish ports and hopping ships looking for one with a friendly crew. I finally get back in and discover an *Azoan* ship in need of a wizard. I could hardly fathom my good luck. Better yet, the *Emmiran* also needed refitting and would not be ready for two months, giving me enough shore leave to make a proper visit to Nickel. I knew I couldn't walk up the drive and present myself at the front door, but I had no idea it would be so bad. What do I find left of the man I knew aboard the *Nabasca?* This battered mess, all torn to shreds inside and out and more blue than pink below the neckline. I told him I would not stand for it. Whether he loved me or no I was taking him away from that wretched place, and I set about making plans to do it.

"I could not, of course, simply spirit him away. Being the son of an Earl that would cause us problems. I needed to extract him, but in such a way that no one would think to pursue us. A disguise, I knew, would be in order, and what better way to disguise a man than to dress him up as one of your Kyrish ladies? They wear such complicated outfits and makeup—even more than Azoan gentlemen—I knew Nickel would be unrecognizable. I was able to contract, through a sympathetic soul in

Redling, the services of an understanding tailor who made the clothes for Nickel's new wardrobe—I did not dare enchant them, as I worried even the scent of magic would arouse suspicion.

"It was actually Nickel's idea to fake his own death, but as we both agreed it would not be convincing without a corpse and as we would not consider using a real one, I had to come up with the simulacrum. We originally planned to stage the murder the night of our departure, so as to provide no time for the police to catch on . . . but . . . well . . . "

"Some crisis occurred," Felpz finished.

"You saw the simulacrum," Medrova said grimly, and gazed sadly at Lord Nickel, whose shoulders drooped.

"I may look all right now," he said quietly. "But when Med found me I could barely breathe."

"That awful old man had hit him with a poker. An *iron poker.*" Medrova's soft, foreign voice pitched up in anger and he clenched his fists. "His own *father!* I could have banished him to the outer darkness—the one with *thorns* in it—I really could have!"

"I'm glad you didn't," Nickel said quietly. "He is my father."

"From my point of view that makes it rather worse," Felpz said, folding his arms. "However, I'm glad you restrained yourself, Medrova. It would have made things difficult for me."

Medrova muttered a word I didn't recognize except I fancied it was an insult.

"Med insisted on getting me out immediately, even though the *Emmiran* wasn't due to sail for another two weeks. I've been living as Miss Summers during this time, and we had expected to depart at dawn. We still intend to, unless you mean to stop us."

"You may *try,*" Medrova said, with a grim smile.

Felpz only leaned back in his chair and laughed. "My dear young men," he said. "Such a thing is furthest from my mind. Not only do you have my sympathies, but I could never bring myself to wreck such a brilliant scheme. No, at this point I only wonder what you intend to *do* when you get to Azo. Lord Nickel, surely you must realize none of your titles or rights will hold any power there."

"I realize this," Lord Nickel said. "In fact, I wish it. They have only brought me misery. I am quite looking forward to being plain and simple Nickel. Have even been considering taking an Azoan name."

Felpz raised his eyebrows and looked at Medrova, who shrugged.

"We will live as best we can," he said simply. "Azo does not offer the same opportunities for men as Kyreland does, but it is getting better. Perhaps we'll find a woman who will take us both. Whatever the case may be, we will not have to *hide* who we are."

Felpz regarded the couple with a placid smile. "Then I can only wish you the very best of luck," he said. "Though with your capabilities, Medrova, that hardly seems necessary. Oh, and you can be sure I shall keep the police chasing their tails for weeks to come. You shall have no fear of pursuit. Unless, of course, *Corianne* has some reason to object."

Suddenly I found myself at the center of attention, not all of it friendly. I glared back at them.

"What?" I exclaimed. "Of *course* not!"

As we disembarked after a leisurely and considerably more amicable dinner, Felpz paused on the gangway and rapped his hand against a plate of wood on which was inscribed the ship's name.

"A more fitting vessel to take them I should not believe exists," he said.

"Why not?" I asked.

"The name *Emmiran*," he said, taking my arm and leading me up away from the docks, "belonged not only to one of their queens—*Azrans* they're called—but to one of the royal husbands. Sumér Emmiran, who became the equivalent of a Prince Consort, was originally a slave from Niérlind. Brought to Azo by centaurian traders he was freed and eventually married Azran Raion. And although our Lord Nickel is giving *up* his title by going to Azo, I cannot help but think he will find his own sort of freedom there."

"Did you suspect Medrova was a man?" I asked.

Felpz snorted and ducked his head. "That was an oversight on my part, I regret to say. The name sounded Hyberian to me, because of the ending. I quite forgot that Medrova is also a traditional Azoan boy's name. It just goes to show you, Cori-anne, that you can live a thousand years and *still* be surprised. Though the revelation didn't change my feelings on the matter. No, they didn't change one jot."

"How do you suppose the earl will react when he eventually finds out?" I asked.

"I am not convinced he will ever find out. Certainly I think the former Lord Nickel would be safer if he did not. No, I think I shall have to make certain he never finds out, and I'm afraid that means you'll have to wait to tell this story until death carries the old man off. Hopefully by that time this country will have progressed to the point that it will be able to accept Medrova for the hero that he is. For he is a hero, Corianne, if not quite the one we were expecting."

That is all there is to the story of Nickel and Medrova. My story, however, continues on a little longer, and finds its end two weeks later, when I once again sat down to lunch with Milky on the upper floor of Valaire's. As I felt I could rely on him to keep the secret—and since I suspected his Mrs Grissom was the selfsame tailor that Medrova had gone to—I told him the entire story of the remarkable man for whom those dresses had been meant. When I had finished he stared at me for some moments over his untouched meal, his mouth agape, and then burst out:

"And . . . he let them *go?*" He seemed torn between amaze-ment and a sort of stunned hopefulness.

"Of course he let them go," I said. "They were clearly madly in love with each other and besides, they hadn't done anything *wrong*. Quite the opposite, I think. Why, I should have liked to have gone straight to Moonfoot and given that horrible old man a right thrashing. To treat your child in such a way—it's *repulsive*."

"Is that what you think?" Milky asked, his voice as stiff as a board.

"Of *course* it is," I said, too caught up in my own emotions to notice. "Why, don't you agree?"

Milky looked down at his plate very suddenly then, and said in a rather choked voice: "No, no, I agree completely. I just . . .

well I weren't sure you or Felpz would feel that way. But I'm glad you do."

I stared at him, hard, my mind slowly fitting together the bits of evidence that had been piling up around my friend for decades. I remembered Medrova's allusion to 'a sympathetic soul in Redling' and all at once they fell into place like the pieces of a puzzle, and I was stunned by the picture I saw.

"Oh, Milky," I said. "Don't tell me *you* would have liked to have been on that ship to Azo as well?"

Milky's head jerked up in surprise. His eyes were red, but he had so far regained control of himself that his voice came out quite normal when he said:

"What? Lady no, Miss Cor! A scratched up old alley-cat like me? I'd ruin their fun. Besides, all my friends are *here*."

I looked at him and felt a great swell of pity for the man, and at the same time a sort of fierce protectiveness.

"Quite right," I told him. "Besides Mrs Grissom and Mrs Dolnir *and* Miss Valaire, excellent guard dogs that they no doubt are, if you ever find yourself in any serious trouble I am sure Felpz would be more than happy to sort it out. Just don't expect him to create a perfect simulacrum of your dead body."

Milky closed his eyes and shuddered. "*Good Lady*," he groaned, lowering his head into his hands. "Let us hope it never comes to *that*."

And to my certain knowledge, it never has.

Following "The Moonfoot Problem," "The Case of Countess Baronia" comes ninth in the second volume of The Adventures of Bouragner Felpz, though as with most stories it can be read on its own. Written in the final days of 2013, it will be followed in the Perihelion 2016 issue of Apsis by "The Goblin's Fiddle."

THE CASE OF COUNTESS BARONIA

AUTHOR'S NOTE

This story contains two names whose pronunciations are not obvious and whose spelling could lead to some confusion. To prevent this, remember that the name Merodite *is a four-syllable word pronounced with an ee sound at the end, similar to the name "Aphrodite." Conversely, the terminal e in* Calamite *adds no additional syllable, and that name ends with a sound identical to the word "might." The fact that both names are spelled with the same three letters at the end is an unfortunate accident, where the limitations of our alphabet have become sorely apparent.*

—GO

Winter 2323

THE YEAR OF 2323 WAS A MEMORABLE ONE in the house of Bouragner Felpz, not for the repetitious alignment of its number but for the sheer volume of cases Felpz handled. Hardly a day went by, it seemed, that he did not field some request for aid or provide consultation on a magical problem. Why then, asks the reader, do I not have volumes worth of stories from this year? The sad truth is that, while Felpz was very busy, the cases that kept him so were not memorable. A misplaced relative here, a cursed tree there . . . Felpz applied himself to all the problems with the same vigorous fervor, and as a result they were usually solved in a matter of hours—if not minutes—and oftentimes without Felpz needing to leave the comfort of his armchair.

I confess I lost track of my friend's activities, being hip deep in a project of my own, until the late fall, when I realized we had somehow contrived to drift as far apart as two people living in the same quarters could. I was appalled, but so busy wrestling with my novel that I had no energy to spare to do anything about it. Once I had beaten the book into some state of presentability, however, I decided to give myself a holiday and determined that Felpz should share in it.

I approached him with the suggestion that we take the month of Chandarmas off—perhaps to visit my daughter and her family—during which time he could read my novel, and I could go over the notes from his cases to see if there was anything of interest worth publishing. To my delight he was of the same mind as I, and we were on the verge of making more substantial plans when our morning was upended by the arrival of Lady Emalta, Countess Baronia.

She swept into our sitting room like a tidal wave, the effect heightened by the frothing white skirts that escaped from under the severe navy-and-teal traveling coat to trail artistically behind her. These surged around her legs before stilling in a flutter of chiffon and lace when she stopped to survey her audience, while her upper body—encased as it was in the aforementioned coat—remained erect and rigid, stiff as a ship's prow. A middle-aged woman, though her features were not particularly striking, now as then I do consider her to have been the best dressed of all our visitors. Everything from the fluttering, light skirts, to the elegant leather boots beneath them, to her coat, to her tasteful hat and her soft gloves was perfectly coordinated on a theme of sea greens and blues, with just enough contrast to keep it visually interesting. The cut of her costume was similarly artistic: it ranged from the soft, flowing tresses of her skirts to the hard lines of her coat and back again to the frills peeking out from her cuffs and collar, altogether enforcing my initial impression of her as a great, white wave breaking on sharp, dark rocks.

"Magician Felpz," she announced in stentorian tones.

The man in question, who was no less strikingly—if less elaborately—dressed in a morning coat of plum silk with a brocade collar and matching slippers, rose to his feet and bowed graciously.

"I am Emalta Tragansea," this impressive woman continued. "You may know me better by my title, the twelfth Countess of Baronia. I require your assistance in a matter most urgent."

"My dear . . . *Lady*," Felpz replied, taking special care of the honorific. "If the matter is indeed so pressing that you have arrived in advance of your card I shall naturally hear your case, but you must allow for the presence of my friend Corianne as well, for you did interrupt our business."

Lady Emalta had the grace to look a little ashamed—but only so far as a dusky blush across her wide cheeks and a slight suppression of her chest. The next instant her natural confidence reasserted itself, and she took another stride into the room, bringing herself into the center of our little world. She stood there, with such erectness and majesty that I forgot my disappointment over the interruption and turned to give her all my attention—as indeed Felpz was doing himself.

"Magician," said this imperious woman, "I shall not waste your time. I *am* sensitive to the needs of others. But my case is of such immediate import that you will no doubt forgive me for intruding so rudely. My situation, therefore, is this: a necklace of great value has gone missing from my house, and I desire you to find it for me."

There was, I'm afraid, a rather impudent *clink* of porcelain as I fairly dropped my coffee cup onto its saucer in surprise. For although I had witnessed my friend take on all sorts of cases, none of them had ever appeared so patently mundane.

Felpz must have felt so as well, for he sank back into his chair with a look of incredulity.

"My Lady," he said, and I could not tell whether he was reining in anger, disappointment, or laughter with his restraint. "I have been asked to do a great many things during my time, but finding a piece of lost *jewelry* has never been one of them."

"I realize my request may seem . . . somewhat below your standard," said Lady Emalta contritely. "But this is no typical necklace: it is an heirloom which has been in my family since the founding of our house. Its worth is beyond that of sapphires. Furthermore, I do not believe it has merely gone missing: I am certain that it was, in fact, *stolen.*"

"The worth of the artifact is unimportant to me," Felpz said with a wave of his hand. "If you believe it to be stolen then surely the *police,* or even a private detective, would be of more help than I. I deal in *magical* conundrums, Lady Emalta, and I am under no illusion as to my ability to act as an agent of the law. No, what you want is a detective, milady, not a magician."

Lady Emalta smiled at this self-deprecating excuse, as if she half expected it. She reached into a pocket of her coat and removed two small velvet bags, one of which chinked faintly as she laid them both on the nearby side table.

"There are two hundred Kyrish crowns in gold, eight hundred in verified bank notes," she announced. "They are yours if you will but come with me to Baronia and consider my case. No, do not argue," she said, seeing Felpz's mouth come open— though I believe it was only in astonishment. "You shall have a thousand more—in whatever form you like—if you do manage to find my necklace. I hope, magician, that this will convince you of the sincerity of my request."

Felpz's eyebrows climbed right up his forehead, pushing wave upon wave of surprised wrinkles ahead of them, as he looked from the neat little bags to the countess and back again. Yet I could see how his jaw had set obstinately, and I could tell he would throw away this unasked-for windfall purely because of the pride he took in his craft.

"Oh, why not find the necklace for her?" I asked him. "It will not be so hard for you. I will come, and we can spend our holiday at the seaside. I daresay it'll be a trifle warmer down there than our dreary Redling winter. Think of it! Reading in the morning, walks along the beaches and the sandy cliffs in the afternoon, and hearty southern suppers in the evening. It will be marvelous. And all you have to do is find the lady's necklace— is that so much to ask?"

Felpz crumpled back into his chair to stare at me in consternation, while the Countess Baronia gazed in open surprise.

Taking a cue from her I held my chin up high, defying either to contradict me.

Neither did.

Which was how Felpz and I found ourselves bundled into a private, first-class compartment on the western express that very afternoon. The skies over Redling were gray and murderous cold, as indeed they had been all autumn, and persisted thus all the way to Greywall, where we switched to the coastal line and began winding our way south. In all, the trip lasted well over six hours, during which time Lady Emalta gave a full account of the circumstances surrounding the disappearance of her necklace. This she did, but not before she also gave us a brief history of the Tragansea family, with which, she assured us, the necklace was inextricably linked.

"It belonged to Amariel Tragansea, you understand," she explained, when we were hardly out of Redling. "She was the wife of Roderick Tragansea, first Count of Baronia. It passes to the eldest daughter of each generation, you see, along with the title of Countess."

"I'm sorry," I said. "Isn't that a bit odd? I thought titles usually went to the eldest child, whatever its sex."

"That is how the modern Kyres do it, yes," Lady Emalta said. "But the Traganseas have always been a matrilineal line, sort of a reverse of that archaic practice of male primogeniture. In fact, when the title was founded that was the fashion, and Lady Amariel caused quite a disturbance when she insisted upon a *female* primogeniture. Now, of course, things have been going this way for so long hardly anyone pays notice to it."

"You were telling us about the necklace?" Felpz said, steering our topic gently back on course.

"Oh, yes, yes of course," said the current countess, rearranging her skirts. "The necklace. It came with Amariel Tragansea and has been passed from mother to daughter down that line directly to me—and I would pass it on to my own daughter, if only I still had it. It has great . . . sentimental value."

"Clearly," said Felpz in a wry tone.

Lady Emalta shot my friend an uncharitable look but made no comment. "I only wish to make its importance clear," she said, with admirable self-control. "So that you may take its disappearance as seriously as I do."

Felpz, who had been sitting slumped against the window, propped his head up on one hand and gazed across at our employer. "Then tell me of it," he said.

"The necklace disappeared two days ago. I regret to say it has taken me that long to get the straight story from the servants, who were greatly confused, and my daughter, who took the whole thing as a practical joke at first. As far as I can tell, after stitching together their disparate accounts, what happened was this:

"The last time I saw the necklace, it was in its box on my dresser, where it had been since my mother's death. I noted it particularly when I was dressing for dinner that night, as my maid—Liriel—had been asking if she could take it out and clean it. Its box has a glass front, you see, with a steel frame and lock, so although it is quite secure it can also be admired. Lately, however, it has begun to tarnish a little from lack of attention, and I gave Liriel the key to the box so that she might clean it before I went down to dinner.

"Now, from my perspective it was a perfectly ordinary, quiet evening. No guests in the house, and so my daughter and I dined alone. Falling into a lengthy conversation we were both late to our beds, and when I returned to my rooms I noticed at once that the box containing the necklace had been moved. Thinking only that Liriel had failed to put it back where it belonged, I went to correct its position. That was when I discovered that the necklace which should have been inside it was gone.

"I summoned Liriel, to ask her what was taking so long, but when she arrived she was as mystified as I. She had been planning to clean it the next day, she explained, and had not so much as touched the box during supper. Then I began to feel a twist of anxiety in my gut, and asked her what she had done with the key. She assured me she had it safe about her person, but when asked to produce it was unable to do so.

"Well, this as you can imagine upset the poor girl something awful. Being newly employed in my service she had been eager to prove her worth, and such a disastrous failure on her part was a crushing blow. I do think she expected to be sacked on the spot, but it was her utter and abject despair that convinced me of her innocence. I sat her down and had her recount the events of her evening exactly as she could remember them. I took notes," the countess assured us, producing a sheaf of papers, "so I might repeat her story to you.

"According to Liriel, after she had finished her own supper she sat up in her room working on a piece of mending I had assigned to her the day before. She had only one visitor during that time, our new improver who came in to borrow a needle and thread. She also answered a call from the housekeeper about breakfast for the next day, but other than that she did not leave her room. She insisted she had the key on its chain around her neck the entire time and offered to scour the steps between her room and the housekeeper's quarters in search of it—thinking, no doubt, that the chain might have broken and the key dropped off without her knowledge. I pointed out that this was a futile effort, as clearly someone had *already* found the key, and used it to make off with my necklace.

"At this point I called my daughter in and explained the situation to her. She is a feisty young woman, and I've known her to pull practical jokes before. I hoped, I suppose, that she had conspired with her own maid to play a trick on me, but she was just as surprised as I had been—and a bit more quick to pin the blame on Liriel. She was convinced, however, that *someone* was playing a very naughty trick on me and had the entire staff out and lined up so that she could lecture them. No one volunteered any information, which led me to believe that they either knew nothing, or that someone had indeed stolen my necklace. Perhaps both, if it had been done by someone from outside the house. Further adding to the mystery, not a single soul had been seen in the vicinity of my rooms that entire evening. It was as though a ghost had been through and spirited the thing away.

"Nevertheless I had the police out the next day, and though the detective they sent was quite energetic and eager to help, she was unable to uncover any more evidence than we had. Which was why I determined to enlist *your* aid, magician. Since it seems the mundane methods of investigation are utterly powerless to help me."

Felpz considered our client from his post by the window, with thoughtful expressions drifting over his face.

"Is there any reason to believe this *might* be the work of a ghost?" I asked.

"None that I can think of," the countess admitted. "I only meant it *seemed* that way."

We both found ourselves looking expectantly at Felpz after this exchange, but the man gazed out the train's foggy window into the ominous winter sky, and had no answer for us.

The weather lightened noticeably after our change of trains and grew steadily sunnier the farther south we went, so that by the time the sun set it was sending strong rays of gold across a pale blue sky, and I was most sorry to see it go. We finished the final leg of our journey in darkness, lit only by the yellow lanterns of the station and the harsh electric torch wielded by the driver who awaited the countess's return.

I was a little disappointed in our timing, since the House of Baronia lay at the center of Old Baronia, the last holdout of what had once been the most powerful kingdom of ancient Kyreland. Its crooked streets and pale-gold stone houses were much admired in the rest of the country, and I did long to see it with my own eyes. But I consoled myself with the assurance that I would have plenty of time for sightseeing after Felpz had sorted out the matter of Lady Emalta's necklace.

The House of Baronia itself was raised somewhat above the town in the manner of the old castles. It had originally been one itself, but long ago its wall had been torn down to supply building material for the town, and now only a single tower and part of the courtyard of the original structure remained, the rest having been renovated by a Tragansea two centuries earlier. It perched on a headland of stone overlooking the sea, and was something of a jumble, being built across many different levels so as to accommodate the natural terrain.

In the dark, from within the carriage, I could see little but got the impression of a high, turreted building with many lights around its base, the towers standing as dark silhouettes against the starry sky. Even through the padded walls of the coach I heard the wind howling in its heights, and smelled in faint gusts the tangy swell of the ocean nearby.

We were greeted at the front door by an iron-faced man and a distraught young woman who ran down the steps and pulled open the door of the coach all in a rush. She was a wild, pale-faced thing with dark hair that had contrived to wriggle out of the tight bun it had been put up in, falling haphazardly around her ears.

"Milady, *milady,*" she was saying as the countess gathered her sea-foam skirts and swirled out of the coach.

Such was her concern that for a moment I took her to be Lady Emalta's daughter, but then saw the plain black dress she wore, and concluded this must be the maid.

"Never fear, Liriel," the countess was saying, confirming my suspicions. "You were in such a state last night I didn't think the trip would do you any good. And look, I have brought help—Mr Bouragner Felpz, the magician from Redling, is here to find the necklace."

The maid's large, dark eyes turned to Felpz, pleading.

"I *didn't* take it," she said to him, her voice a whisper.

Felpz gave her a keen look, and after a moment he gave a little shrug. "No, no, I believe you did not," he said. Then, to the countess, he went on: "I would like, however, to question the remainder of your staff. Particularly this new boy—the, er, *improver,* you called him? And if you have a picture or photograph of the necklace, that would be helpful. I'll need to know *what* I'm looking for if I am to find it, after all."

"Yes, of course," Lady Emalta said, and turned to the iron-faced man, who nodded and retreated up the steps without a word.

By this time the maid Liriel had composed herself enough to take the countess's travel case, and a pair of footmen had trotted up to unload our bags. In this way we were ushered up the steps to the front door of the hall and inside, where we found ourselves in a veritable blaze of lights. This area was clearly part of the old castle, for the ceiling stretched up above us in a high arch of stone, which had been hung with strings of electric lights. The walls were decorated with tapestries and portraits, and the stone floor covered in a magnificent ultramarine carpet. In the center of this stood a young woman—hardly more than a girl, but with such poise and confidence that she projected the bearing of someone much older.

"Welcome back, mother," she said, dropping a neat curtsey. "I take it your errand was a success?"

"Merodite, my dear, come meet the magician and his assistant. Mr Felpz, this is my daughter, Merodite."

Felpz, however, had wandered over to the far wall and was studying a line of oversized portraits that ran the entire length. These showed, upon closer inspection, woman after woman, beginning with a painting so dark and stained with age that the subject was barely discernible.

"A pleasure, I am sure," Felpz said distractedly, not taking his eyes off the paintings. "You'll forgive me but . . . who are *they?*"

"They are our ancestors, magician," said the countess, a trifle coldly.

Ignoring her tone Felpz went to stand under the nearest and pointed up. "And this one?" he asked.

"That is Amariel Tragansea," Lady Emalta said. "Next is her daughter, Corialla, and . . . "

"Next is *her* daughter, so I see!" said Felpz, sounding delighted. He moved away down the line, leaving me to pay my respects to Lady Merodite, who was looking a trifle sour.

"He may have a brisk manner, but he means well," I assured the young woman, but she did not appear impressed.

"My lady," Felpz called from some ways down the hall. "Are *you* in this collection?"

"Indeed I am," said Lady Emalta tiredly. "At the very end. Merodite . . . " but Felpz had already turned and hurried off. Gracefully, as if this had been her intention all along, the countess turned to me and finished her sentence. "Merodite has a portrait too, but it hangs in a different part of the house. Only countesses are hung in the hall. We have a separate room for the Lords of Baronia as well."

"I'm sure Felpz will be pleased to learn that," I assured her.

However, once he had been down the line of portraits and back again, Felpz showed no desire to see any other Tragansea family members. "The necklace," he said. "I am so sorry for letting myself be distracted. To find your necklace I need to know what it *looks* like. Have you a detailed drawing or even a photograph I could work from? Also, the box in which it was kept. That would be helpful."

"Both will be supplied," Lady Emalta assured him. "If you'll come through into the library, that will doubtless be more comfortable."

In due course we were led out of the hall and up a flight of marble stairs, through a high wooden door and into a round, comfortable room lined with books. Here a wide table sat in the center, covered in a crimson cloth with matching upholstered chairs set around it. A footman was just laying out a tray of tea and coffee and arranging a trolley filled with cakes nearby. Having had nothing since the rushed dinner between trains at Greywall I felt my attention drawn inexorably to that trolley, and could not understand how Felpz kept himself away from it, marching up and down the length of the table while we waited for the requested items to be brought. He condescended to receive a cup of sweet, milky tea, of which he took two sips and no more, while I piled my plate high with scones and, after the tea, took a serving of coffee.

I had only begun upon my plate of refreshments when Liriel entered, bearing in her arms a silver box with a glass lid and a small, framed picture. These she laid by the countess's elbow, bobbed a curtsy, and then went to stand demurely in the shadows by the door.

Hastily brushing away my accrued crumbs I leaned over to get a better look as Felpz opened the box and examined the picture.

The box was roughly the size of a large, thick book and had, as I have said, a glass lid. This was framed in silver, cast into the shape of breaking waves. In fact, the whole box was decorated along similar lines: the sides showed waves crashing upon a shore, flecks of foam and seaweed artistically fashioned into feet. Though the metal was blackened with tarnish in the crevices, the raised surfaces were brilliantly polished. All in all it looked to me like a much-loved artifact that was nonetheless seldom used.

The picture, in its elaborate, gilded frame, had a similar feel. Felpz turned it over in his hands and examined the back of it before looking at what the picture actually showed. When he saw it, he gave a small, inward sort of nod, and passed it to me.

It was another portrait of a woman, and showed her face and neck down to the point where the latter was crossed by a necklace, thus giving her the appearance of being a floating, disembodied head. It was, if I am any judge of such things, a very good little painting, and the woman it depicted bore a remarkable resemblance to Lady Emalta—if perhaps a trifle more austere.

"Another one of your ancestors?" I asked her.

"My own mother," replied the countess, tersely. "Lady Istel."

"Mark that she wears the necklace, Corianne," Felpz told me.

Mark it well I did, for it was a remarkable thing: at first glance it appeared to be a string of pearls, but upon closer inspection these resolved themselves into tiny, perfect skulls. Glinting from each eye socket was a shard of diamond, and the artist had rendered the reflected light such that some of the skulls appeared to be staring back at the viewer.

"That is the most unique and beautiful thing," I told Lady Emalta, though in truth I found the piece rather unsettling. Some of the skulls struck me as being of a sour disposition, and I did not like the way they looked at me.

"Many have thought so," said the countess with a stiff bow of her head. "You see why I wish to have it returned?"

"Yes," said Felpz, who had picked up the box and was sniffing it curiously. "I am beginning to see why, though it might have helped, of course, had you told me right away that your family has *merfolk* ancestry."

At hearing this I looked up from my study of the portrait sharply, in time to see the two noblewomen freeze. But while young Merodite appeared purely surprised—and perhaps a trifle disbelieving—Lady Emalta's hands grasped the tablecloth convulsively, and I saw a trace of fear in her eyes.

"Why ever should you believe *that?*" she demanded, coldly.

"The legends about Amariel Tragansea coming out of the oceans are just that—*legends!*" said Lady Merodite, with a nervous glance at her mother.

"So it *was* Amariel Tragansea. I wondered, you know," Felpz said with a twinkling smile.

"Mother, what *is* he talking about?"

Lady Emalta unclenched one hand from the tablecloth and lifted it to silence her daughter. The young woman obediently fell back in her seat, but her eyes were alight with curiosity. When the elder woman remained mute, glaring at Felpz with pursed lips, it was he who answered the question.

"That necklace," he said, gesturing at the picture I still held. "And this box. Both are of merfolk make. I have seen their like before, and it is most . . . distinct. The portrait of Amariel in your hall also contains certain clues, though she had disguised herself well enough that I could not be sure if she was a mermaid, or merely the daughter of one. You told me yourself that you are a direct descendant along the matrilineal line from her, therefore I reason, *you are both*, if only the slightest bit, part mermaid. Although, unless new sea-blood has been introduced in the interim since Amariel, it is likely the two of you are more or less human by this point. But I think you may find yourselves quite unable to *drown,* if it ever comes to that, and you may experience a slight ringing in your ears if a ship ever wrecks upon these shores."

Merodite laughed at this, but her mother's face remained closed and grave, and Felpz looked across at her with a pleasant, expectant expression. Eventually the ice of her countenance cracked, and she spoke—in a resigned tone—the following:

"It is not a topic I like to discuss. The legend—and it is as Merodite says, a *legend*—tells that the first Count of Baronia stole that necklace from a grotto, and that Amariel came out of the sea and offered to be his wife in exchange for it. In the way of tales this came to pass, and Amariel ruled Baronia well, but was ever found to be wandering the beaches in the moonlight, and would on occasion disappear—only to return in the morning, sopping wet and smelling of the sea.

"But all old families have granules of mythology embedded in their history," she said with a stern frown. "Who is to say this one is true?"

"I do," said Felpz. "At least, I hope it is true. It would explain, for a start, why your necklace is currently *at the bottom of the ocean.*"

This caused a great stir, and even I found myself surprised.

"You found it already?" I asked.

"I have been casting my consciousness outwards as we have been speaking," Felpz said dryly. "The necklace was not hard to locate, once I knew what I was looking for. It quite *reeks* of magic, did you know? I hope you were never so foolish as to actually wear it."

"It is on the *bottom* of the *ocean*?" Merodite said, flabbergasted.

"Not far west from here," Felpz said, but he did not take his eyes from Lady Emalta, who had grown pale at his words.

"All the portraits in the hall," he continued, fixing the lady with his stare. "The ladies in them are depicted wearing this necklace—it was too difficult to make out in detail, but I am satisfied the necklace they wear is this one—all of them, save the last. You. You have kept it in this box—quite wisely, I must say. Was it by chance, or do you know more of its powers than you have told us? Tell us now, Lady Emalta, for it may shed some light on why the necklace was stolen—and who it was that took it."

Lady Emalta rose from her chair in a majestic flow of seafoam skirts. For a moment I thought she would sweep out of the room in a great huff, but she only took to pacing up and down the length of the table, one hand fisted on her breast as though she fought some internal battle.

"The truth is I know nothing for certain," she said at last, drawing up to stand next to Felpz. "That is part of what vexes me so. For I only know what I have seen with my own eyes—all else is supposition based on old and questionable legends."

"Then tell me what you have seen," Felpz requested patiently.

"What I saw," said the countess, a faraway look about her face. "What I saw was my mother, day after day, wearing that necklace. She would never take it off, not even to sleep or to have it cleaned. But rather than become tarnished or dirty—or even wear down and break—the necklace only looked more and more spectacular. Yet at the same time, my mother grew more and more frail. By her forty-second year she was so decrepit that people thought her a woman twice her age. By forty-three she was bedridden—and *still* would not take off the necklace—and by forty-four she was dead, the necklace gleaming at her throat, shining with a radiance that was not to be believed unless you saw it. I can prove nothing—the doctors said she died of natural causes—but I am convinced that the necklace stole her life away. So I had it removed and put into that box, where it has remained these past twenty-five years."

"You never told me of this, mother!" Merodite said.

"Like I said before I know none of this for certain," the countess snapped. "It has been something of a superstition of mine, and I do not like to admit to it."

Felpz tipped the box closed with a soft *snap,* and held up the portrait for a better look.

"And this is she? Your mother, Lady Istel?"

The countess gave a curt nod.

"Well, well," said Felpz with a sigh. "This is a trifle messier than I had anticipated. Though I may yet get it sorted in short order. You are a very astute woman, Lady Emalta, and quite right: I rather fear the necklace *was* responsible for your mother's death, and that you kept it safely locked in this box— which has a pretty strong containment charm on it—was most fortunate for all your family."

"What, do you mean to say the thing was cursed?" Merodite asked.

"Not cursed," said Felpz. "It merely . . . *is.* Being created by merfolk it has certain . . . properties. There is magic in it which, though harmless to merfolk, has serious detrimental effects on anyone who is *not* a merman or a mermaid."

"But our ancestors have been wearing that necklace for *ages,*" Merodite protested. "I never heard of it giving any of *them* problems."

Felpz did not answer immediately but smiled kindly at the young woman, while her face went from flushed to pale and her expression from incredulity to shock as she realized what her words implied.

"It would not have," Felpz said at length. "As long as they had sufficient mer-blood in them, the magic would not affect them. It seems, however, that with Lady Istel the line has become sufficiently humanized that it is now susceptible to the necklace's magic."

Lady Emalta came around and sank into a chair.

"Then what are we to do? Once we have it back?" she asked.

"Put it away in the box again, I should think," said Felpz.

"But why—" Lady Emalta began, but was cut off by a commotion at the door.

This had been growing slowly for some time, beginning with the frequent opening and closing of the door as servants came, saw us engaged, and went. This escalated to hushed conversations in the hall outside, which in turn grew more heated, until at last the iron-faced butler came into the room and bowed.

"Apologies m'lady, ladies, sir," he said. "Something dire has happened; I must speak with you at once."

Lady Emalta drew an indignant breath, but something about the man's manner piqued Felpz's attention, and it was he who responded first:

"What have you found?" he asked.

This startled the butler somewhat. He took a half step back before he regained his composure. He looked shaken, I now realized—almost sickly.

"It was what we *didn't* find at first," he began, his voice a wheeze. He coughed. "I assembled the staff, as you requested m'lady, so that the magician here might interview us. Come to find the improver, Combs, was *missing*. It then came out he had not been seen since your necklace was stolen. We've been searching the house all this time."

"Well?" said Lady Emalta. "Did you find him?"

The butler's iron face cracked, but he pulled himself together. "Yes, m'lady, we just found him. And . . . it is with the deepest regret . . . I must inform you that he is *dead.*"

"Dead!" cried Merodite. It was not even a question.

"*Dead?*" repeated Lady Emalta, incredulously.

Felpz rose in a swirl of purple coat and stood there, very still, while we all looked at him. Then he gave a little twitch, as if shaking himself out of a dream, and said: "In the under-cellar." Then he took off out the door, brushing past the butler and the servants beyond, and was gone.

"What did he mean '*in the under-cellar?*'" Merodite asked in the confused silence left in his wake.

"I expect that is where they found his body," I said wearily, heaving myself out of my chair. I made it all the way to the door before the other two women started after me, they were so taken aback.

"Lead the way," I told the butler.

The under-cellar turned out to be located at the very bottom of that great house, set deep into the bedrock. At high tide it was easily below sea level, though it was so well insulated by stone and mortar that nothing could be heard of the outside, and it was easy to believe you were deep in the heart of some isolated mountain.

Though our way was well lit—first by electric torches and later by gas lamps—the stairs were roughly cut and very worn, and I soon grew weary of them. Natural curiosity, however, spurred me to pass my usual tolerance for physical exertion.

I was rewarded, at the end, by a scene out of nightmares. In the dance of dark and light thrown by the lanterns we eventually came upon a small storeroom where Felpz and a male servant crouched over a fallen form on the stone floor. Something dark was puddled beneath it, and I found I had to steady myself against a nearby wall.

"Magan, notify the police," I heard Lady Emalta say in a choked voice, and there was a hushed *"Yes m'lady,"* and the patter of feet away up the stairs.

"Who found him?" Merodite asked, pushing her way into the room.

The unknown man by the body stood up, revealing himself to be a dirty but fair-faced young man. Hardly out of his teens, I thought.

"That would be me, milady," he said, with a respectful touch of his forelock. "It was a mad errand, only we'd searched everywhere, and Magan was ready to send to the village to see if he'd run off to visit his mum, and I thought . . . well, there's *one* place we haven't looked, might as well check that so's there'd be no door unopened and . . . " he trailed off dejectedly, looking down at the boy on the floor.

This one was truly a boy, still with the soft, smooth face of youth, evident even contorted by death. I felt my heart ache for him, and more so for the poor woman he'd left behind, but whatever emotional upheaval my soul intended to experience was put on hold when Felpz leapt up and went over to what appeared to be a solid brick wall and began pawing at it.

"Felpz," I said heavily. "*What* are you doing?"

"Salt water," replied Felpz, not turning away from the wall. "That is not blood—he was strangled—it is *salt water.* How did *salt water* get here?"

"How do you know—*oh . . .*" said Merodite in a small voice.

Cautiously I came forward, and indeed the dark liquid was not blood—it only gave the impression of being dark because of the bad light. Now I saw it was too thin, too transparent to be blood, but the pitiful figure on the floor was enough to keep me at bay. I did not try to ascertain for myself that he had been strangled, but trusted my friend's assessment.

Felpz was murmuring to himself, strange words I only half caught, but understood them to be in some mysterious language.

"Magician, what are you—" Lady Emalta began, but then there was a *snap* in the air, as though my ears had popped, and a grinding sound as a section of bricks fell away under Felpz's hands. Their movement revealed a small, dark passageway, out of which a draft of cold, wet, salty air blew, along with a faint rushing sound.

In that grim little room all was silent, and when Felpz turned away from the wall his eyes were gleaming.

"It is an escape route," he said. "Built into the very foundations of this house. Oh, Corianne, I must thank you for convincing me to take up this case. It is proving *most* interesting."

"Would this have anything to do with Amariel Tragansea?" Lady Emalta asked, sounding resigned.

"I think it has everything to do with her," Felpz said. "This portal leads to the sea. What more perfect way for the merfolk employed by her to slip away home for their holidays, without revealing their true nature? It's been sadly neglected, I fear— you have not employed mer-servants for many generations, it seems—but it still responds to the correct words. Now, however, it has served as an escape route for our thief."

"Thief *and* murderer," I reminded him.

Felpz glanced back at the body on the floor, and he sighed. "No, I do not think this was murder. Not as it could be described by you or I. This was a tragic and entirely avoidable accident. One that, I hope, will never be repeated."

With these words he turned to the wall again and climbed into the hole, shoulders first.

"Felpz!" I called after him, indignantly. "What are you *doing*?"

There was some thumping from within the tunnel, and eventually Felpz's head reappeared. "I am going to retrieve Lady Emalta's necklace," he said, innocent as a babe. "Expect me back by morning. Good night!"

His face disappeared into the darkness, and no amount of calling was able to bring him back. After a couple of minutes, distant but distinct, I heard a splash echo up the tunnel.

"He is a most *peculiar* man," Merodite said faintly, and though none of us replied verbally, I think we were all of her mind.

The remainder of the night was no less busy, if rather more mundane. First a constable and then a detective arrived and had to be shown the body. I left after giving my own limited statement and allowed the head housemaid to lead me up to my room. This was a comfortable apartment in the modern wing of the house, and it was so far removed from that cold, eerie cellar that I put myself to bed quite easily. Though my mind was initially plagued by the events of the day—the fate of the boy had deeply upset me—soon it all faded into pleasant blackness, and I slept.

The morning came, and with it the cries of seabirds, which served to shake me from my rest rather earlier than I would have wished. I had begun to dress, and to push my hair into some sort of order, when there was a knock at the door, and the maid, Liriel, put her head in.

I confess I was surprised to see her, but more surprised, I think, at the sight that was revealed in the morning light— which had, I could only assume, been invisible in the artificial light from the torches the night before.

The girl was older than I had first thought, and there was a strong ovality to her face that caused the features to slope somewhat toward the center. Her dark hair had been bravely pinned up under a cap, but a few wriggling wisps still escaped around her ears. The most peculiar thing of all, however, was that her skin had the faintest greenish tinge in the corners and the crevices of her face. It was enough to make me hesitate before addressing her, and to forget the words she had greeted me with.

"I'm sorry," I said. "My mind is all in the clouds this morning. What did you say?"

"Beg your pardon, ma'am," said the girl. "But breakfast is ready in the dining room, and the countess is requesting your attendance. The magician is not back yet, and she wants you to find him."

"Oh . . . " I said. "Well, I'm afraid I can no more bid that magician than I can bid the tides of the sea, but I'll come down to breakfast, and see if I can't settle her feathers."

"Very good, ma'am," said Liriel, bobbed, and left.

I went down to breakfast very slowly, for I was still not easy in my mind over the recognition that had stirred within me when I had looked upon the maid's face. I felt, strongly, that I had seen those features before—though in a different configuration. I might have tormented myself over this puzzle for hours had I not passed by the entrance hall en route to the dining room. There I caught a glimpse of the portraits lining the wall, and one about halfway down provided all the answers I needed.

I must have had a strange expression on my face when I entered the dining room at last, for Lady Emalta—assembled in a magnificent costume of burgundy wool with chocolate silk lining and layered skirts of mint and sky blue—greeted me most courteously and expressed concern over the quality of my night.

Marshaling my features into an expression of idle pleasantness, I assured the lady all was well with me, before filling my plate at the sideboard.

"And the magician?" the countess asked, folding her hands over her half-empty plate. "Any word from him?"

"Alas," said I. "I know no more than you do, milady. Felpz goes and does what he will, and I find the best course is to relax and wait for him to bring the answers to you."

Lady Emalta's face pinched, but she swallowed her disappointment and resumed her meal. In time we were joined by her daughter, and the three of us were still seated around the table when there was an almighty hullabaloo from the front door.

I heard it bang, and then raised voices and a thundering of feet. A rushed conversation just outside our door, and then it opened to reveal the butler, Magan, his iron face rust red from exertion and his chest heaving. Nevertheless, he had composed himself enough to speak fluently, though his words were somewhat forced.

"My . . . ladies," he said. "I am pleased to announce that the magician has returned. He is . . . on his way. Up the drive. As I speak. And, m'lady, he has someone with him."

"Someone, Magan?" said Lady Emalta.

"Someone, m'lady," the butler repeated. "We cannot be sure what they are . . . but it looks to be a mermaid. Or perhaps a merman. To own the truth it's hard to tell from this distance. But if you come to the front door you may see for yourself."

Needless to say we all rose—the two fine ladies in a swirl of skirts—and as one made a rush for the door. Coming out onto the front steps I was immediately struck by the majesty of our surroundings—which I had not been able to fully appreciate the night before.

From where I stood the promontory fell away before us in a tumble of pink and gray stone to the village nestled at the foot of the cliff. To our right stretched the sea, cool and misty gray on that winter morning, with the sky fading to a delicate blue above our heads.

The road we had climbed in the carriage the night before was now visible as a dark stripe crisscrossing the tumble of stone, sometimes disappearing behind a crag, and upon it I saw two figures moving. They were well over halfway up the ascent and drawing steadily closer, but it took me a moment to recognize Felpz, and his companion fairly baffled me.

The reason I had difficulty identifying my friend was because he was soaking wet. His hair was plastered down across his head, smooth and shiny as a seal's back, and his normally fluttering coat hung, stiff and dripping, at his side. In its wetness it appeared more black than purple, and this also served to confuse me.

The person he had with him—and I saw now how he clutched their arm and forced them to walk a little in front of him—was as strange a creature as ever I saw. Slinky, with

greenish blue scales that caught the light and sparkled with iri-
descence, they were so covered with spines and fins that it was
difficult to make out the shape beneath it all. They walked with
a stunted, stuttering gait, and relied upon Felpz as much to keep
them upright as anything else.

Quite a crowd had gathered upon the steps of Old Baronia by
the time Felpz and his unusual charge crested the final rise and
trudged across the wide stone terrace before the house. Lady
Emalta and her daughter stood at the head of us, but turning to
the side I saw the butler Magan, both footmen, the servant from
the cellar last night, and the maid Liriel, all crowded around the
door.

Felpz drew up in front of this audience and bowed. He did
so rather jerkily because the person he held made a determined
effort to get away just then. Coming upright once more Felpz
tugged at their arm.

"I said I would return you safely to the sea," he said, a little
snappishly. "The *least* you can do is cooperate."

The creature snarled and shook its arm out of his grasp, but
made no move to flee. Instead, it drew itself up, the fins and
spines around its neck fanning out and revealing its face, which
was a most interesting combination of human and fish. Almost
draconian in its construction, it had an eerie beauty about it,
and glittered from all the fine, translucent scales that served in
place of skin. The eyes were perhaps a little large, and when it
blinked there were not eyelids, but pale membranes that pushed
in from either side. The nose was very small and the mouth
very wide, and the whole face had that same, slanting ovality
that I had noted in the maid Liriel and the portraits in the hall.
It sneered at us, and so fascinated by it was I that I didn't even
notice that it was wearing the necklace of pearl skulls until Lady
Emalta cried out and pointed.

"There!" she exclaimed, half in alarm and half in triumph. "A
thief! I knew it all along!"

A strange gurgling, hissing sound bubbled up from the
throat of the mer-person, and their mouth split asunder revealing twin ridges of sharp, triangular teeth. They were laughing,
I realized with a cold chill, just as they began to speak.

"No thief," they said, their voice as hissing and gurgling as their laugh, but still understandable. "Never a thief. One cannot steal what one already *owns*."

"But that is *my* necklace!" Lady Emalta declared, and looked so fierce saying it that for a moment I was unable to decide who looked more threatening, the woman or the mer-person.

At her words the latter straightened up, the spines across their shoulders lifting to provide an even stronger impression of height and size, and their eyes narrowed to slits—which, due to the arrangement of their membranous lids, were *vertical* slits rather than horizontal ones. It was a truly unsettling sight.

"It was Princess Amariel's necklace," they said, their voice like steam flying from a hot iron. "And you, though you bear her title, hold none of her blood! The necklace rejected you a generation ago. Now the ownership returns to me, and I shall take what is mine: first the necklace, and then the house of Old Baronia."

"You shall do no such *thing*," said Lady Emalta, coming down the steps. "You've no *right*."

"I'm afraid Calamite here has every right," Felpz said heavily. Even in the cold morning air he had begun to steam faintly and was becoming visibly drier. "The rights and legacy of the countesses of Baronia are tied up in this necklace. As has been explained to me, the necklace was a betrothal gift to Amariel Tragansea from a sea lord. She took the necklace, but instead went ashore and married a human. She tied his lands and title to her necklace, so that she could pass them down to her daughters through the piece of jewelry. An ingenious way of circumventing the traditions of the time, but now that the blood of the merfolk has dwindled so far as to be imperceptible in your generation, the necklace can no longer be safely worn by the countesses of Baronia. So Calamite, as a descendant of the original owner of the necklace, has some claim to it. The necklace, and through it, thanks to Amariel's enchantment, all the lands and titles of Old Baronia."

"This is outrageous," declared Lady Emalta, and I had to admit I partly agreed with her. "He killed *Combs!*"

"I killed no one," hissed Calamite. "The necklace saw to the boy. You've your own human frailty to thank for that."

Lady Emalta looked so angry at those words that I thought fire would leap from her eyes. Seeing her so, however, only made the mer-person chuckle.

"Don't be so angry," it said. "I agree it would be unfair to pull your home out from under you, as a riptide sweeps a swimmer out to sea. Which is why I propose a compromise: give me your daughter to wed, and our children can carry on the line—yes, and the necklace as well."

Lady Emalta turned white in fury and shock, but it was Merodite herself who replied.

"I shall *never* in a thousand *years* marry anyone as despicable as *you!*" she cried, her eyes flashing like thunder. "Neither shall I let you steal mother's necklace! We may be humans, but we're still *Traganseas*. We are the ladies of Old Baronia, and we will not give it over to you!"

Calamite laughed again. "If you want it, you may come and take it off me. Though I highly doubt that will do you any good," and the creature smiled at us, broad and satisfied and so smug it truly began to wear on my nerves.

"Felpz," I said. "Can't you *reason* with him? Er, it?"

"I have spent all *night* attempting to negotiate a mutually acceptable compromise," Felpz said wearily. "Convincing Calamite to come ashore was the most I could do. Even now, I dare not take the necklace by force. Were I to touch it, I very much doubt you would ever get it away from me again, and this would prove disastrous for all parties."

"Oh, *yes,*" Calamite fairly cackled. "The necklace has a power. In the hands of the merfolk it is tamed, it is *obedient*. To a human it is unquenchable lust and a consuming fire. To see it is to desire it; to have it is to die for it. So you can take me as the new Lord Baronia, or you can take the necklace back—and in doing so, throw away your lives."

I could have slapped it, spines and all, I was so frustrated. But it was Merodite—young and impetuous, with all the pride of her ancestors behind her—who strode down the steps, across the short expanse of gravel, and took hold of the creature by its neck and began to pull at the necklace.

Her mother and I both shouted—inarticulate noises of protest, as we were too surprised for proper words—and

Calamite, far from allowing the necklace to be taken, grappled with Merodite and bared its teeth.

The young woman might have come to grief then, had Felpz not intervened. He pushed an arm roughly between the warring parties, and there was a sharp *snap* of raw magic that sent the two staggering backwards from each other.

There was a twinkle in the air, and something landed with a delicate *clink* upon the ground. I blinked and looked more closely, and realized that the snap I'd heard had not just been from Felpz's magic: the clasp of the necklace had also broken, and in Merodite's contortion as she stumbled backwards it had flown out of her hand and now lay among the rocks, gleaming and shimmering.

What came over me then was the strangest feeling. As I looked upon the necklace I felt a great rush of desire within me, while at the same time the reaction left me cold in the pit of my stomach. A sour taste grew in my mouth, and altogether I felt quite ill. Where the necklace had looked eerily beautiful in the painting and upon the mer-person's neck, now it appeared the most horrible and evil thing imaginable, and I wanted nothing more than to crush it beneath the heel of my boot.

Judging by the reactions of the crowd, however, I was alone in this revulsion. When I chanced to look around, I found them all gazing at the thing as though they were besotted. Even— and this was most terrifying of all—Felpz himself, who clung to Calamite as though they were an anchor.

It was Lady Emalta who came forward, stumbling a little, and picked up the necklace. She cradled it in her hands reverently, an odd light dancing in her eyes.

"Best put it away now, my lady," Felpz said in a strained voice. "You had the strength to shut it away once. Shut it away once more. The box!" he barked. "The silver box! Why does no one have it?!"

But Lady Emalta said nothing, and no servant went to fetch the box. Instead, as one in a trance, she put the necklace round her throat and held it there—for the clasp was still broken.

"*Mine,*" she said, her eyes shining and shimmering. "I am Lady Emalta Tragansea, Countess of Baronia. You have no claim and no power. *Go back to the sea!*" She pointed with her free arm, forcefully, towards the cliff.

Calamite sneered at her, at all of us, and then shrugged. "I shall be back," the mer-person said. "Upon your death I will return. Again and again I shall. And I won't have to wait long— the necklace will see to that!"

The creature took three lunging, awkward strides, and then cast itself into the air beyond the cliff's edge, whereupon it disappeared.

My first instinct was to run and see how it navigated the tumble of rock that lay between it and the sea, but at that moment Lady Emalta gasped, clutched at her neck with both hands, and fell to the ground.

We all rushed towards her, but Felpz reached her first.

"Ease up, my lady, let it go," he was saying, and I saw with horror that the necklace had tightened considerably around the woman's neck. Her skin was standing out around it in angry red, and she was clearly suffocating. Her mouth worked, forming words for which she had no air, and her eyes bulged.

"Yes, this is exactly what Calamite hoped would happen," Felpz said. He looked up, cast around, and for a moment settled on me. "Corianne," he said. "I cannot risk touching the thing. You'll have to take it off her."

"No!" I cried, for I had the sudden unshakable knowledge that were I to touch that horrible thing I would be sick.

"Oh, will you both stop dallying and *help her!*" someone shouted.

To my surprise it was Liriel, the countess's maid. She who had stood behind me quietly for the whole ordeal had now come forward and was gently lifting the countess's head into her lap. "Have *none* of you worked a clasp before?" she said, her pale little hands running around to the back of the older woman's neck. There was a neat *click*, and then the necklace came away and Liriel was scrambling backwards, holding the artifact as though it were a live snake.

As abruptly as a candle being snuffed the sickness in my stomach left me, and Felpz's face lost that panicked, strained look. The crowd fell away as Merodite came forward and took her mother's hand, and the countess coughed and gasped and drew in much-needed air.

Through it all Liriel stood with the necklace in her hands, its skulls faintly gleaming—but only as much as any pearl would in that bright winter sunshine. It appeared to me nothing more than a curious bauble now, and I could not imagine why it had elicited such strong feelings.

"Could I trouble someone for its box?" she asked faintly. "It's put away on milady's dresser. Ordinarily I'd go, but I don't like to leave her now."

Felpz himself went for the box, returning in a matter of seconds. The necklace was placed in it, and the lid sealed. Then at last Felpz seemed to relax. He handed the box respectfully back to Liriel with a short bow, looked around at us, and said:

"That turned out as well as could be hoped. Is there any breakfast left? I am *famished.*"

"You must thank Liriel not me," Felpz said later, after he had breakfasted. Lady Emalta had been put to bed, but was now sitting up and insisted on seeing us. We were seated in her room along with Merodite, and Liriel herself was standing modestly by the door.

"If it pleases you, milady," said the young woman, her face still downcast. "Think of it as reparations. It was my weakness that allowed Combs to get the key off me in the first place. If I hadn't been so wrong in the head over him I should have noticed what he was up to."

"Oh, I imagine he would have got it eventually *some way,*" said Felpz magnanimously. "Merfolk are notorious for getting what they want out of humans. Including myself, I confess. When I brought Calamite to Old Baronia I hoped that they could be reasoned with. I see now I was overly optimistic. Without Liriel's intervention I shudder to think what would have happened. You'll want to give her a raise, I believe. A promotion, too. You'll need someone to be the keeper of the necklace now that you yourself cannot handle it, and it seems Liriel is more than a match for the task—she is, after all, more than meets the eye."

"Traganseas aren't the only ones with family legends about merfolk," Liriel said modestly. "It's quite common 'round here, actually."

"Oh, *good*," wheezed Lady Emalta. "Do you know if any of them contain eligible bachelors? I've been thinking, you see, about what the creature said, and it was right about one thing: perhaps Merodite *should* marry someone who, if not a *merman*, is at least closely related to one."

"*Really*, mother?" said Merodite, aghast.

Felpz shrugged. "That is a possibility, I suppose. In the meantime, however, I recommend entrusting all duty concerning the necklace to Miss Liriel. Now, I believe our task is complete. Corianne, I promised you a holiday, and I do not see any reason to delay."

So it was we left the three women there, and I am happy to say the following two weeks proved to be as enjoyable and excitement free as ever I could have hoped. Felpz read my novel, and I compiled this neat little account of our adventure, which now needs only one or two words to make it complete.

It is my understanding that Merodite did not marry a man of merfolk descent, but chose instead a decent gentleman from Greywall who took the eccentricities of the family he married into very much in stride. It is Liriel who keeps the necklace to this day, and she is training a young boy—the orphan of a fisherman father and a mermaid mother—to be her successor. Lady Emalta remains a steadfast fixture at Old Baronia, and Calamite has remained in the sea.

As to the exact powers of the necklace, Felpz and I compared notes about our experiences the following week.

"The machinations are simple," he told me. "The necklace makes itself irresistible to anyone without sufficient merfolk blood. It then proceeds to kill them. Because it is magic, however, and powerful magic at that, what it would have done if brought into contact with *my* magic. . . . " He trailed off and shuddered. "*Perish* the thought."

"But I felt no desire to put it on!" I pointed out. "Quite the opposite, in fact."

"You are a rather special case, dear Corianne," he said, twinkling a smile at me. "I was counting on that, not being certain of

Liriel. You have, after all, a knack for subduing powerful magic. Look at the effect you had on that fairy when you were but a girl, or the demonic lamp you still keep in your bedroom with no ill effects. No, I was—and am—confident that you would have had no trouble with the necklace of Amariel Tragansea."

"You flatter me," I said with a wry grin. And I was very flattered, and deeply touched that he trusted me so. "However, I must say I'm glad I never had to touch the thing."

"As am I, dear Corianne," said my friend heartily. *"As am I."*

NOTE ON THE GENDER OF CALAMITE

In my first draft of this narrative I identified Calamite as male—as most people had assumed based on its behavior. Felpz corrected me, however, and explained that the creature did not have a human gender. Merfolk, it seems, are more fluid in these matters than humans, and unless explicitly stated, they should properly be referred to by gender-neutral terms. Though some merfolk will take on the characteristics of human males or females and then may be gendered accordingly, this is a conscious change and one they make the same way they can take on legs, lungs, and other aspects of humanity. So Amariel is female because she felt that presentation was the best way to achieve her ends. Had Calamite succeeded in marrying Merodite they would undoubtedly have made a similar adjustment. Since that did not come to pass, happily, I have chosen to render to them in their natural, ungendered state.

Bouragner Felpz will return in
"The Goblin's Fiddle"

The sixth spoke in the first wheel of the Driving Arcana saga, "Mission-ary Man" follows "God, or Aliens" (Apsis Fiction: Perihelion 2015). It was written in January 2014, and will be followed in Perihelion 2016 by Spoke Seven: "Sons of Fire." Previous spokes can be found in Apsis Fiction *issues 1.1–2.2, and the first three have also been collected in the volume,* Driving Arcana: Rotation One.

MISSIONARY MAN

Pearson, Kansas

ANDREW BELL WAS SMALL FOR HIS AGE and he knew it. He felt even smaller than usual seated at his mother's enor-mous kitchen table. The vast expanse of hard-scrubbed wood stretched out in front of him, striped with afternoon sunlight from the kitchen window. He was grateful for it, however, be-cause it kept the man on the other side a safe distance away.

This man was only the latest in a string of well-brushed men in neat dark suits who had been through his mother's kitchen ever since the *incident,* and in Andrew's experience, they were mostly well-intentioned people who were unable to listen to the words Andrew said.

It didn't stop them asking questions, though.

"Who was the first person you saw about your condition, Mr. Bell?" the latest man asked.

This man was different, Andrew had to admit. He was white, for starters, and while the others had all called him Andrew, or even *Andy,* this man spoke to him as though he were an adult. It was all "May I speak with you, *Mr. Bell,*" "How are you doing today, *Mr. Bell?*" It was enough to convince Andrew to come down to the kitchen when his mother called, instead of leading them on a mad chase all over the house and into the backyard like he had done with the others.

"I already told you that," Andrew's mother said. "We went and saw Dr. Chaser over in Wichita—"

"Thank you, Mrs. Bell," said the man. "I appreciate your information, but I would like to hear what young Mr. Bell has to say."

And Momma, by some miracle, fell silent. Andrew was shocked. Nothing and no one had been able to get Momma to be quiet ever since the incident if she didn't want to. It gave him the tiniest spark of hope that things would be different this time, and that gave him the courage to speak.

"Yes, Mr. Bell?" said the man. He had muddy blond hair neatly trimmed, and a sprinkling of stubble across his strong, squarish chin. He looked, Andrew thought, rather like Captain America, if Captain America forgot to shave for a couple days and traded in the red, white and blue spandex for a priest's black coat and collar, and the star spangled shield for a white cowboy hat. This, which was now hanging neatly beside the front door, had positively shone in the sun as the man had crunched up their driveway in his leather cowboy boots.

"I wen' an' saw Dr. Chaser, yeah," said Andrew, then kicked himself for not finishing his words. That made him more nervous, which made him begin to stammer. "H-he s . . . said ah . . . ah . . . said ah ah ah I am fine. Buh . . . buh buh but Momma say no so she brung in Mr. Palm."

"Mr . . . Jeremiah Palm," the man said, producing a small book and making a notation. "The local priest? What did he do?"

"H-he he he say I un g-got got demons inside me—"

"Demon, darling," said his mother. "Just one."

"Could be more than one," the man disagreed cheerfully. "Dual possessions are rare, but they do happen. What sort of demons did he say you had?"

"A bad kind. Devil spawn an' darkness," said Andrew. "He ah . . . had me eat salt an' it brought my dinner back up. I kept blowing an' blowing, so I thought all the demons got blown outta me, but he say they still inside so he put me in a bath an' wrapped my head in towels."

Andrew shivered. The water had been cold and the towels had gotten soaked. He could hear Mr. Palm's chanting and feel his mother's hands holding him still, so he couldn't reach up and yank the towels off. He'd begun to choke, struggling to breathe. He'd thought, certainly *this* would get the demons out of him, but when the towels were finally removed Mr. Palm had declared the demon only weakened, and told his mother he'd have to come back next week.

"I see . . . " said the man, making a little mark in his book. "And . . . how many times did this happen?"

"I forgotten," said Andrew. "Once a week since Chrissmas? I dunno how many weeks that is, but is a lot, innit?"

The man nodded gravely. "And you still have demons in you?" he asked.

"Don' I must?" asked Andrew. "Momma says I scream at night an' paint my walls in blood. Ya *seen* it, I know. I don' remember doing any of it, but is *there* every morning an' it *scares* me."

"Yes," said the man, "they're meant to." He gave Andrew such a sympathetic look that suddenly he knew—he *knew*—that this man not only believed him, but understood how he felt. "Well," he went on. "I think you've been through enough. Lets get those demons out of you right away, what do you say?"

"Will it need wet towels?" Andrew asked.

"None at all," said the man, smiling broadly. He had perfect white teeth, just like Captain America should, Andrew thought. "You don't even have to move. Sit tight, this will only take a minute."

Getting up, the man came around the table and gently pushed it away from Andrew, so his chair now stood alone in the middle of the kitchen floor.

"Comfortable?" he asked. "Need to use the bathroom?"

When Andrew nodded, and then shook his head, the man smiled reassuringly and opened his briefcase. Inside Andrew glimpsed a lot of little bottles on silver chains, a couple knives, leather pouches, and several flasks of dark liquid. Removing one of these and a large brush, the man unscrewed the lid and began painting a circle around Andrew's chair.

"Wha's that for?" Andrew asked.

"Well," said the man. "I'm going to draw the demons out of you, carefully, so you don't get hurt. Once they're free, however,

I need to make sure they can't just run off and jump inside someone *else*."

"So the circle is to protect *us?*" asked Andrew's mother.

The man, bent over the floor and concentrated on his work, didn't answer at once. He finished the circle by painting a smaller circle that joined the two ends, inside of which he painted a little sigil, like an *S* with an extra squiggle and some dots. Then he opened a pouch and sprinkled some powder around the legs of Andrew's chair.

"Right," he said, replacing the bottle, brush and bag and getting to his feet. "Whatever happens, don't leave the circle. Got that?"

Andrew nodded.

"The circle is for protection," the man said, turning to Andrew's mother. "But it's to protect *him,* not us."

Momma stared at the man. Andrew tried to understand. He knew something had changed about his mother since the incident, but it had never been so obvious as it was now. Her face was still Momma's face, but it was the wrong expression. Her eyes were too wide, too bloodshot, and her breathing was too fast. Her teeth bared in a humorless grin; she began to laugh.

"You-huhuhu have the *wrong* idea, Mr. Freeman," she said.

"No," said the man with a sigh. "Stop messing around, Lashka, and come out."

"You-huhu *summon* me?" said Andrew's mother. Or, rather, the thing *inside* Andrew's mother. Andrew found he had to admit, it hadn't really been his mother since the incident.

The man held out his hand, as if offering it for the taking. "I do, Lashka, I summon you."

And then . . . then Andrew's mother began to laugh in earnest. Her mouth opened wide—wider than it should have. Her skin turned blue, and some *thing* crawled up her throat and out her mouth. It crouched on her tongue a moment and then leapt at the man.

Almost too fast to see, the man snapped his hand back and thrust the other out. He held something in it that glinted like crystal, and the thing dissolved into a thick, blue-black smoke in midair. This billowed out, cloaking first the man, then Andrew's mother, before rushing to fill the room.

All except a narrow pillar of air around Andrew's chair, which remained clear as day.

Peering into the smoke, Andrew heard a grunt of pain, a hastily bitten-off swearword, and finally a triumphant *"Gotcha!"* Then there was some confused thumping, the sound of someone running into the table, and then a grinding as the window over the sink was pushed open. Almost at once the smoke began to clear, and a moment later the shape of the man was visible, bent over Andrew's mother and gently fanning her face.

"Doing okay, Mr. Bell?" he asked, his voice a little hoarse.

"Is Momma okay?" Andrew asked.

"Yeah—she should be," said the man. "Could use a drink of water though, I think. Would you mind? I don't know where you keep the cups. Oh, you can get off your chair now. Demon's gone."

"They said the demons was in *me* though," said Andrew, cautiously climbing down off his chair.

"Nope," said the man. "Only one demon, and that was in your mother. All you've got inside you is a whole bunch of bad memories. Which, I can assure you, no matter what you may hear people say, aren't nearly as bad as a *real* demon. Easy there, Mrs. Bell. Looks like there was a bit of an accident, but no harm done. Can you manage to sit up? Your son is bringing you some water."

Somewhere on the outskirts of Denver, Colorado

CLAYMORE DREAMED. This was unusual: she had gotten rather good at *not dreaming* and usually shut dreams down before they got too strong, if she couldn't avoid them entirely. This one, however, was persistent. It had dogged her sleeping mind for the past two weeks, and it was becoming difficult to get any rest with all the waking up she had been doing to escape it. So, finally, worn out from a day of riding and an evening listening to Jill and Selene bicker, Claymore allowed herself to sleep. And to dream.

In her dream she was walking through a thick dark wood. Unless she was floating. She had become her name: her legs had fused into a long, gray blade; her arms were quillons and her hands were quatrefoils.

She was lost. This she knew. More than that, she had lost everything else. She was alone. Even Bellatrix and Unicorn were gone. Though, if she had become a sword, perhaps Bellatrix was now a woman and Unicorn was a unicorn. She could see them clearly in her dream, though she knew they were not there. Bellatrix made a tall, narrow, sharp-looking woman, and she wore a gray dress that glinted like metal. Unicorn was a huge, dark shadow behind her. Big as a Shire, graceful as an Arabian, she held her neck in a proud arch. Her horn was made of anodized aluminum and glimmered faintly in the reflected light from Bellatrix's dress.

Claymore could see them, knew the feel of them, but could not find them in her dream. The wood closed in thickly about her, and she did not know where to go.

A light bloomed behind her, and Claymore turned her stiff neck to find a deer standing over her. No, not a deer . . . a *stag*. He was white as fresh snow, and the two magnificent antlers resting on his head had a translucency like ice. Colors shot through them, brilliant like a rainbow.

He stood over her for a moment, and then with a leap took off through the wood.

Claymore followed as best she could. The stag knew the wood. He knew the way out of it. And he would lead her, if she could but follow.

She shot through the wood after him, keeping the pale leaping body always in her sight. She was gaining on him, she was closing on him. She could not stop.

I am a sword, and he is a soft, beautiful, innocent animal, she realized with a sense of horror. Then, grappling frantically for control of the dream, she remembered something else: *I am going at him hilt first. I will not hurt him.*

They cleared the wood just as Claymore reached the white stag, and for a moment the two were suspended in air over a dark city while the wood crowded away behind them.

Then the white stag gave another bound—across thin air this time—and shot away into the sky. Claymore watched him leaping among the stars, toward the face of the moon, even as she fell.

"I think it's a demon," the moon said.

"No it's not," said Claymore.

"What do you mean it's not?" asked Jill.

She opened her eyes, and like the lights going up at the end of a play the dream vanished. Bellatrix was at her back, and Unicorn she knew was parked just outside their motel room door. Claymore was gone, replaced with Clara, and the stag remained only as a memory of snow-white fur and a brilliance shot with a rainbow of colors. Selene was staring at her from across the other bed, Jill's computer balanced on one leg, with an amused expression on her face.

"Didja just fall asleep on us?" she asked.

Clara rubbed her face, assuring herself that she did have *hands*. She was also pleased to find that her legs had gone back to normal.

"Sort of," she said. "There was a dream that wouldn't leave me alone."

Selene raised an eyebrow, and Jill, who was sorting through newspapers at the little desk, shot her a curious look.

"So you mean in your *dream* it wasn't a demon?" she asked.

Clara nodded. "It was a white stag," she said.

Selene chuckled. "Well, it *sounded* like you'd been listening, which if you had, you'd admit this is pretty quintessential demonic activity. Listen here . . . " she straightened the laptop and began to read. "A boy in Pearson, Kansas, was reportedly found asleep in a pool of blood late last year. Afterward he began exhibiting signs of extreme stress, disorientation and schizophrenia. Doctors have been unable to determine the cause of his illness, and his mother hired a priest to perform an exorcism.' Now, compare that to *this* report, also from Pearson, of an outbreak of graffiti defacing local storefronts. They've also had an increase in cases of rabid dogs and other animals."

"Graffiti doesn't mean—" Jill began.

"*Look* at the graffiti and tell her," Selene insisted, shoving the laptop at Clara.

Taking the computer, Clara scrolled through the collection of pictures and felt an uncomfortable prickling in her gut. They were all of comfortable, modest buildings, some with wide windows, others with inviting expanses of brick wall. All of them had been decorated with copious amounts of red and black paint which, to an untrained observer, might have been a disordered jumble of lines, circles and dots, but to Clara they spoke volumes.

"This is a master *unbinding*," she whispered, tracing a finger over the first one. "This is the sigil of Lashka the Tormentor. And *this* . . . is that a partial *odegra?*" She raised her face to Selene. "How is this town not *crawling* with demons?"

"For all I know, it *is,*" Selene said grimly, taking the computer back.

"Okay, okay," said Jill, waving a hand. "Someone explain to me how demons work, and how they're different from gods and angels and stuff."

Clara and Selene exchanged a look. The look said, "Oh, won't *you* please take this one?" at which Selene groaned and rolled her eyes.

"So, near as I can tell," she began, "demons are non-corporeal entities that can manifest within a person's mind. That's what we call a *possession*. They can also manifest in—that is, *possess*—an inanimate object. They are generally pretty nasty, and the best thing to do is stay as far away from them as possible."

"Unless you are an exorcist," Clara added.

"Or us," said Selene, with a dark grin. "They can't be killed—not in this dimension, anyway—and they have all sorts of powers over their environment that makes fighting them a royal pain in the butt."

"They exist in a strict hierarchy," Clara took over. "The exact structure is unknown, but it is generally accepted that there are an infinite number of lesser demons, somewhere on the order of thousands of greater demons, and several hundred legendary demons. Also, theoretically, there are maybe a handful of elder demons, but these have never been directly observed. The greatest power you can hold over a demon is to know its true name, but this in itself is risky, since their name is intrinsically linked with the demon. To know its name is to invite the demon into your mind. You have to be strong enough to keep control of the demon at all times, otherwise it will consume you."

"Interesting," said Jill. In place of her computer she had pulled over the motel notepad and was scribbling on it.

"As for how they relate to gods," Clara sighed. "It's complicated."

"That never stopped me before," Jill pointed out.

"It's sort of like this," Selene said. "*Gods* feed off human belief. No belief, no god. The entity *behind* the god can still exist, however. These are the entities that make up the class of beings *we* refer to as angels, demons . . . and gods."

Jill nodded. "So basically, what makes it a demon or an angel or a god . . . all depends on how we perceive it?"

"Pretty much," said Selene. "And by their behaviors. There are certain things a demon will do that an angel won't. But yeah, it basically comes down to: are they nice to us or not? And whether or not they have a cult following."

"It would be useful," Jill sighed. "If there was a clear way to organize these different entities."

"There a number of ways of categorizing demons," Clara remarked. "But most of them have to do with their culture of origin. It's not the best, however, since demons aren't cultural—it's just that different cultures have seen them differently and so perceive them to be different."

"So what you're saying is . . . "

"Take a demon like . . . oh . . . *Lilith*," said Selene. "Everybody likes Lilith. She's primarily a Judeo-Christian demon, but the actual *spirit* behind her *isn't*. It's more likely that she's similar to Echidna—in fact they may be the same person."

"Hold on, hold on," said Jill. "Lilith, Echidna . . . those are both *mythological characters*."

"Yep," said Selene. "And, like a lot of them, they existed—just not in the way the stories make it out. Most gods and stuff, when you start to dig a bit, turn out to be real things that humans have plastered all these names and legends on."

"So . . . what about other monsters? Gorgons and trolls and ogres and things like that? Are they demons too?"

Selene wagged her head from side to side. "It's hard to tell, actually. Since, the way we use the term, a *demon* is just a malevolent spirit that can't manifest corporeally. *If* they could, they might turn out to be a gorgon or something like that. But they can't, so we don't really know."

"Demons are wide and varied," said Clara. "It is likely that the things we call demon contain multitudes of different entities."

"But mostly, when a hunter says *'demon'* they mean a nasty piece of work that possesses people and causes all kinds of trouble." Selene explained. "It's like . . . fish. Fish all live in water and stuff, but there's *tons* of different *kinds* of fish, and some are so different that you'd never guess they were both fish. *And . . . "* she continued, warming to her metaphor. "There's even things that *look* like demons, but aren't. Same ways not everything you find in the sea *is* a fish."

She sat back, smiling proudly, while Jill continued to scribble notes.

"This is hardly conclusive," she said with a frown. "But it's a place to start. Very well. What do you propose we do about the demon in . . . " she leaned over to check the computer screen, " . . . Pearson? Would it be possible to study it up close?"

Selene laughed nervously. "Sure . . . I mean, same ways you study a *tornado* up close. Wait until it goes away and then examine the wreckage. Or, in this case, wait until we *make* it go away."

Jill's mouth twisted in disappointment. "So . . . there would be no way to . . . well . . . *catch* it for study?"

"It's possible," Clara said, while Selene's jaw dropped. "But unwise. Many have sought to harness demons, to use their power for their own ends. It . . . never ends well."

"I don't *want* to use its power!" Jill exclaimed. "I just want to understand how it *works.*"

Selene and Clara looked at one another despairingly.

"Look," said Selene. "We'll go sort out Pearson, and you can take whatever you can from *watching us work,* and collect whatever evidence is left over. If, after that, you still want to have a pet demon . . . well, we'll see."

Jill pursed her lips, but didn't press the issue.

They stayed only one night at the hotel outside Denver, and left early the next morning.

*   *   *

After spending the last several months in mountains of varying dryness, the great open *flatness* of Kansas took a little getting used to. Jill, who had never considered herself a mountain person, still found herself surprised by the sheer amount of sky that stretched over them as they chugged along Interstate 70. It was enough to wonder, if she didn't keep a firm hand on the wheel would Arcana float off into that great blue ocean? She couldn't help smiling inwardly at the flight of fancy, and shook her head. Jill was fond of reason and logic, but that didn't mean she couldn't indulge her imagination now and then.

Arcana, big and red and loud, ate up the miles as they traveled east, following in the wake of the sleek black form that was Clara riding Unicorn. They traveled across a sun-bleached asphalt road that cut a straight line between the flat green plain and the blue arc of the heavens.

Stopping for fuel on the outskirts of Pearson, Selene left Jill in charge of cleaning the windows while she headed into the foodmart. She returned a few minutes later, a frown on her face and a folded newspaper in her hands.

"Something wrong?" Jill asked, shaking the excess fluid off the window scraper.

"Take a look," said Selene, passing Jill the paper in exchange for the squeegee. She got up onto Arcana's front bumper to reach the middle of the windshield. "That article lists no less than *four* probable cases of demonic possession. Oh, yeah, they're *calling* it the flu, but look at the symptoms!"

"Archie Davis, 27, claims to have hallucinated walking on his ceiling and biting the ears off the neighbor's dog . . .'" Jill read. "'Said neighbor, Julie Christopherson, denies having seen the man on her property, but reports her dog did get in a fight that left it with a mangled ear.'"

She looked up at Selene incredulously.

"Keep going," said Selene.

"'Two minors have been admitted to Pearson Memorial Hospital with extreme cases . . . ' what are *extreme cases?*"

"Probably vomiting pea soup and spinning heads," Selene remarked casually. "Or something along those lines. Keep going, though, it gets better."

"'Laurel Fletcher, 32, was diagnosed after *painting her children black and locking them in the attic?*'"

"All fun and games now, but just wait until they start eviscerating each other," Selene said grimly.

Clara, who as always finished refueling first, had wandered over and now stood, reading the paper over Jill's shoulder.

"We should begin with the woman Fletcher," she said. "She appears to be the prime host."

"Can't argue with that," said Selene. "You thinking straight up exorcism or should we try to catch it?"

"I don't have any lamps with me," Clara said. "We can salt the earth to prevent a repeat possession."

"One problem," Jill pointed out. "How do we *find* her?"

Selene laughed at that, and even Clara managed a sort of smile.

"If she's got a demon in her, hon, she'll be *easy* to find," Selene said. "Now let's find us a room so I can set up my gear."

The room was provided by the Happy Pear Inn, and Selene's gear turned out to be a greasy, wax-stained cloth and a bunch of candles. Clara hunted down a paper map of the town and spread it out on the bed, then sat down at the little table where she opened one of her panniers and unpacked a bottle of dark liquid, a roll of brushes, and several pieces of cloth—they looked to be torn squares of old jeans.

"More magic?" Jill asked, a little tiredly.

"If it helps, you can think of it like a test," Selene said, spreading the cloth on the floor and sticking the candles to it. "These are moth-wax candles; they don't burn with physical fire. They will, however, react to demonic activity. Do we have any oil? I need it to prime the map."

Wordlessly, Clara produced a small tube and handed it to Selene.

"Thanks." Selene took the tube and squeezed a generous dollop onto her hands, which she began to rub into the paper. "The oil makes the candles read the map as if it were the place it represents," Selene explained as she worked. "Don't ask me *why.*"

"I see," said Jill. "Then what is Clara doing?"

Clara had laid out her little squares of cloth and was now painting things on them. They were unrecognizable to Jill, save in the most abstract sense. One of them looked a little like an A.

"This is not magic," said Clara. "It is *protection*."

"Since demons aren't physical, they can pass through walls and armor and things," Selene explained. "So to protect yourself from them, you need to make . . . erm . . . non-physical walls."

"Place this under your clothing," Clara said, handing one of the squares of cloth to Jill. "Make sure it lies flat."

This was easier said than done. Jill retreated into the bathroom to solve the problem, and by the time she returned Selene had lit the candles and was holding the oil-soaked paper map over them.

Jill made an involuntary move to look for a fire extinguisher, but Clara held up a hand to stop her.

"It's moth wax," she said, as if this explained everything.

"I don't understand," Jill said, creeping cautiously forward.

"We're not sure we do either," said Selene, but absently, as she was concentrating on moving the map over the flames in a systematic pattern.

Sure enough, the paper wasn't burning, though Jill could see the light from the candles shining through it. Then, sparks. A glow of orange and yellow.

"Got one!" Selene cried, as a small portion of the map caught fire. Before Jill could become alarmed, however, the fire died out, leaving a dark, burnt circle behind.

Only for another fire to start up at a different place on the map.

"Two . . . " said Selene.

And another. And another. And another. This last was the biggest of them all, and left a hole in the map the size of a quarter.

"Damn," said Clara.

"What does that mean?" asked Jill.

Selene lifted the map away and blew out the candles. Laying the paper back down over the bed she took out a small flashlight and began examining the surface of the map.

"Put simply, sister, it means we're gonna have our hands full."

*   *   *

"We'll take the one on Pleasant Drive first," Selene explained as they packed. "That'll likely be the lead demon. Get rid of that, and the smaller ones will probably hightail it out of here."

Jill followed mutely in the woman's wake. The manner of her two employees had changed so dramatically that, for once, she'd managed to rein in her curiosity and desire for knowledge and simply let them work. Almost as if in gratitude, neither of them had suggested she stay behind. So she drove while Selene dug through her duffle bag pulling out strange little artifacts and tying them to her wrists and ankles. They weren't crosses or other religious paraphernalia, as far as Jill could see. They looked more like twisted little bones.

The house on Pleasant Drive—as indicated by the huge scorch mark on the map—looked ordinary enough in real life. A comfortable house with a wide lawn, it was missing only the white picket fence to be something out of a suburban fairytale.

"Stay in the truck," Selene said, opening the door as soon as Arcana stopped.

"But—" Jill began.

"*Trust* me on this one," Selene said, sliding her legs out. "If we find anything you can safely study, we'll bring it back to you."

And Jill was forced to accept that. Leaning on the steering wheel she watched as the two women—looking almost like a humorous double-act, Clara was so much bigger than Selene—walked up the path and boldly rang the doorbell.

After a moment the door cracked open and a conversation, inaudible to Jill, took place. Then the two women were permitted inside, and the door shut behind them.

In the truck, Jill prepared for an interminable wait and so was surprised when the door opened less than ten minutes later and Selene and Clara re-emerged, looking puzzled.

"That was fast," Jill remarked as Selene opened the door and climbed in, pulling out the map and spreading it open on the dashboard.

"It's clean," she said with a frown.

"What?"

"I mean, there's no demon in there anymore. Sure, there *was* or this wouldn't have pinged," she tapped the scorchmark. "But *apparently* it left on its own."

Jill frowned. "I take it that doesn't happen very often?"

"Often?" said Selene. "Try *never*. There's something fishy going on here."

"I recommend we check the other houses," said Clara. "It could have moved on."

"Hells yeah," said Selene. "Let's try the one over on McCormack Street next."

McCormack Street held a modest block of apartments. Jill parked across the street and watched Selene and Clara approach Number 12A like a pair of lions stalking prey. After a considerably longer conversation (during which the occupant refused to take the chain off the door), they returned with nothing but puzzled expressions, and in Selene's case, mounting frustration.

"It's like the thing keeps jumping hosts right before we get there," she said. "No doubt that guy *had* been possessed—he had the look. But I didn't pick up *any* signs of possession, did you?"

This to Clara, who shook her head gravely.

"Well, let's try Fifth and Cottonwood," Selene sighed.

Fifth and Cottonwood found Jill waiting in the truck for almost an hour, but as it turned out, this was only because the little old lady who lived there felt compelled to invite Selene and Clara in for coffee and cake and proceeded to tell them all about the nice young man who cured her migraine that morning.

"I think I have heard my fill of handsome young men with miracle cures in neat, black suitcases," Selene said, rolling her eyes. "What's next?"

Next turned out to be a small cottage on the back lot of a larger house on the outskirts of town, where a prickly young couple informed Selene and Clara that the gas leak in their home had been fixed two days ago, thank you very much, and the pair came away with nothing.

After that it was a trailer. Clara went to talk to the inhabitant on her own, while Selene crept around the back.

"I found his stash," she confessed as she climbed back into the truck. "But no demon."

At last they found themselves in front of a small bungalow on a dingy street. The yard was mostly dirt and littered with children's toys, and there was a battered Honda sedan in the drive.

"What are we at now?" Selene asked tiredly as they trudged up to the house.

"This is our sixth," Clara replied, indomitably.

"Right," said Selene. "Let's get this over with."

She knocked on the peeling front door, and from within came the sound of small feet pattering on tile. A moment later the door opened, and the two women found themselves staring down at a small boy of maybe ten or eleven. He had very large black eyes set in a dusky, umber face, which was in turn surrounded by a halo of frizzy black hair.

"Can I help you?" he asked in a small voice with a hint of a stammer.

"Yes," said Selene. "Can we talk to your parents?"

"Or," said Clara, leaning her head down over Selene's shoulder. "Can you tell us if you've seen any demons around lately?"

"*Clara,*" Selene hissed, elbowing the larger woman in the ribs.

Unfazed, Clara peered down expectantly at the little boy, who was staring back up in shock.

"What we mean is . . . " Selene began, but then the boy began to speak.

"Momma had a demon in her," the boy said, quickly and quietly. "Demon did bad things. But the man came and got it outta her. He like you . . . " he pointed at Clara, then leaned conspiratorially toward Selene. "*White* man," he explained. "But wears black all over. An' a white hat."

"Did this man have a *name?*" Selene asked shrewdly.

The boy shook his head. "He ah . . . like a missionary. Missionary man."

"Like a priest?" Clara asked.

"He no priest," the boy said, drawing back inside. "No priest helped Momma."

"And the demon is totally gone now?" Selene asked.

The boy nodded.

"Well, that's good," Selene said. "Glad to hear it. Thanks, uh . . . kid. Yeah. You don't have to tell your parents we were here."

The boy nodded gravely and withdrew into the house, and Selene and Clara walked back down the drive in thoughtful silence.

"Let me guess," said Jill as Selene climbed back inside. "No demon?"

"Nah, there really *was* a demon in that house," said Selene. "It's not there anymore."

"What happened to it?"

"I think it got exorcised . . . or . . . " Selene frowned and gave a small shudder. "It jumped hosts."

"How do you mean?"

"Sometimes a demon gets bored of one person, and hops onto a new host. Sometimes it kills its old host, sometimes it just leaves them alone to live with the trauma."

"So you think the reason we haven't been able to find any *actual* possessed people . . . is because the demon's *moved on*?" Jill pressed.

"That's *one* possibility," Selene said, spreading the map out and tapping a spot near the center of town. "This is our last hit," she said to Clara, who had come to stand outside the window, helmet on but with her visor raised. "If it's not there . . . "

Clara nodded. "I'll lead you in," she said, flipping down the visor and striding off to her bike.

Downtown Pearson was in a sleepy, mid-afternoon lull when Arcana pulled up across from a dusty shop with TATTOO above it in red-and-purple letters. The door stood open like the black mouth of a cave, but nothing moved inside.

Clara was already there. Having parked Unicorn around the corner she was now approaching the little parlor slowly, with one hand outstretched as if she expected to run into an invisible barrier. Inside Arcana, Selene checked her gun—"Special cartridges for the special occasion"—and the talismans hanging from her wrists before jumping down into the street.

"You think this is the one?" Jill asked, coming around the side of Arcana to peer skeptically at the shop.

"It's the last place on the map," Selene said, a little shortly. There was a smell just on the edge of her senses, like something foul and wrong, that she had begun to associate with demons. In the other places it had seemed old and stale, but here it was definitely fresh.

Whatever it was, smell or no, Clara could sense it too. She had one hand up behind her shoulder, resting on the hilt of her sword. Selene bit back on the urge to remind her not to harm the human host; Clara was a warrior, a hunter like herself; she didn't need Selene telling her how to do her job.

The silence of the afternoon was broken by the purr of an engine as a white sedan turned onto the street and rolled to a gentle halt directly in front of the tattoo parlor. There was the muffled sound of music, which shut off a moment after the purr of the engine ceased, and a creak as the driver's door opened and a long leg, encased in a black trouser with a black cowboy boot on the end of it, reached out to rest on the asphalt of the road. A hand on the window frame followed, and a trim, square-shouldered masculine body stood up, adjusting the pair of aviator sunglasses perched on his face as he ducked out of the car. He reached back in a moment later and re-emerged carrying a white cowboy hat, which he placed jauntily over the crop of short, golden-brown hair that decorated his head.

He wore a black suit and a priest's collar, the little snip of white at his throat being the only bright thing about his clothing, apart from the hat. Even under all this, Selene thought, he looked like the kind of generically handsome model one found in clothing magazines or on television shows. His jaw was too perfect—strong and angular without being overly square and blockish—and when he smiled at them in passing he flashed dimples and perfectly straight, white teeth. He walked with an easy, rolling step that showed off his long, well-formed legs and kept his back straight and his shoulders broad and confident.

He was altogether unreal, a perfect specimen of the sort of beauty not usually found outside of a cinema, and this unrealness fixed Selene and Clara to the spot as they watched him stroll up onto the sidewalk, swinging his black briefcase, and disappear inside the tattoo parlor. There was a tinkle of a bell, and the sound of low male voices.

That sound brought Selene to her senses. Either that man was the exorcist—in which case he'd just walked into a demon's lair without a spotter—or he was some poor missionary about to get his ridiculously well-formed butt handed to him. She started across the street, called to Clara—who seemed to be distracted by the man's car of all things—jerking her into action.

They made it to the door of the shop this time, at the same time there was a deep and bone-shaking *thud* from within, and *something* whipped past them, ricocheted off Arcana's side, and billowed up into the sky like oily smoke before shooting off across the town.

Hardly had this happened when there was the crash of a door from within, and the man came pelting out again. He had a greasy smudge across one chiseled cheek, and his glasses had been knocked off, but he fairly leapt into his car, tossing the briefcase into the back seat, and peeled off into the street with a screech of tires.

All this happened so fast that Clara and Selene were still more or less where they had been when they'd felt the *thud,* though Jill had wandered halfway across the street in her confusion.

"*Stay* where you *are!*" Selene shouted at her, and rounded on Clara.

"It was an Impala . . . " the woman whispered. She still didn't move.

"A *what?*" Selene said.

"That car, *his* car," said Clara.

Selene, who had only registered the car as *generic, white, sedan* glared at her in consternation.

"Chevrolet Impala, named after the antelope," Clara continued, raising her face to stare at Selene, her crystalline eyes wide and bright. "*He's* the white stag . . . " she whispered, and took off down the street in the direction of Unicorn.

Seconds later, with a deafening engine roar, she came skidding around the corner and shot off down the street with a scream of rubber on pavement.

"What on earth . . . " Jill murmured, coming to stand next to Selene, "was *that?*"

Others had sensed the disturbance as well, and now a few cautiously curious heads were poking out of doors and windows.

"Honestly, I have no idea," Selene said under her breath. She shrugged expansively when one of the heads turned to stare questioningly at her, smiled and waved. "She said something about that dude being a white deer and then just took off. No idea what she was thinking. I mean, *you* know Clara."

"No, no," said Jill, waving her hand. "I mean the thing that came out of the shop."

Selene lowered her hand, and the plasticky smile faded from her face. "That was a shadow," she said. "It's what we can sometimes see when a demon leaves its physical host."

"So the demon's not *in there,* anymore?" Jill asked, indicating the tattoo parlor.

"We'll see," said Selene. She glanced around the street, frowned, and turned back to Jill. "Spot me, will ya?"

"How do I do that?" Jill asked, but gamely.

"Just . . . keep an eye out. You see anything fishy, give me a holler."

So Jill waited, fidgeting, by the door while Selene crept inside. The lights had been blown out, so she walked, crablike, with her flashlight trained along Elvis's barrel.

The shop was long and narrow and deserted except for the form of a man on his back on the floor. He was pasty white and bald, wearing a denim shirt, jeans, and the kind of pretentious leather vest with artistically frayed edges. Switching the flashlight to her mouth, and keeping her eyes moving around the room the whole time, Selene checked his pulse. It was steady, and the man was visibly breathing. Taking his right arm she pulled at it gently until it was raised above his head, then she grabbed a fistful of leather vest and dragged until she'd rolled him onto his side, his head resting on his raised arm. She hooked a foot behind his left knee and pulled it forward until it met the floor, preventing him from rolling onto his face. She then checked the back area, the office, and the tiny bathroom. Then she ducked back into the office and used the landline to call an ambulance. Then she left.

"Nothing here," she said to Jill, who was waiting anxiously outside.

"No what?" came the predictable reply.

"Get that map out again," Selene said, pocketing her flashlight and holstering Elvis. "And my candles. We gotta find out where that demon went."

"What about Clara?"

"I would bet good money she's already there," Selene said with a wry grin.

Clara leaned as far as she dared into the turn, and *there* was the flash of white. They were headed for the highway, which meant she could catch them. She leaned forward into the wind as Unicorn picked up speed, banked for another turn (behind her someone honked) and found the white Impala in her sights once again. Whether its driver knew he was being followed was uncertain: he made no attempt to lose her but pulled onto the highway and headed out of town.

Wind whipped up along the road. It buffeted the car, but Clara sliced clean through it. A partially disassembled cardboard box was sent cartwheeling across the road only to be crushed beneath the car's tires, then thrown up into the air once again. Leaning serenely to the side, Clara dodged it by inches and closed on the car. Looking past it, now she could see the billowing black cloud that ripped through the air in front of them, so faint it could be mistaken for a shimmer on the air. With her experienced eyes she could clearly see the miasma that trailed behind the disembodied demon like thick exhaust.

They cleared the town, and the demon jerked suddenly sideways—as if it were a puppet pulled by a string. Almost as abruptly the white sedan turned down a road, hardly more than a dirt track, kicking up a huge cloud of dust, its rear wheels skidding along the turn. Thrown wide, Clara cut a sharp track through the sparse grass growing on the shoulder and tailed the car all the way down the road, where it ended in an empty lot behind a dilapidated warehouse.

* * *

The man was out of his car before it completely stopped, sprinting across the dirt toward the small cairn of stones he'd constructed earlier. Now they were belching a stream of truly angry-looking smoke: flames licked like orange tongues in its depths, and it took only a very little stretch of the imagination to see a face glowering out from the dark cloud. This dwindled to a narrow funnel above the cairn, one that was narrowing further by the second.

Shaking in his hurry the man threw out an arm, a single flash of white cuff visible beneath the black sleeve, and something else swung forward: the smooth round bodies of rosary beads, suspended in the air before the outstretched hand.

The beads touched the edge of the cloud, and he felt it connect even before there was a shriek like ripping stone and it condensed inward, pouring itself into a shape somewhere between a man and a spider. Legs flicked out, clawed at the man's face, but he jumped backward just in time.

Words drifted forth from the shape, clawed their way into his mind, biting, ripping. Mentally he brought up his guard to resist them, and then—

Then they were drowned out by other words. Ancient words. Foreign and yet familiar, they rang clear in his ears from the throat of a living being, and against every instinct he turned his head from the demon to look toward their source.

He saw an impossibly tall woman appear out of the swirl of dust, standing astride a muscular, black motorcycle. A long leg kicked over the back of the bike, and she approached, one hand held awkwardly behind her shoulder. The reason for this pose became apparent when she brought it around and in a flash of cold steel plunged the broadsword into the shadow.

For a moment the shadow swallowed the sword. Then there was a crack like a thunderclap, and bolts of lightning shot through the haze, jumped about within it, and eventually found their way to earth. They took the last of the smoke with them, leaving the man staring down the length of the woman's sword, which glinted brightly in the sun.

She put him in mind of a modern black knight, right down to her tinted visor, though clad in leather instead of steel. Slowly she lowered her sword, and from behind the helmet a voice emerged—the same voice that had spoken before. This time it spoke words he understood, though once again their meaning escaped him.

She said: "I come hilt first. I will not harm you."

And sure enough, she had turned the sword around in her hand so the blade pointed behind her, and all he saw was the smooth round end of its pommel.

For his part the man pushed the rosary back up under his sleeve, and then extended his free hand.

"That's good, I think," he said. "Ariel Freeman. Thanks for the assist."

This gesture seemed to perplex the woman, who stared down at his hand awkwardly. Eventually she reached forward with her free hand and took his in a light, careful grip.

"Claymore Nordstern," said the black knight.

They stood there for a moment, connected by their hands, until the tentative silence was ruptured by the growl of a truck's engines, and the huge red pickup lurched into view at the head of a billow of dust. A dark-skinned woman with an impressive mane of black hair stuck her entire upper half out the passenger window, and shouted over the sound of the engine:

"Okay, I've had about enough of this god-forsaken snipe hunt. You stay right there, mister, and tell me who the hell you are!"

The man was surprised, but not offended. He tipped his white cowboy hat respectfully, and laughed at the expression on the new arrival's face.

"So you're, like, a demon *specialist*?" Jill asked, much later. After an awkward round of introductions. After Selene had carefully inspected the contents of Freeman's briefcase, the trunk of his car, the little cairn of stones, and finally proclaimed him to be "legit."

The sun had set on them, and a bright spring night rolled over the sky. Freeman had set up a small bonfire and produced a six-pack of warm beer and a foil-covered tray.

"The lady I saw this morning insisted on giving me a casserole," he explained sheepishly. "There's no way I can eat it before it goes bad."

So they had eaten cold casserole around the bonfire and drunk warm beer. That was, Selene and the man drank the beer. Jill sipped reluctantly at hers, and Clara just sat on the opposite side of the fire and glowered at them through it.

Selene had begun to grill the man—Freeman—on his activities. He answered readily enough, with the good humor that was apparently his natural state, and they discovered they had been only a little behind him in their circuit of the town.

"Seems like you were practically stalking me," he said, with a sly grin. Selene punched him lightly on the shoulder. The man swayed with the blow and didn't take offense. Indeed, he practically radiated amiability.

At last Jill posed her question.

Ariel Freeman tilted his hat so he could scratch his scalp under it, letting a few locks of golden-brown hair escape, glinting in the firelight.

"Exorcist is the more generally accepted term," he allowed, but nodded. "Same thing, though. I always liked 'infernal plumber' but people tend to take that the wrong way."

"And what sort of priest are you?" Jill asked, gesturing at his clerical collar.

Freeman paused with the bottle halfway to his lips, then gave a sort of shrug and took a swig from it before answering.

"Not a priest," he said. "A minister. Was, anyway. Baptist."

"Was?" asked Jill.

Freeman shrugged and grinned sheepishly. "There was a time in my life, earlier, when I was confused about a lot of things. I believed in a perfect and just universe created by God, and I saw it as my duty to protect that." He shrugged again. "Like you do."

"Yeah-huh," said Selene knowingly. "And now what? You just keep the collar for the casseroles?"

Freeman cocked his head at her, but he was grinning. "Not so much for the casseroles. But it does help you get in the front door. Also . . . well, people just don't ask so many questions of priests. I think mostly they're afraid I'll try to convert them. And I'm not a complete fraud," he added. "I still *believe*."

"Yeah . . . but in *what?*" Selene asked.

For the first time the man frowned. He looked at Selene shrewdly, before pushing his gaze on to the other two women.

"Have any of you actually *read* the bible?" he asked.

Jill was obliged to shake her head, and Selene rolled her eyes, but Clara nodded gravely.

"Okay." Freeman drained his beer and set the bottle aside. "It's like this. You read the bible—and I mean *really* read it—and you have to come to one of three conclusions." He held up the same number of fingers to illustrate. "Proposition: our world was created by a benevolent, omnipotent god. But if you read the bible several things become clear: firstly, *bad things* happen. Our world isn't perfect."

"You don't need the *bible* to tell you that," Selene pointed out dryly.

Freeman shook his fingers at her. "Yeah," he said. "True enough. But here's something you only learn from the bible: God is an insecure bastard. He changes His mind. Makes mistakes. He lets some really messed-up stuff happen."

"People say that is because the Nameless God has a great plan that encompasses everything and is beyond the scope of our experiences," Clara intoned from beyond the fire.

"Yes, that's *one* of the three conclusions," Freeman said, with a nod of his head.

"Another option is that there is no god," Jill pointed out practically. "That the bible is a work of fiction created thousands of years ago and mutilated by centuries of translations, rewriting, and political bias, and frequently used as an excuse for people to do what they wanted to do in the first place."

Freeman nodded. "That's two," he said. "And the third . . . is that everything in the bible is true . . . except for the bit about god being omnipotent."

"I'm sorry," said Selene. *"What?"*

"If you look at the events of the bible," the man said, "you could see how they could all come to pass . . . *especially* if God wasn't all-powerful. Maybe He's just a bigger, more powerful version of an ordinary guy. One who's trying his best but makes mistakes, has attacks of insecurity, and loses his temper sometimes. Someone who made something amazing, and then let it get away from Him. His creation got too big for Him to handle, and now He's just clinging to its coattails, trying to keep up."

"There is one more option," Selene said, a dark grin spreading across her face. "Maybe your god's a malicious little bastard. Maybe all the suffering and bad things in the world *are* for a reason: he thinks it's *funny.*"

Freeman pulled another beer from the box and expertly twisted the cap off. "And you know," he said, bringing it to his mouth. "I just can't decide which of those last two I believe in. It's one or the other. Point is I believe in *something.* I don't know what that makes me, but I'm not what you'd call an atheist."

"Atheists can believe in things," Clara said softly.

"Nuh-huh," said Selene. "That's the whole *point* of being an atheist. It's that you *don't* believe."

"I think," Jill cut in with finality, "that it's less important what you *call* yourself and more important what you *do.*"

"I'll drink to that," Freeman said, raising his beer. When he had finished he wiped his mouth on the back of his hand and stared into the fire for some time. In the quiet left by the lull of their voices the only sound was the crackle and pop of the flames.

"So about you," he said, sloshing the remainder of his drink around the bottom of his bottle. "You're on a bit of a quest then?" He nodded at Jill. "Like a modern-day Brothers Gunn."

Selene snorted, and Clara frowned.

"It's not like that," the large woman said, but Jill cut her off.

"I've heard of them before," she said. "But I've never gotten a clear explanation. Who *were* the Brothers Gunn?"

Ariel Freeman shot an incredulous glance toward Selene. "You haven't told her?"

"Oi," said Selene. "Most of what we know about them is legend. What do you want me to do? Sing her their song? Buy her those stupid novelizations that came out in the eighties?"

Freeman's face twisted in disgust. "Okay," he said. "The novels *were* awful. But the song is good. Matches up with all the historical facts we could dig up. The Brothers *Gunn,*" he continued, turning to Jill, "were a pair of hunters. David and Adam. Very interesting couple. Got up to no end of hijinks and died *several* times. Helped stop an apocalypse . . . once. Nearly brought one on once or twice. Adam was an antichrist, you see."

"Hold on," said Jill. "*An* antichrist?"

Freeman nodded. "There's one for every generation. They don't usually amount to much, otherwise . . . *poof* . . . old John's prophecy would've come true a dozen times over by now."

"You mean Armageddon?" Jill said.

"I do mean the great *reboot*," Freeman said, nodding.

"So what happened to them?"

Freeman smiled. He was rather ridiculously good-looking, Jill noted with detached interest. Like a benevolent, golden angel. He rolled his head back to look at the stars, the fire highlighting the sharp curve of his jaw and the faint dusting of stubble there. After a quiet moment, he began to hum. It was a rudimentary melody, but it made both Selene and Clara sit up a little straighter. Then to Jill's surprise, Selene joined in, this time fitting words to the tune.

"Somewhere out there the wayward sons, Jimmy's amber-eyed boys, are blown by a Kansas tornado—they landed who knows where . . . "

The song had the simple rhythm and cadence of a folk song, and Selene—though she had a pleasant, throaty voice—was a somewhat hesitant singer. Then Freeman picked up the words and Jill realized she was listening to an immensely talented musician—albeit one rather out of practice.

"David was born in forty-nine and Jimmy was his dad. He hollered high, he rolled strong. He drove his mother mad," he sang in a reassuring baritone. *"Adam was born in fifty-three and Jimmy was his dad. Though he was quiet, before one year, his mother she was dead."*

Then Selene joined in and they both sang together . . .

"Somewhere out there, the wayward sons, Jimmy's amber-eyed boys, are blown by a Kansas tornado, they landed who knows where . . . "

Selene dropped off, but Freeman continued.

"Adam ran off to college, but that there didn't last. David came a-knockin' on his door, and they blew town but fast. They say David loved no woman, but he took them all to bed. Adam loved but one (it's true) but in a year she was dead."

"I don't like what happens to women in this song," Jill remarked dryly.

"Oh, it gets worse," Selene assured her as Freeman launched into another verse of *Somewhere out there the wayward sons . . .* "Proper old-boys club, they were. And white as lilies. No offense," she added, with a nod to Clara, who shrugged.

"Adam had been dead two days before David sold his soul," Freeman sang on.

"Life don't come cheap," Selene chimed in.

"A year he had skirting the Pit before he took the plunge . . . "

"Hell's river runs deep."

"Oh, Adam went near crazy, he took a demon's hand. As he danced to the devil's tune he sang 'they don't understand.' Somewhere out there, the wayward sons . . . "

"Can you possibly skip the refrain?" Jill cut in. "What happened next?"

"Oh?" said Freeman. "It's kinda important to the ending, and leaving it out makes me lose my place."

"Next is the bit about the angels," Selene prompted.

"Oh, right," the man cleared his throat. *"It took seven angels to raise David from the Pit. One broke his back, one broke his bonds, and one, he broke his heart."*

Now Selene joined in, and gustily. *"Oh, those seven angels, where have they gone? One died in thunder, one died in ice, and one, he broke his heart. When those seven angels raised David from the ground, one was lost, one was found, and one, he broke his heart."*

"That's nine angels," Jill pointed out.

"The one who broke his heart is mentioned three times for some reason," Selene said. "He became kind of important later on, you see. Anyway, after that there's another bout of the refrain, and then . . . "

Freeman took over.

"They said Adam raised the Devil, they say David closed the gate. They say the angel with the broken heart was bent on tempting fate. They say Adam beat the Devil, they say David went to ground, and the angel with the broken heart was lost and never found."

"And another refrain," Selene cut in. "And then there's rather a lot of cryptic verses about boxes and the various crimes the brothers got up to and from the sound of it our poor angel had a bitch of a time."

"He did," Freeman added.

"Anyway," Selene continued, "after the bits about the blood of hell and earth and how the boys lost their angel and how the angel found his heart too late and one last bit with the Devil, it ends with . . . *They drove their bird into a storm, they stopped the world turning. They were strong and silent, and they vanished in the storm.*"

"That's not how it ends," Freeman protested.

"Oh right," said Selene, mock-slapping herself on the forehead. "We get one more reiteration of that lovely refrain and then . . . "

"Then there's the ending, but I can't start up on it now, I have to sing the whole thing," Freeman admitted.

There was an awkward silence, and then from the other side of the fire came a soft and haunting voice, and it took Jill a moment to realize it was Clara singing.

"So if you pass a weeping angel, best stop and pay your leave, for he's waiting on his amber-eyed boys—Jimmy's wayward sons—but they are blown by a Kansas tornado . . . "

Then Selene chipped in, singing louder and faster, and Freeman joined her, clapping his hands along with the beat.

"They are blown by a Kansas tornado—"

"They are blown by a Kansas tornado!"

"They are blown by a Kansas tor-NAY-dooooo . . . "

The other voices faded out, and left Clara's alone to finish, softly, delicately . . .

" . . . and they landed, who knows where."

"Am I to take it they went to Oz?" Jill asked, once it was clear the singing was good and done with.

"One would like to think that," Freeman said, finishing his beer. "Truth is, last anyone saw of the Brothers Gunn, they were driving their car—a black Ford Falcon, hence the lyric about their bird—along a road in Kansas when a tornado whipped up and ran right into their path. The car was found—upside-down in a tree two miles away—but the boys never were. So . . . they landed *who knows* where."

"And the angel?" Jill asked.

Selene shook her head, but Freeman spoke up.

"Oh, he's still around. In a graveyard not far from here, actually. But you wouldn't know it to look at him."

"How do *you* know so much about the Brothers Gunn?" Selene asked.

The man shrugged innocently. "I made it a special study. Mostly to figure out what *not* to do . . . " he added with a grin.

"Now, that I *will* drink to," Selene said, raising her own beer and clinking it with his.

Clara, Jill noticed, was silent even for her usual stoic self, and remained so as the fire was put out and the other three bedded down for the night.

Jill spread herself out in Arcana's bed, staring up at the stars and wondering about demons—Freeman had promised to lend her some of his "souvenirs"—with the melody of the song still stuck in her head. In the end the words *they are blown by a Kansas tornado* morphed smoothly into dreams, and she slept.

It was Clara's voice that woke them, when the dawn was still dim and gray. Her words were indistinct, but spoken so sharply that they roused Jill from her fragile slumber. Feeling gingerly over the side of the truck, she found the surface moist with dew and withdrew her hand at once to wipe it on her sleeping bag before carefully propping herself up.

"Say what, Clara?" she asked blearily.

Clara didn't answer her right away. Jill heard her talking, but it seemed she was speaking to someone else. The words, " . . . and you're *sure* that's the shape the blood made?" drifted over and Jill rubbed her eyes, coming more awake by the second.

Clara was kneeling in front of a small black boy, who had just straightened up from drawing something in the dirt. An old bicycle, two sizes too big, lay on the ground behind him.

Beside the remains of the campfire Selene and Freeman were coming to life, shaking themselves out of their cocoons of blankets. Selene staggered over, but Freeman lounged with the ease of a cat, smoothing his tawny hair before jamming the white cowboy hat down over it. He stretched, and fairly strolled over to where Selene and Clara stood by the boy, staring down at the ground in consternation.

"Mr. Bell," he said, tipping his hat to the boy. "How can I help you?"

The boy stammered something, but Selene picked up her head and rounded on Freeman.

"You *missed* one," she said, and jabbed her finger at the dirt.

By this time Jill had pulled her shoes on and was staggering toward the little group, her sleeping bag wrapped around her shoulders like an oversized feather boa.

"Hold up, hold up," she said. "What's happened? How did you know to find us here?" she asked the little boy.

"Went looking for you," said the boy, not meeting her eyes.

"I told him to find me here if there were any problems," Freeman sighed, and pointed at the ground. "By the look of *that*, our work here isn't done yet."

On the dirt was scratched a symbol, unfamiliar to Jill, like a circle with a sort of twisted tree in the center. Unless it was a giant eye.

"*Our* work?" Selene protested.

"Of course I will assist you," Clara announced.

"Great," said Freeman, flashing her a dazzling smile. "Demon first, then a shower and breakfast, maybe? I still owe you for yesterday."

"Like hell you're going in there without a spotter," Selene said. "Jill will want to come anyway. Here, kiddo, we'll put your bike in the back and give you a ride home. Don't suppose your ma is around this time?"

But the boy—whom Jill realized must be Andrew Bell—nodded. "She stuck," he said quietly.

"Well then," said Freeman brightly over Selene's curses. "No time to waste."

Jill helped Selene hoist the bicycle into Arcana's bed, made sure Andrew Bell was safely buckled in the back, and then climbed in only to find Selene already in the driver's seat.

"What's happened?" she asked as the other woman started the engine and began turning the huge truck around.

"Missed one, didn't we?" Selene said shortly. "Our boy back here"—she jerked a thumb at Andrew Bell—"his ma was one of the folks that preacher man exorcised. Only the demon's not *gone*. Or there was more than one. Anyway, he found that sigil in blood on his ceiling this morning and hightailed it out here as fast as he could."

"So, now what?" Jill prompted.

"Now we follow our leading lady and gentleman," Selene said, gesturing as first Clara on her bike and then Freeman in his car, peeled out of the dirt lot. Arcana followed at a more sedate pace, maneuvering cautiously through the thick dust the other vehicles had left in their wake.

The sun was just peeking over the horizon when they arrived at Andrew Bell's house, which looked much the same as it had the day before. Except . . . not. As Clara rolled Unicorn to a stop a safe distance away she became aware of a faint miasma that hung over the building, fuzzing its edges and making her nose itch.

Ariel Freeman—she kept thinking of him by both names for some reason—had parked around the corner and now came strolling toward her at his strange, rolling gait that was deceptively fast. He had his hat tipped at a jaunty angle and his black briefcase swinging, but he paused when he came in sight of the house, and sniffed the air experimentally.

"You smell that?" he asked, coming even with Clara.

"No," said Clara. "But I can see it."

Ariel Freeman shot her a penetrating look from under the brim of his hat, his light green eyes focused briefly on hers, then turned back to the house.

"What do you think?" he asked.

"I think one of the demons you exorcised yesterday might have left a door open behind it," Clara remarked.

"That's what I was afraid off," Ariel Freeman said. Kneeling on the pavement he set down the briefcase and opened it. Clara couldn't help staring a little as she found herself looking at a perfect anti-demon kit.

There was silver, and blood-ink, a battered copy of the Red Book of Sigils, and a jar full of small, twisted bits of iron that looked like they had been melted at some point. A similar—if fainter—miasma hung about that jar, save that where the one cloaking the house was oppressive and dark, this one was light and golden.

"Something wrong?" Ariel Freeman asked her.

Clara blinked, breaking her line of sight to the artifact.

"Sorry?"

The man grinned nervously. "You look like I've done something to royally piss you off. Everything okay?"

Clara stared down at the man, then realized that could be construed as glaring, and shook her head.

"It's just"—she pointed at the jar of twisted metal—"is that holy shrapnel?"

"You have a good eye," Ariel Freeman said, picking up the jar and rattling its contents. "Picked these up myself after an angel sighting in Arizona five years ago. They're too potent to wear full time, so I just keep them for emergencies."

Clara nodded. She didn't ask if this was an emergency—that was something only Ariel Freeman could decide.

Their stilted conversation was given a merciful death by the sound of Arcana rolling up to the house. Selene got out almost as soon as the vehicle had stopped and marched over to them.

"Right, so what's the plan?" she asked.

"Well, I go in," Ariel Freeman began.

"*We* go in," Clara told Selene. "Can you hold a perimeter?"

"I can shoot whatever comes out of the house," Selene said dryly.

"Do you have bullets that work on demons?" Ariel Freeman asked. Not accusingly, just with natural concern.

Selene laughed. "I got something that'll *make* them work," she said with a sly grin.

The exorcist inclined his head respectfully. "Great, perfect." He reached into his briefcase, took out a small string of beads like greenish pearls, and wrapped it around his hand. Closing the case he gestured with his beaded hand and made a slight bow to Clara. "After you," he said.

Clara did glare at him then, having heard enough mocking *ladies first* jokes in her life. Ariel Freeman saw the look, and gave her a short, small smile—somehow worse than his huge blinding one, because this was personal; it was just for her, and it said, *I realize how that must have sounded and I'm sorry; please don't hit me.*

"Your eyes are probably better than mine," he explained.

"If you say so," Clara said.

She advanced on the house as if it were a wild animal. Drawing her sword as she reached the edge of the lawn she saw Jill and the boy Andrew staring out Arcana's windows.

"You should be further away," she told them.

"I told them that," Selene called, climbing up to sit in Arcana's bed. She had her shotgun out and was tying a soaking-wet rag around the barrel. A heady, golden miasma hung thick about it, and with a jolt Clara realized the cloth must have been soaked in holy oil. Where Selene had managed to get it Clara would have loved to know, but the curling, twisting presence in the house was only growing stronger.

Still, she insisted on waiting until both Jill and Andrew had withdrawn to the far side of Arcana, then with a nod to Ariel Freeman she pushed the door open.

Or tried to. It was locked. Selene could probably pick it, but she didn't want to take her off guard duty. Clara tested the deadbolt, got a feel for the wood under her hand, and then concentrated very carefully on her left arm—the one that held the door handle. Then she opened the door.

Splinters went flying as the bolt ripped through the soft wood and one of the hinges gave out. Clara carefully set the door to the side and stepped into the small living room.

The miasma was thick in here, and now she could smell it as well. The ceiling was dark with a thick, reddish ooze that dripped in puddles on the carpet, and from these puddles rose the heavy scent of burned Dacron and brimstone.

Ariel Freeman stepped forward into the room and made a wide sweeping gesture with his beaded hand. Then he repeated the motion, slower this time, but keeping his hand low to the ground.

"She's in the basement," he said. Then gave a wry smile. "As usual."

Clara appreciated the joke but didn't laugh. She was all too aware of the oppressive presence of the demon, stronger than any she had faced alone before.

Well, she wasn't exactly alone now, but she had yet to construct a firm grasp of Ariel Freeman's abilities. She only hoped he'd had the sense to be warded against non-consensual possession. She didn't ask, either, because considering his profession he probably would have found the question insulting. So she only nodded and began searching for the stairs.

They found them without much trouble, and she was pleased to see Ariel Freeman lay down a holy shard at the top of the stairs. It was wrapped in a silk handkerchief to prevent anyone touching it directly, but Clara could still see the glow of its power through the thin cloth.

Taking a small flashlight from a pocket of his coat he led the way down the stairs until they ended in the concrete floor of the basement. Clara heard him locate the light switch, and then the click as he flipped it, but the darkness remained.

"Hello there," he said pleasantly, and turned up the power on his flashlight, aiming it at the ceiling so its beam was reflected back down, filling the whole room with a soft, diffuse light.

The demon was there, twined around the form of a woman standing very still in the center of the floor.

Her eyes were directed at the ground, and they were blank and unseeing. Her body had a contorted, scrunched-in look, as though the bones and muscles were trying to force themselves into a form that the human body simply couldn't take.

"Mrs. Bell?" Ariel Freeman asked, experimentally.

The woman's head twitched, but her eyes didn't move, and her expression didn't change. Clara felt a sinking feeling in her chest: the demon was so closely wrapped around the woman that she wouldn't be able touch it without harming the human host.

Ariel Freeman, however, seemed perfectly confident.

"Right Mrs. Bell, you just stand there. No need to . . . move. Just relax, and this will be over very, very soon . . . "

As he spoke, Clara noticed the man was carefully running the pale beads through his fingers, stroking them gently with his thumb.

The demon turned to watch him. Clara could see its eyes, like two points of darkness that made her own ache, tracking Ariel Freeman as the man began to circle slowly around the woman.

"Claymore?"

The sound of her true name sent a thrill of nerves through Clara's body, before she realized it was Ariel who spoke, and she forced herself to calm down. She had given him that name, it was only to be expected that he would use it.

"Here," she said, trying to keep the hoarseness out of her voice.

"If you want to light up that sword of yours, now would be a good time."

"I can't use it without harming the woman," Clara told him tightly.

"That won't be a problem in a moment," came the reply.

Clara chanced a glance at the man, and saw him looking back at her, steady and confident. Half his mouth tipped up in a grin, showing a flash of perfect white teeth in the dim light. "Trust me," he said.

Clara inclined her head, eyes narrowing, and carefully drew her sword. She didn't want to risk alarming the demon, so she laid her free hand along the blade and traced the words onto the cool metal. When she felt the hum of power in response she gave Ariel Freeman a short nod, then lowered the blade to a less threatening position.

"Little girl . . . " came a voice that hissed and breathed like the gasping of a dying animal. Clara felt the demon's eyes; its gaze burned on her skin, then faded as it turned its attention to Ariel Freeman. "Little boy . . . you are very . . . confident . . . for so delicate a . . . creature."

"Oh, I'm sure I'll grow on you," Ariel Freeman replied with easy self-assurance. "We'll have a *lot* of time to get to know each other, once I've got you safe in a lockbox, that is. So why don't you let Mrs. Bell go, and we can talk about what it is you think you're doing here."

The demon laughed, sending waves of nausea through Clara's body. She stomped down on the feeling, consciously loosening the muscles in her shoulders and widening her stance.

Ariel Freeman seemed unaffected. He raised his beaded hand, beckoning, and smiled at the demon—or rather, at the human woman the demon had possessed. Clara wasn't sure if she could see the demon itself.

"I won't ask again," he said, closing his eyes briefly. When he opened them his face had gone cold and hard as a piece of marble. A tendon in his jaw tensed, and he grimaced briefly. Then he shouted, the words racketing out of him and shooting around the room like an angry animal.

"*Ashkazural,* I hold your name and I summon you!"

The demon screamed—a physical shockwave that shot through the room, through the walls, through Clara and Ariel, and sent a shower of dust and plaster and other, less pleasant debris, down from the ceiling. It leapt from the woman, toward Ariel, bounced off him and streamed for the door—where Clara intercepted it with a decisive slash of her sword.

She felt the energy sing along the blade, rush through her arms and rattle around in her chest, before it dissipated into the air, leaving a strangely clean, bleached smell and a faint ringing in her ears.

Ariel had dropped the flashlight in the blast, having been knocked down by his impact with the demon, but was now getting stiffly to his feet.

"Mrs. Bell?" he asked, sounding as though he'd just inhaled a lungful of smoke.

"Son of *God . . .* " came a bleary, drunken voice. "What are you doing in my *basement?*"

Ariel Freeman just laughed, warm and rich, and a little bit wheezy.

Clara sheathed her sword with an inward sigh of relief, and went to help Mrs. Bell to her feet. The woman was shaken but seemed uninjured. It was difficult to tell in the uncertain flashlight, so Clara gently wrapped an arm around the woman and began leading her tenderly up the stairs.

It was slow going, the woman still being wobbly on her feet, and with every step Clara noticed how the stairs creaked, how there seemed to be more cracks in the wall, and how—did the ceiling always sag like that?

They reached the threshold, and Clara turned to find Freeman still at the bottom, curiously looking around the room.

In that instant Clara felt a strange wave of energy flow through her. It felt bad, like a deep ache in her bones, and she heard an ominous crack.

"Freeman! *Move!*" she shouted.

Ariel Freeman looked up at her, puzzled. At the sight of her expression, however, he began to climb the stairs. Slowly, though. Too slowly.

A step gave way and things jerked back into motion.

There was no time to think, so Clara didn't. She gave Mrs. Bell a shove, didn't bother to watch the woman land, and fairly dove back down the stairs.

She reached the man just as the ceiling came down around them.

Outside, Jill tapped a finger against Arcana's side. She'd heard muffled shouting, felt a tremor like a small earthquake, and seen Selene tense, alert. But nothing happened. Nothing came out of the house. Eventually she grew bored and climbed up into the bed alongside Selene and the boy Andrew.

"Can I ask a question?" she asked.

Selene jumped, but nodded after a moment.

"Why the rag?" She waved at the piece of dripping cloth tied around the barrel of her shotgun.

Selene glanced at back at her, and without taking her eyes off the house she explained: "It's holy oil. Hard to come by, but effective. Not holy water, which only works against some types of demons. What it does is give the slugs that pass through the barrel a charge of power, which lets them damage noncorporeal monsters. Like demons."

"Fascinating," said Jill. "Why is it so hard to come by? I should think any church . . . "

She was cut off by movement at the front door, and a bedraggled woman staggered out. She clutched the door frame for support, her chest heaving, then took another step—but without the support of the house she staggered and fell.

"Momma!" cried the boy, and tried to climb down out of the truck. Selene caught him by the arm, shook her head, and pushed him back.

"If it's really your momma," she said, "I'll bring her back." She swung her legs over the side and slid to the ground, landing lightly on the asphalt. She approached the fallen woman with her gun down, but still ready.

Jill saw her kneel, check the woman's pulse, turn her face skyward, look at her eyes, and finally press two fingers briefly to her forehead. Then she seemed to relax and took the woman gently under the shoulders and supported her down the rest of the drive.

She sat her on the curb but kept looking back over her shoulder at the house, which remained silent.

"Watch her," she said to Jill. "I don't know what's happened in there, but I don't think it's over yet."

Jill nodded, all too aware that there was no sign of Clara or Freeman. She hopped down, using the running board as a foothold, and went to support the woman's shoulders while Selene turned back to cover the house.

It was dark and hot, and what air they had was filled with plaster and brick dust. But after the shock of the collapse had passed, Ariel realized that he had not been crushed to a bloody pulp, and in fact all his limbs were perfectly intact.

"Are you injured?" came Claymore's voice, strained, and very near his right ear.

Ariel tried to raise his head and felt his hat catch on something. He realized he was crouched in a very small space with nowhere to go, and thanked his lucky stars he wasn't claustrophobic.

"Not that I can tell," he gasped, choking on dust. "You?"

No answer. There was a creaking sound and the squeak of leather as the woman moved above him. He was aware of a pressure that had been on his back shifting, and realized it was one of her arms. She must literally be spread over him like an umbrella.

"What happened?" he tried.

"I do not believe the demon was vanquished," came the reply, now slightly muffled, as if Claymore was looking somewhere else.

"Oh," said Ariel, his heart sinking. "It trapped us."

"It tried to kill you," said the woman. "Now please be quiet. I have to concentrate."

*   *   *

There was a sound from inside the house like rocks tearing apart. Jill, Selene and Andrew all jumped, and Andrew's mother even turned her head, dazed though she was, toward the front door. A billow of whitish smoke came rolling out, but Selene relaxed as soon as she caught a whiff of it: it was ordinary plaster and dust, not brimstone.

Two figures materialized out of the smoke, solidifying into Clara and Freeman as they staggered out. Their dark clothes were covered in white and red dust, and there were splinters stuck in the shoulder pads of Clara's jacket. Freeman was holding his hat, disappointedly trying to bend it back into shape, but he gave up and squashed it back on his head when he saw them.

"What the hell *happened?*" Selene asked, lowering her gun.

"Demon was uncooperative," Clara replied, wiping debris off her shoulders and shrugging.

"Is it gone now?" Andrew Bell asked with wide eyes.

Ariel Freeman opened his mouth. Jill thought he was going to say something reassuring, like *yes,* but instead all that came out was a puff of black smoke.

The man frowned, coughed, and then doubled over, choking.

Jill froze, uncertain what to do, but Clara reached over and pressed a steadying hand against his shoulder, before giving him a firm whack across the back with her other.

Something came loose in Ariel Freeman's throat, welled in his mouth, and then fell to the pavement with a *splat,* where it began to steam faintly.

"What is—" Jill began, but Selene had already jumped down, ripped the rag off the barrel of her gun and spread it over the puddle of black liquid, as though she were mopping up spilled milk.

"Don't *tell* me you got your ass *possessed,*" she snarled, glaring up at the man.

Ariel Freeman looked back, his eyes unfocused. There was a drop of the same black liquid rolling down his chin as he shook his head.

"C-car . . . " he whispered, and then swallowed, painfully.

Clara looked up, spotted the white sedan, and then scooped the man up, bridal style, and carried him across the street.

"Is mister going to be all right?" Andrew Bell asked, clearly torn, but he did not let go of his mother's hand.

Selene didn't answer. She'd grabbed her duffle bag and vaulted out of Arcana's bed to follow Clara. Jill, reaching in back for her sample kit, paused.

"I don't know," she said, frankly. "But we'll do our best to take care of him."

"Take him to hospital!" the boy called after her as she made her way across the street.

Clara had set Ariel Freeman down in the shadow of his car, leaned him carefully against the rear wheel, and after fishing in his pocket she found his keys and opened the car's trunk.

"Where is your asphodel?" she asked, fingers reaching unerringly for the handle to lift out the false bottom, revealing a small space crammed with bottles, books, and an assortment of bladed weapons.

There was an impatient tap on her leg, and she looked down to see that, through all this, Ariel Freeman hadn't let go of his briefcase.

Leaving the trunk Clara opened the case and immediately saw the little bottle of grayish-yellow powder in the middle of the top rack. She pulled it out and popped the top off, looked around for a cloth or rag, and found Ariel calmly holding out a small white handkerchief.

His eyes were focused now and seemed steady, but Clara noticed how he was keeping his jaw clenched shut and how there was black liquid oozing out of his right nostril. His breathing was rapid and whistled through his nose in an alarming way.

Clara poured a generous amount of asphodel into the cloth, folded the ends over to make a neat little package, and even remembered to re-cork the bottle before she presented the bundle to Ariel.

The man opened his mouth—and a torrent of thicker black liquid poured out. Clara pulled his shoulders forward so most of it went onto the pavement, but a significant amount had already run down the side of his face, soaking into the fabric of his collar and staining the little white snip an ugly brownish-purple.

"Breathe," Clara said quietly.

This got her a few gasping breaths. A shaky laugh. Ariel reached for the packet of herbs, but his hand was trembling so badly Clara was forced to steady it with her own as he placed the folded cloth in his mouth and bit down with relief.

Clara took one of her own rags and gently wiped the side of the man's face, where the liquid had already begun to congeal and harden. She folded it over so a relatively clean side was presented, and held it up to Ariel's nose.

"Blow," she told him.

Ariel snorted out through his nose obediently, and a distressingly long string of black, tarry goo came away with the cloth.

"What's happened? Is he *possessed?*" Jill asked, her head appearing from over the side of the trunk.

"Nah, sister," said Selene, even as Ariel shook his head vehemently. "I thought so at first, but this looks like he's been *hooked.*"

"Hooked?"

"It happens sometimes when a demon tries to possess someone, but can't—for whatever reason. If that someone, say, knows the demon's true name." She looked at Ariel, hard, before continuing. "Well, the name *is* the demon, and the demon *is* the name. That's why knowing a demon's true name is so powerful. But if the demon is strong enough, they can turn the tables on you."

"They can manifest inside your head," Clara said.

Ariel ripped the little packet out of his mouth, spat—spittle and black goo—and shook his head.

"I spoke its name," he said, his voice thick and hoarse.

"I did not keep it," Clara assured him, and he gave a sigh of relief.

A sigh that turned into a violent coughing fit. Clara didn't ask this time before sticking the packet of herbs back in his mouth.

"What's *that* for?" Jill asked.

"Asphodel," Clara said, shortly.

"Helps alleviate the . . . er . . . symptoms," Selene said.

"We need to get him to a sanctuary," Clara said.

Jill opened her mouth, saw the looks on Clara and Selene's faces, and decided not to ask what a sanctuary was.

"The nearest sanctuary is in New Mexico," Selene said. "We'll never make it in time."

Ariel Freeman shook his head violently and removed the packet. Of course all that came out of his mouth was another torrent of black slime. Now Jill noticed its smell—sharp like iodine but with an undercurrent of rotten plants.

"Not . . . not . . . " His words were drowned.

Clara, her brow bunched and her cold blue eyes glaring, moved a hand behind the man's neck and traced a pattern there, as though she were trying to soothe him.

And amazingly, it appeared to work. Ariel Freeman let out a short gasp and shuddered. He raised his head and looked wonderingly at Clara.

"Thank you," he said, smiling weakly.

"I did not know if it would work on a human," Clara replied.

Ariel shrugged and turned back to Selene.

"If you can get me to the Angel's Graveyard, I think I can take it from there."

"The *Angel's* Graveyard?" Selene repeated. "But no one knows where that is!"

"I do," Ariel said. "I found it. It's not far. Load me up in the back, I'll give you directions."

"I'll stay with you," Clara declared. "I will return for Unicorn later."

"Fine, *fine*," said Selene, waving her hands. "Jill, you better follow in Arcana. We might need the arsenal."

Jill, who had been pondering whether she wanted to take a sample of the black goo, looked up alertly.

"Where are we going?" she asked.

"The Angel's Graveyard," Clara said.

"You *remember* the song, right?" said Selene. "The one with the broken heart. Supposedly, he's *still here,* in a way."

Clara installed herself in the back seat of Ariel's car, laying her sword down on the floor, and pulled the man in beside her. As Selene started the engine she cast a look back at Unicorn, sitting resolutely at the edge of the street, and her mouth hardened. Then her line of sight was cut off by Arcana pulling in behind them, and then the view was fading. She caught a glimpse of the woman, Bell, her arms around her son, as they watched them leave in bewilderment.

Perhaps it was best for them. They would be confused, and haunted for some time, but whatever was left of the demons that had plagued them was now confined within the man next to her on the back seat. The best thing they could do was get him away from them.

"Talk to me, missionary man," Selene said, weaving slightly on the road as she shoved the seat forward and adjusted the mirrors. Clara braced one leg against the back of the passenger seat in order to hold Ariel steady. The man groaned, his eyes fluttering closed, and a thin trail of black ooze ran down from his nose.

"Get on the highway," he said, wheezing a little. "Head south. It's in Dodge City. Suburbs."

"Got anything more specific?" Selene asked. She *didn't* say "In case you can't talk by the time we get there," and Clara appreciated it.

"It's called Mercy's End Cemetery." He had to pause and cough. Clara braced his shoulders between her knees and started making a fresh packet of asphodel. "End of Mercy Street. Can't miss it."

"You got that, Jill?" Selene asked, driving one-handed as she held her cell phone up to her face.

"Copy," came the answer, a little fuzzily. "That's about . . . two and a half hours away."

"Well, no time to lose," Selene said, and hit the gas.

They made the highway in no time, speeding southeast once they cleared the last of the lights, and Clara was just daring to hope, daring to imagine something other than an ugly death for the man in her lap, when they passed the "Now Leaving Pearson, come again!" sign, and the car's engine abruptly stuttered, stalled, then died and refused to start.

"What the ever-loving—" Selene let out a string of curses as she tried to restart the machine.

Ariel's eyes opened, very wide and bright in the dimness of the car. Clara noticed the green of them was shot through with bolts of amber. They were also red around the edges, and the tears that sprang from them were ugly, dark and brown. Raising a shaking hand he took the packet from his mouth and whispered, "It's gaining on me."

"*Pus buckets!*" Selene shouted, guiding the car to the side of the road as they coasted to a halt.

Arcana rolled past a moment later, its right turn signal blinking, and stopped with a crunch a few feet ahead.

"What's happened?" Jill demanded, climbing down.

Selene, who had popped the hood and gotten out, shook her head.

"Demon's messing with the car. Doesn't want us to leave."

"But we need to get him to this sanctuary, right?" Jill said, frowning.

"That *was* the idea," Selene said. "But if this demon's strong enough to meddle with machines without being fully manifested we are in *big* trouble."

"We can't just . . . er . . . load up in Arcana?" Jill asked.

"Probably wouldn't get far . . . " Selene admitted.

"But worth a try?"

Selene glanced back into the white car. Clara met her gaze, and then took matters into her own hands as she grabbed her sword, pushed open the door and began dragging Ariel out.

"Open up the back," she said as she strode past, Ariel draped limply in her arms. "Get his briefcase. Don't forget to lock his car."

"Clara, the demon will just shut down Arcana—"

"It's worth a try," Clara said through clenched teeth.

Selene didn't argue. She went back, pulled Ariel's briefcase out of the back seat, closed and locked all the doors, and then jogged forward and hopped in next to Jill.

"All right," she said. "Let's try this."

Arcana coughed ominously when Jill went to start him up, and in the back Ariel rolled his eyes heavenward. Clara took his meaning, and figuring it couldn't hurt, whispered a short prayer.

With a heavy growl the diesel engine came to life, and the truck shuddered as Jill pulled gently onto the road.

"Now's not the time to drive like a granny," Selene said. "That man needs a sanctuary *ASAP.*"

"This is no time to get pulled over, either," Jill replied primly, and insisted on driving exactly the speed limit.

But she drove. She drove, and Arcana *did not stop.* Out of Pearson, mile upon mile, the black tread of the highway falling away behind them as they crawled under a blue sky that became increasingly overcast as they drove into the rising sun.

In the back, Clara went through Ariel's supply of asphodel and dug into Selene's, keeping the packet fresh. She refreshed the words on his back once, but dared not do it again when she felt how hot his skin had become. The black goo flowed freely from his nose and eyes, puddling on the floor when Clara failed to wipe it away in time.

In the front, Jill had Selene put the address for the cemetery into her phone's map app, and kept eyeing the directions as they told her they were two and a half hours away . . . two hours away . . . one and a half hours away . . . It was a lucky thing they'd filled the tank so recently; Jill suspected they could not afford to stop.

Arcana himself appeared to be running smoothly, yet the way in which Clara and Selene had been acting made her more sensitive to the truck's performance. Perhaps because of this she noticed at once when the engine began to rev faster every time she put her foot on the gas.

Had Arcana always handled that way? Was this just her nerves? Even if it was new, it certainly wasn't *slowing them down.* Jill had, true to her meticulous nature, been maintaining the vehicle faithfully and saw no reason to suspect a mundane mechanical malfunction, yet she made a mental note to have it checked out the next time she brought the truck in for service.

The sky was an ominous swirl of black and gray by the time they entered the outskirts of Dodge City. Jill had the headlights on as she slowed and got off the highway, squinting at the directions on her phone's screen. In the back, Ariel moaned as they swung right abruptly.

Coming to a stop at an intersection Jill flicked a finger over the map, trying to get an idea of where they were going. The light changed, and Jill eased Arcana forward while still squint-ing at her phone.

The truck had barely rolled two feet before it took off like a rocket. The engine blared. Jill found herself thrown back against the seat and Selene swore. Ariel let out a pained moan and Clara grunted.

"Now is *not* the time to start a drag race!" Selene shouted.

"That wasn't *me!*" Jill screamed back. She had taken her foot off the gas at the first wild leap and slammed her other down on the clutch, but even though they were slowing down the engine revved faster and faster.

"It's the demon," announced Clara.

"*Runaway,* more like," hissed Selene.

Jill had already put the truck into sixth gear, but she kept her foot on the clutch until they had pulled off the road and come to a complete stop, engine practically *screaming* by this time, like an animal in pain.

"Don't forget the parking brake," Selene said, and Jill remem-bered to set it before she slammed her foot down on the brake pedal, took a breath, and then let out the clutch all at once.

The huge truck shuddered, jerked, and the engine died with an ugly gurgle. In the silence there was the faint hiss of steam, but everything else was still and calm. Almost apologetically, Jill put the machine back into neutral and patted the dashboard.

"Sorry, big boy," she whispered.

"Are we there yet?" came a wavering voice from the rear of the cab.

"Almost," replied Selene, hopping out and pulling the back door open. "We're gonna have to hoof it from here. Can you walk? No, stupid question," she admonished herself when she laid eyes on the man. Ariel's mouth was stained black, and there were tears like dirty water running from his eyes. "Clara, can you carry him? That's probably *also* a stupid question . . . "

Clara merely rolled her eyes as she gently lifted Ariel out of the back seat, being careful to keep his head elevated.

"Can you get my sword?" she asked, and obligingly half knelt so that Selene could slide the blade into the sheath she wore strapped to her back. Then she looked around. "Which way from here?"

"Keep heading north another quarter mile," Jill said, coming around the truck's nose, her phone in one hand and her sample kit slung over her shoulder.

Selene, who had climbed up into the bed and was hastily packing one of her small duffle bags, looked up at the sky worriedly. "And then?"

"Then it's not far at all. Less than a mile."

"Well thank the stars for small favors," Selene said, sliding down. She had Freddie slung casually under one arm, a fresh rag tied around the long barrel, and at her back bounced the sawn-off shotgun, Elvis, similarly treated.

It felt somehow wrong—like an admission of defeat—to leave Arcana there, by the side of the road. Jill shut off the emergency lights and locked all the doors before she left, and kept sending worried looks back toward the truck as they made their way down the street.

Which was largely empty—probably thanks to the evil-looking sky—which was just as well. They made a truly bizarre spectacle: Clara in her black biking leathers carrying what was clearly an injured man in her arms as if he were a child, and Selene with her guns. Jill in her jeans and backpack was probably the only one who could have passed for normal.

Even walking they almost missed Mercy Street—something had come through and ripped the sign down, and it was only because Jill could track their location on the map with her phone that they knew to turn right when they did.

Here they quickly passed into a residential district, the street lined with conservative homes huddling behind scrappy lawns with pickup trucks in their driveways. They passed only one other person—a dog-walker who crossed the street well before their paths met and studiously avoided looking at them.

The wind, which had been gusting fitfully since they'd left Arcana, strengthened, growing to buffet their faces, as if pushing them away.

"Let me guess, demon again?" Jill gasped as her hair lashed her face.

"No . . . " whispered Ariel, his voice barely audible. But his eyes were bright and alert, and they focused intensely on Jill as he answered. "This is from the angel. It means he doesn't want to be disturbed."

"Too bad for him," said Selene, and quickened her pace.

The sky was downright inky, and the clouds crouched low above them by the time they reached the end of the street. Here they had to slip between two houses and through a rusty gate before they at last emerged into a rundown cemetery. A sign above the main gate—which was fused open by all the tangled weeds growing around it—declared that this was Mercy's End Cemetery, and a white piece of cardboard had been tacked under it, on which had been written: "Closed Permanently: Do Not Enter"

"Some sanctuary," murmured Jill.

The place did appear more depressing than comforting; many of the gravestones were chipped, crooked or knocked over. What flags or fake flowers remained were bleached from the sun, and only added to the pervasive atmosphere of abandonment.

Ariel, however, perked up the moment Clara carried him under the sign. He writhed in her arms until she grudgingly let him down, but allowed himself to be supported as he staggered off between the headstones.

The cemetery was filled with trees: scraggly oaks whose boughs drooped and whose leaves from the previous fall still lay upon the ground in thick mats. The hanging branches, the new spring buds still small upon them, clattered in the wind like bones rattling.

"So, you said the Weeping Angel is *here*?" Selene asked the man, who had come to a stop in a wide path between the headstones.

Ariel Freeman didn't answer. He swung his head about, as if scenting the air, then turned and staggered off down the avenue, Clara at his side.

There were a number of statues in the cemetery, Jill noticed. Most of them were high up on pedestals, smaller than life-size. Some appeared to be ordinary humans, but a few had half-unfolded bird wings.

Through a gap between the trees Jill thought she saw some-one standing over one of the graves, and gave an inarticulate shout. The sound alerted Selene and Clara, who turned to look, and Ariel let out a feeble laugh.

Jill looked again, and found it was not a person, but another statue. Trudging through the leaves she saw it was set on a low pedestal, made of a dark brownish stone that was strangely free of lichen or moss. The figure was that of a man in an old-fashioned coat with a long scarf draped over his shoulders. He had a sloppy mop of short hair, and stood with his eyes down-cast, staring at his empty hands which were held palms out, hanging limply in front of him.

Staggering out of Clara's grasp, Ariel collapsed at the foot of the statue, resting his back against the pedestal and closing his eyes in relief.

"Do you require any other assistance?" Clara asked.

Without opening his eyes, Ariel shook his head. "Just time," he said.

Feeling worried and helpless, Jill took a turn around the statue, and frowned when she saw its back: sprouting from the man's shoulder blades were the stumps of what must have once been wings, but the material had been ripped, twisted, as though the appendages had been torn off. Coming around to his front again, Jill finally took a good look at his face, and was surprised to see a discoloration of the stone beneath his eyes: greenish, freckled with white. It lay in two streaks from each eye down across the cheeks, in the exact path that tears would follow.

"*If you pass a weeping angel, best stop and pay your leave,*" Selene whispered at her side.

"From the song?" Jill asked.

Selene shrugged. "You'd be surprised how much of the old songs and legends turn out to have a grain of truth to them. Though, to be honest, I never believed the bit about the angel until now."

"Is he . . . uh . . . a real angel?" Jill asked. "Looks just like a weird statue to me."

Selene tilted her head to one side. "That's hard to say," she admitted. "It's pretty clear the Brothers Gunn *did* have interac-tions with angels. It's not too much to believe that *this* is one of those angels, but . . . well. Things happened toward the end.

Weird things. Ultimately, I'm not sure if their angel was *still* an angel by the time they disappeared."

"Is that why he's a statue now?"

There was a raspy cough from by their feet, and the two glanced down to find Ariel Freeman looking back at them.

"If he wasn't an angel," the man said, hoarsely, "then how'd he turn himself into a statue?" He managed a weak smile, one that vanished a moment later when he started coughing.

"Selene," Clara said, her voice harsh.

Selene came around, and saw immediately what had warranted the change in Clara's tone.

Black liquid was pouring out of Ariel's mouth, streaming from his eyes, and where it pooled on the ground it steamed, smoke that rose white before going black as the sky above them.

Ariel gulped, trying to stop the flow, but Clara put a hand on his back, forcing him to keep his head bowed.

"Let it out," she said gently. "Let us worry about it."

"You don't—understand . . . " for the first time, his voice sounded not only hoarse and weak, but actually frightened. "This—demon—shouldn't be this strong. Think—there's—more . . . "

A vicious wind whipped through the cemetery. It lifted the damp, half-rotted leaves and flung them into the air. The trees creaked, and above them in the burgeoning clouds a fork of lightning flashed. The smoke hung in a thick haze all around them, and within it Jill thought she could glimpse a solid shape growing.

"Selene . . . " she began, reaching to tug at the woman's sleeve.

Selene, however, had already seen the shape, brought her gun to bear, and fired.

There was a horrible, soundless *scream*. It sang in Jill's bones and made her ears and eyes hurt. Unthinking, she clapped her hands over her ears and shut her eyes.

Clara, who had been kneeling beside Ariel, was on her feet in an instant, sword in hand, and she shouted the words aloud into the smoke.

Below her, Ariel retched, shuddered, and lay still. The pool of black liquid had almost entirely evaporated, but now the smoke was twining around them with almost solid tendrils. The wind howled, and somewhere a branch cracked threateningly.

"What are they trying to do, create a Hell Gate?" Selene swore, firing off another shot into the smoke. The bullet left a streak of clear air behind it, through which could be seen the barren trees and banked leaves, but the vision was quickly swallowed as more smoke poured in.

All of a sudden the shapes in the smoke became a great deal more solid. They moved like tigers, or maybe like sharks, and slipped past Clara's blade, aiming for the man on the ground. In response the large woman threw herself bodily in the way, and there was an electric crackle in the air as the demon connected. She dropped to one knee, apparently winded, and buried a hand in the thick bed of leaves. Above her, Selene was firing shot after shot into the smoke.

Then there was a *bang* of an entirely different variety, and with a crash one of the oaks let fall a huge branch, which landed barely a yard from where their group was huddled.

Jill opened her eyes to find herself staring into Ariel's face. The man's eyes were closed now, his skin dangerously pale and his lips stained black. His tears had dried in a dirty streak down his face, and with a jolt she realized he wasn't breathing.

She looked up and around instinctively for help, and found her gaze landing on the statue of the angel.

The angel, whose face was now turned up and away from them, looking out upon the scene surrounding it. Surely it hadn't been like that before? Surely, it had been looking *down* . . .

But even as she watched, Jill saw the angel move. The stone shifted, shimmered behind the haze, and slowly the face turned down upon them again. Its eyes were open now, and Jill swallowed when she saw they were dark, empty hollows.

Something she had read once about angels—you weren't supposed to look at them. But it was too late for that now, and Jill continued to stare, transfixed.

The angel frowned, and turned his hand over, palm down.

It was a little motion, but done with such finality that Jill felt a shiver run through her body.

The next instant the winds ceased. The shapes in the smoke disappeared, and the smoke itself lifted abruptly. Above them the clouds hurtled up and away, lightening from black to gray, from gray to gray-blue, until a beam of strong midday sun broke through and lit the entire cemetery in hues of gold and green.

The angel shut his eyes.

For Ariel, the haze of fog and pain and the screaming in his head faded slowly. Like recovering from a bad fever, he felt weak and cold and incredibly gross. His mouth tasted awful and his face felt crusty. He did not quite trust his mind not to seize and clench every time he tried to think, and he kept expecting the demon's name to muscle itself to the front of his mind and sit there, grinning at him. It took a moment of careful prodding before he was satisfied this was not the case, and after another moment he was surprised to realize he no longer remembered the demon's name at all. There was no blank space, no scar where it had been. It had been lifted out of his mind, cleanly and carefully, like a splinter being removed from a wound.

He inhaled. That cleared the fog further. Above him someone said, "Never mind, I think he's okay," and Ariel cracked an eye open to find three concerned faces peering down at him.

"Oh, yeah," he said, and was surprised at how easy it was to speak. His throat hardly felt sore at all. "I am *fantastic.*"

"You're unbelievable, is what you are," Selene said. "And you look *awful.*"

"We all gotta have grungy days," he replied. "Though I gotta say, demon slime makes for terrible eyeliner. Zero of ten, would *not* recommend."

"Are you always like this after near-death experiences?" Jill asked.

Ariel sat up gingerly, expecting a rush of dizziness. Instead, he only felt his head clear further. He was feeling stronger by the minute. Cautiously he put a hand to his face and began picking dried slime off his cheek. It caught on his stubble, and he winced. "Nah, sometimes I can actually *be clever.* Are you ladies all right?"

To his dismay he saw Jill's face harden. He looked around, feeling a tightening of fear in his chest, but the woman appeared perfectly fine, as did Selene. For a moment he panicked, but then his eyes landed on Claymore, who was stomping through the leaves a little way off, clearly hunting for any residual demonic presences.

"Then what—?" he began, but the small woman cut him off.

"*Arcana,*" she said with a heavy sigh. "My truck. I've probably blown his clutch even if that demon of yours didn't destroy the engine. I hope you have friends in Dodge, because we're gonna be here a while."

It was a beautiful spring afternoon, and in the abandoned cemetery two figures in black sat on a mossy stone bench. They would have been sharing a beer, but Claymore refused every time Ariel offered.

"You should be drinking water," she only said.

"I'll get to that," he said, taking another sip from the bottle. "For now, I need the alcohol. Helps put some distance between . . . things." He grinned at Claymore, who only looked back, blankly. Ariel shook his head and sighed.

"I'm sorry," he said.

Claymore's left brow twitched. "For what?" she asked, sounding genuinely confused.

"For whatever it is that's making you look like you just ate a lemon," he said. "I can't think of anything I've done, but if I have, I'm sorry about it."

Claymore turned to look at him. Her eyes were cold and blue and glittered in the sunlight. She frowned, the motion crowding her forehead with wrinkles. Then, like clouds passing, her expression cleared and she turned away, sighing faintly.

"You have done nothing," she said in that abrupt way of hers. "This is just . . . the manner of my face."

"Oh? So my presence is not like sandpaper on an open wound to you?"

Claymore actually smiled at that. Not a big one, and it was gone almost as soon as it appeared, but it was there nonetheless. She shook her head.

Ariel sipped his beer and the two sat in companionable silence for a time.

"That's good," he said eventually. "Thanks."

Claymore's shoulders dipped and rose, and she tipped her head to one side. "I did what was required," she said. "Thank *him*." She gestured toward the statue.

Ariel looked over at the stone angel. According to Claymore, Jill had seen it move. Ariel couldn't be sure if it was in the same pose as before—hadn't the hands been different? He couldn't remember. Admittedly, he hadn't been in a position to get a good look at it before. Now he could clearly see the streaks of discoloration on the angel's cheeks, and the mangled stump of his right wing was just visible over one sagging shoulder.

"Do you ever wonder what happened? You know, what broke his heart?" he asked after a while.

Claymore did her little inverted shrug again. "Lots of things, I expect," she said.

Ariel laughed. "That's what everyone says. 'What broke his heart?' 'Oh, *things*, you know . . .' But, like, what exactly? Was it that Adam turned out to be an Antichrist? Was it his rebellion against Heaven? Saying someone has a broken heart implies an unhappy romantic relationship, but if you look at actual records there's no sign of anything like that."

Claymore frowned. "Didn't he have a wife, once?"

Ariel nodded. "Twice, actually. Once from before he was woken, and once when he turned human and lost his memories."

"That happened more than once," Claymore pointed out. "Which time?"

"Uh, the second, I think. But in both cases it wasn't really *him*. Not all of him, anyway. That was the man, Calvin McGovern, not the *angel* inside him. Nah, I think it must have been something else."

There was a crunching sound behind them, and the two turned to find Selene wading through the leaves and fallen branches. She had a crooked grin on her face, as though she had been eavesdropping and wasn't sorry about it.

"Innit obvious?" she said, coming up next to them and putting her hands in the pockets of her jeans. "The angel was in love with *David*. Right from the start."

"David Gunn?" Ariel echoed, arching an eyebrow at her.

Selene cocked her head at the despondent statue. "It's all there if you care to *look*. Not even forty years of straight whitewashing could hide it completely. *Besides,* that there," she jerked a thumb at the dejected angel, " . . . is *definitely* the look of someone who tried to date someone in the closet."

Ariel finished his beer and grinned blindingly up at Selene.

"Glad to hear it," he said. "I was beginning to think I was the only one who thought so."

It was Selene's turn to stare blankly down at Ariel. Claymore interrupted the awkward pause by asking: "What is the damage to Arcana?"

Selene gave herself a little shake. "What? Oh, would you believe it? *Nothing.* Needed some more oil, but that was all. No damage to the clutch *or* the engine. It's giving Jill fits, but I told her, I said: 'Jill, you just saw a statue come to life and banish a demon—now you have problems with your precious truck being miraculously unharmed?' And do you know what she said to me? She said: 'Yes, Selene, because *this* doesn't make *sense.*'" Selene rolled her eyes. "She's got him down by the gate now, on the phone with that professor of hers."

Claymore, however, was frowning thoughtfully. "I will go take a look," she said, and stood up.

"Have fun with that," Selene called to her retreating back. Turning to Ariel she went on. "Anyway, we can take you back to your car any time. Unless you want to grab something to eat. Me and Jill already did."

Ariel lifted a hand to stem the flow of words. "Just a sec," he said, getting slowly to his feet. He went over to the statue of the angel and, after looking into its face for a moment, gently laid one of his hands over the angel's stone fingers. He closed his eyes briefly, and murmured something almost inaudible. Selene thought it was Latin.

"If you pass a weeping angel," he said by way of explanation as he came away, "best stop and pay your leave."

"Aye," Selene said. She threw a ragged salute toward the statue. "Better luck next time, ya poor bastard."

They walked slowly back together through the leaves and tombstones. Ariel, though he claimed to be fine, still looked greenish and wobbly.

Then Arcana came into view, parked on the far side of the gate. Its hood was up and Clara was leaning over the engine, inspecting something in its depths. Jill was next to her, waving her arms and exclaiming over something.

"Can I ask you a kind of personal question?" Ariel said while they were still out of earshot.

"Sure," said Selene. "Mind, I might not answer."

"Of course," said Ariel with a laugh. Then his face sobered. "What is she?"

Selene sighed. "She's this crazy chick we picked up in Santa Cruz. She's *obsessed* with finding the *reason* and *science* behind what we do. What we fight. Me and Clara, we just work for her. It's aggravating, sometimes, but we—"

"Not Jill," Ariel said. "Claymore."

"*Clara*?" Selene returned. Her eyes narrowed. "What *about* her?"

Ariel stopped, forcing Selene to pause and turn back.

"A *house* fell on us," he said quietly. "Or a lot of its floor. I was under her. I couldn't see, could barely move. But she just sort of . . . *burrowed* us out of there. Like a mole. Only I looked back when we got out and there were two-by-fours that had been snapped like twigs, shattered pieces of concrete and bent rebar. It looked like a *bulldozer* had been through."

Selene raised a heavy eyebrow.

"Clara's . . . very strong," she allowed.

Ariel smiled and shook his head. He started off toward the truck. "I'm just saying. If you're ever in a tight spot and all hell breaks loose? I'd stick to her like glue."

"Son," Selene said, turning to follow him. "You don't have to tell me that."

The late afternoon sun lit the white sedan by the side of the road like a beacon, flashing so bright it was impossible to miss. Arcana lumbered past, executed a hasty three-point turn before trundling back along the shoulder. The truck stopped. Jill, Selene and Ariel got out and made their way over to the car. While Jill wiped down the back seat, Ariel checked the car's fluid levels, before climbing in and starting the engine.

"All good?" Selene asked.

"As ever," Ariel replied. "Thank you," he said to Jill, who'd extracted his white hat from the back seat.

"You're not going to explain what just happened?" she asked.

"You mean about the angel?" Ariel asked, slipping on a pair of aviator-style sunglasses.

"No, I mean about the demon," Jill said. "How did it hook you? Why was it so strong?"

Ariel's lips pursed and he swallowed. "To tell the truth, I don't know why. It *shouldn't* have been that strong. Then again, maybe I slipped up. I'm only human, after all." He smiled, dazzlingly.

Jill was unmoved. "Very well then," she said, and produced a card from her wallet. "If you ever find yourself in a similar . . . *situation*. Or if you discover anything particularly *out of the ordinary.* . . . Give me a call."

Ariel took the little white card, studied it, then smiled and stuck it in his hatband.

"You know, usually I'm the one handing these out at the end of the day."

"Well, the world is full of surprises," Jill said dryly. But she got out her phone. "Do you want to give me a number, anyway?"

Ariel did.

"Now, if you'll excuse me," he said, almost apologetically. "I'm going to find myself a nice, cheap hotel room with a hard bed and a hot shower. I recommend you do the same." He pulled his shades down far enough to wink at Jill, gave one last flash of his remarkably straight, white teeth, and pulled his car onto the road, and away.

Clara was dozing in the back seat when Jill and Selene returned.

"I gotta say I agree with him," Selene admitted. "I'm all greasy, and I shudder to think what Clara's got on her."

"First stop, Unicorn," Jill reminded her.

From the back came a mumbled agreement.

"Surprised you didn't come out to say good-bye to him," Selene chided. "I think he *liked* you." She leaned around to find Clara's eyes had cracked open.

"No need," she said. "We will see him again."

She shut her eyes and turned toward the window as Arcana shuddered to life. In her mind she felt a dream, but it was receding, like the sound of light hoofbeats fading away into the distance. Somewhere out there the white stag was running. Clara let it go.

*

Well he's a man with a missionary collar
He's a man with a missionary's pride
But if you ask for absolution baby can't you see
He's no gentle preacher he'll take you for a ride
Whether he's been lost, whether he's been found,
Believe what you want to once he's in the ground
Doesn't matter if he loses or wins
'Cause he's got it coming
'Cause he danced with a visionary sin
He danced with a visionary sin
A visionary sinner, he comes in like the tide
A man on a mission, he's got nothing to hide
A rod and a spoiled god
He's a man with a vision
of the world on fire.
There was a man with a vision and an angel lost at sea,
His visionary sin it was going to be
The best and the worst and the
only true reality
Oh listen to the roar as the tide recedes
recedes
recedes
recedes
recedes . . .
Well he's a man with a missionary collar
He's a man with a missionary's pride
(Missionary's pride)
But if you ask for absolution baby can't you see
He's no gentle preacher
preacher
preacher
preacher

preacher . . .
It don't matter, lose or win
Oh honey (He danced with a visionary sin)
See what you done (Visionary sinner)
Take a step back from that door (Visionary sinner)
(Visionary sinner) He danced with a visionary sin
(He's got it coming to him now)
Visionary sin
—Visionary Sinner/*Technorhyme*

The Arcana crew will return in
"Sons of Fire"

Escape Velocity

Apsis Fiction 3.2: Perihelion 2016 will appear in December 2015. In it you can look forward to:

"Sons of Fire"
"The Goblin's Fiddle"
"The Silver Chimera"
"Chronostrophe"

and more!

Find the entire library of *Apsis Fiction* issues at

heliopauseweb.com/fiction/apsis-fiction

Apsis Fiction is a Heliopause Production; written, illustrated, edited and designed by Goldeen Ogawa.

More from Heliopause

The Adventures of Bouragner Felpz, Volume I: A Study of Magic

Driving Arcana: Rotation One

Professor Odd Novellas:
#1: The False Student
#2: The Slowly Dying Planet
#3: The Promethean Predicament
#4: The Elder Machine
#5: The Dragons of Geda
#6: The Monster's Daughter

Coming soon:

#7: The Dogs of Canary Island, and
Professor Odd: The Complete Season One
Driving Arcana: Rotation Two

heliopauseweb.com

About the Author

Goldeen Ogawa is a self-taught writer, illustrator and cartoonist. In her spare time she rides her bicycle and sings. She lives in California.

About the Text and Design

The body of this book was typeset in Elysium using LaTeX.
Cover art and design by the author.